BROWN GIRL GHOSTED

BROWN GIRL GHOSTED

A novel by

Mintie Das

HOUGHTON MIFFLIN HARCOURT

BOSTON   NEW YORK

The text was set in Goudy Old Style.

Art by Samya Arif

Library of Congress Cataloging-in-Publication Data
Names: Das, Mintie, author.
Title: Brown girl ghosted / by Mintie Das.
Description: Boston : Houghton Mifflin Harcourt, 2020. |
Audience: Ages 14 and up. | Audience: Grades 10-12. |
Summary: In Meadowdale, Illinois, sixteen-year-old Violet deals with mean girls,
racism, murder, and being spurred by immortal Lukas to accept being an Aiedeo, a
hereditary warrior queen charged with protecting the world.
Identifiers: LCCN 2019029202 (print) | LCCN 2019029203 (ebook) |
ISBN 9780358128892 (hardcover) | ISBN 9780358131304 (ebook) |
ISBN 9780358343455 (audiobook) | ISBN 9780358343110 (audio CD)
Subjects: CYAC: Murder—Fiction. | East Indian Americans—Fiction. |
Race relations—Fiction. | Supernatural—Fiction. | Immortality—Fiction. |
Mystery and detective stories.
Classification: LCC PZ7.1.D33545 Bro 2020 (print) |
LCC PZ7.1.D33545 (ebook) | DDC [Fic]—dc23
LC record available at https://lccn.loc.gov/2019029202
LC ebook record available at https://lccn.loc.gov/2019029203

Manufactured in the United States of America

DOC 10 9 8 7 6 5 4 3 2 1
4500790407

To Dede, Mommy, and Ita,
thank you for haunting the crap out of me
until I finally wrote this book.

BROWN GIRL GHOSTED

Prologue

Smart Girl. Funny Girl. Good Girl. Bad Girl. Nice Girl. Mean Girl. Happy Girl. Angry Girl. Brave Girl. Scared Girl. Best Girl. Daddy's Girl. Mommy's Girl. American Girl. Indian Girl. White Girl. Brown Girl.

One

Day 1: Alive

DEAD PEOPLE *ARE* SCARY. Even if my nanny has spent my entire life trying to convince me otherwise. Granted, at sixteen, I'm too old to have a nanny. But that is beside the point at this particular moment, as I find myself staring down at the corpse of Dr. Jenkins.

He'd been Meadowdale's most popular pediatric dentist. I hadn't seen him since losing my last baby tooth but I remember the way his face turned bright red when he laughed. That and the fact that he always commended me for being able to open my mouth wide enough to accommodate his sausage fingers.

I glance down at Dr. Jenkins's hands, which are folded one on top of the other and resting across his expansive belly. It is the kind of unnatural pose that you never see people in unless they're dead. His ruddy complexion is plastered over with thick, waxy makeup, and his eyes and mouth are glued shut. The result is a Dr. Jenkins that looks like an eerie, artificial version of his living self. Like those creepy wax figures I saw once at Madame Tussauds.

"Kiss him again," Naomi Talbert commands in a cool, low voice that sends goose bumps up my arms. Here we are in front of a cadaver and still, Naomi manages to be the most menacing thing in the room.

All twelve of us girls from the Meadowdale High School poms team, unaffectionately known as the Squad, stand around the doublewide pine rose casket where Dr. Jenkins lies. I can bet that at least eleven out of twelve of us desperately want to be anywhere but here in the parlor of the Talbert Funeral Home. But what we want hardly matters since Naomi, cheer captain and all-around head bitch, summoned us for an official team meeting at her house.

I draw a circle with the tip of my sneaker in the moss-green carpet. This isn't the first time that I've seen a dead person. Up until three years ago, I saw them quite frequently. Thankfully, not in the same wacked way as that poor boy from *The Sixth Sense* who was haunted by dead strangers 24/7. My visitors were merely dead relatives who came and went. These days, they don't visit at all. Or at least, that's what I've convinced myself of.

Naomi narrows her steel-blue-gray eyes at Madison Kingsley. "I said kiss him again."

I've also seen my fair share of dead bodies here in this very parlor and that one time when we snuck downstairs to the morgue. I used to be a frequent guest at Naomi's house, back in the days before popularity, boys, and the amount of Instagram followers you had determined if you were good enough to be Naomi's friend. In fact, in that first year that the Talberts moved to Meadowdale, I was one of the only kids who came over. It seemed that most parents and their children weren't too keen on sleepovers with the dead. But that quickly changed as the Talberts rose through the town's social ranks and became Meadowdale royalty with Naomi as the celebrated princess. Nowadays, everyone is just dying to hang with the Talberts.

I shoot a quick glance at Naomi. This morning, she posted a photo of herself wearing those ridiculously tight white jeans she has on and it had already gotten 4,200 likes by lunchtime.

There's no denying that Naomi fits the mold of the classic hot girl: thick, wild honey-golden mane, lush lips, curves in all the right places, and firm where it matters. She looks like the love child of Gigi Hadid and a pair of Daisy Dukes.

But high schools around the world are filled with beautiful girls. It wasn't solely good looks that had catapulted Naomi into a league of her own. It was that girls like Naomi had discovered their power and staked their claim to the top prize before the rest of us even realized we were in a competition.

"No way am I doing that again!" Madison shouts as she wipes her mouth with the back of her hand for the umpteenth time.

I exchange eye rolls with Jessica Chang, who is standing on the other side of the coffin. Madison is a freshman and therefore new to the Squad. She doesn't know that there is no point in taking the high road or standing your ground because no matter what, Naomi always wins. She isn't just *a* mean girl. Naomi is *the* mean girl.

What Madison has to do in order to keep the little social cachet she's accumulated in the two weeks since school started is suck up her pride and let Naomi humiliate her. That way the budding sociopath will be satisfied (at least temporarily) and we can all finally leave.

"Madison, we're not going anywhere until you do as I say. I told you to kiss him for thirty seconds and you like barely did it for five," Naomi counters as though her argument is completely logical.

I sigh. Why does every moment with Naomi feel like a scene from a Lifetime movie? One where the mean girl murders the new pledge in a hazing gone too far and the rest of her minions have to help cover it up.

At some point or another, we've all been subjected to Naomi's tests. Madison is actually getting off kind of easy. Last year, Naomi forced a new recruit to spend an entire hour inside a closed casket.

I arch my neck slightly to peek into the showroom across the hall. Glossy coffins in all makes and models sit out in full display like shiny new automobiles at a car dealership. When he'd renovated this place a few years ago, Mr. Talbert had poured so much money into blinging out the main floor with crystal chandeliers and gold accents that he'd dubbed it "the bank."

I've always thought it was like putting lipstick on a corpse. No amount of designer wallpaper can hide the creepy fact that there's an actual morgue downstairs.

"Please don't make me kiss that old dead man again," Madison begs. Her freckled chin begins to tremble.

I wince. Doesn't Madison know that crying only makes it worse? Hasn't the girl watched *Karate Kid*, *Heathers*, or any

1980s Molly Ringwald flick? Maybe Maddie isn't an '80s girl, but, come on, she's certainly seen *Mean Girls*.

Those films might have been made way before my time but I firmly believe in applying history (at least movie history) to the present. Basically, any situation that I find myself in can be referred back to a book, movie, or TV show. Who better to help me navigate the perilous world of high school than Judy Blume or John Hughes? This doesn't mean that I've managed teenage-hood unscathed. Far from it, actually. But at least I'm still alive, and survival is all I'm hoping for right now.

Big, sloppy tears roll down Madison's face, forcing me to look away. I don't need a movie to tell me that I should do something to help the girl. The nausea that is making me want to hurl my lunchtime nachos is enough of an indicator that every single aspect of this situation is wrong. However, the warning bell going off in my head reminds me that any action that sets me apart from the herd will draw a lot of attention.

By doing something, I risk becoming the heroine. Heroines are leads and I have already determined that the safest way to get through high school is to play an extra—just be part of the background and *blend in*.

Of course, blending in with the predominantly white cast of Meadowdale isn't so easy for a brown girl. To be accurate (I'll put it in food terms, since that's usually what most people use to describe girls who look like me), I'm a caramel frappuccino with a peanut butter swirl. My brown comes via India.

No, I'm not going to have an arranged marriage. No, I didn't escape the squalor of Mumbai like that boy in *Slumdog Million-aire* (*Jai ho, bitch*). No, I don't need to wear a red dot on my fore-head. No, I can't show you how to wrap a sari. No, I don't know Priyanka Chopra or Mindy Kaling or "that one girl from the Bollywood video." And yes, I speak English and I understand every single word that you just said about me.

"The longer you stall, the longer you have to kiss him the second time, Maddie," Naomi hisses.

I realize that we live in the age of Beyoncé, where brown, black, and everyone in between is accepted and even celebrated. However, that applies to the world out *there*, the la-la land of social media and diverse metropolises like NYC, LA, Toronto, and London.

My reality is Meadowdale, Illinois, population thirty-two thousand, smack-dab in America's heartland. A town that feels like it cropped up in the middle of a cornfield and has more cows than people. Meadowdale is three hours away from Chi-cago, one hour from a decent mall, and light years away from everything else.

It isn't that Meadowdale is intolerant. For the most part, it's okay to be a minority here. As long as you act just like everyone else. That means I have to work harder and be better than all of them just to prove that I am *exactly like them*.

I'm junior-class vice president, in the honor society, and on the student council, tennis team, and poms (bottom of the pyramid and back line, but nonetheless). I maintain a 3.7 grade point average but make sure not to reach 4.0 because everyone hates a brownnoser. Most important, I am the perpetual nice girl, never too much and adapts easily. Except that there is nothing easy about it.

Madison's sobs drown out the Muzak playing from the overhead sound system. In this particular situation, no matter how hard Madison cries, blending in means that I should do nothing at all.

"Naomi, I think Maddie has had enough," Tessa Price mumbles as she looks down and pretends to study a lock of her bleached-blond hair extensions. I'm all about DIY beauty but her hair looks so fake that I wouldn't be surprised if she'd just glued pieces of straw to her head. She's skinny to the point of being skeletal and her voice is quiet and wispy. "Can we just drop it and go on with our cheer meeting?"

Tessa is Naomi's BFF which makes her VP, wingman, and number two. She is generally perceived as the good cop but runner-up is mostly a ceremonial position with lots of perks but very little influence. To Tessa's credit, she's usually the only one of us that makes any effort to check Naomi on these all-too-frequent occasions when she goes full-on Regina George. Naomi gives Tessa the kind of withering stare that would turn most mortals into stone, then raises a perfectly waxed eyebrow. "Who cares what she wants? That's—"

"You're not supposed to be in here," a deep male voice barks.

I jump and turn in the direction of the voice. In the doorway is a tall guy with a short blond buzzcut wearing an ill-fitting black blazer that appears to be at least a couple of sizes too big for his lean, muscular frame. His intense green eyes peek out from behind his thick dark-rimmed glasses, which look like the kind of fake prop that I used in the costume department for last year's school musical.

"Who's the hottie?" Jessica coos not so quietly. A few of the other girls chime in with their own catcalls and stupid remarks.

I also can't help checking him out but for a different reason. A weird sensation like déjà vu washes over me. I am fairly certain that I've never met the guy but there is something oddly familiar about him. Maybe because he's an unsettling mix of *American Psycho* and Ryan Gosling.

"He isn't a hottie. He's, like, my dad's pathetic intern," Naomi says, letting her disgust drip from every word.

"A creepy hottie," Jessica purrs. "Even better."

Naomi ignores her and turns her attention to the intern. She plasters on her best fake smile. "Since you're new, lackey boy, I'll let this one slide. But just so you know in the future, this is my house and I can go anywhere I want."

Naomi's delivery is classic diva. All that is missing is the hair flip. I try to read the guy's face for some kind of reaction but there isn't even a tiny crack in his icy demeanor.

"You can go anywhere you want upstairs in the private living quarters. Not here with the bodies," he counters. He is talking to Naomi but I feel like his eyes are on me, which makes me jittery. I'm not used to guys noticing me, especially when Naomi is around. Though the way this guy is checking me out doesn't feel like he wants to ask for my digits.

Naomi digs her platform heels into the carpet. "I don't take orders from the help."

"And I don't tolerate petulant children." Then he makes a gesture that is too fast for me to catch.

But Naomi sees it. Her cheeks flame with rage. "It was you . . ." she mutters, but she doesn't finish her thought. Instead, to my utter shock, Naomi begins to make her way toward the door. In the nearly ten years that I've known Naomi, I've hardly ever seen her obey anyone so easily.

We all follow her without saying a single word.

As I reach the end of the hallway, just before the staircase, I turn around. That same strange feeling comes over me again. The guy is still standing in the doorway and I swear that he is staring right through me.

Two

LUKAS MAKES A SMALL INCISION near the femoral artery of the cadaver. His eyeglasses slip down the bridge of his nose. He darts his head from side to side to make sure that there is no one else here in the morgue with him. At least, no one alive. Then he rips off the glasses and carelessly tosses them onto the worktable next to him.

He picks up a clear plastic tube. The cadaver's blood is drawn from her body through the tube and into the sink; as it circles the drain, a tinny metallic smell fills the room. He breathes it in. Just a whiff of blood sends his adrenaline pumping. Lukas eases the tube farther into the cadaver. Rigor mortis has already started to set in and it feels like he's breaking through ice. He waits until he hears the *pop* sound of the cadaver's insides before settling back down onto the stool.

The tools for preserving cadavers have changed but one fact has remained the same throughout time: Humans die. It is the one certainty in his line of work.

Lukas shakes his head. He can't afford to let the darkness set in right now. After a moment, he refocuses his attention on the cadaver. These days, he usually gets stuck playing a tech mogul or hardcore hacker. But in this godforsaken village, neither was relevant.

He actually quite enjoys pretending to be a mortician or, as Naomi put it, a "pathetic intern." Although when he'd been given this assignment, he didn't think it would be such a pain in the ass. More specifically, he didn't think that Violet would end up being such a pain in the ass.

Lukas rips off his latex gloves. Since the day he became immortal, at the age of nineteen, what he has always been and what he will always be is a soldier. His only true function is to win the war at any cost.

The Aiedeo sent him here for just that reason. In the centuries that he's worked for them, he's rarely seen them make a misstep. That's why they've become as powerful as they are. He also knows that he's one of the best soldiers working for them, which is why it's baffling that they're wasting him on Violet.

It was supposed to be such a clear-cut assignment. The Aiedeo are a legacy of powerful warrior queens that protect the world. Violet is an Aiedeo who has apparently gone rogue in the past three years.

Perhaps "going rogue" is an overstatement because that would require Violet to take some kind of action. In the month that he's spent watching her, he hasn't seen Violet do anything at all.

Nevertheless, the Aiedeo need to know if Violet can still be of use to them. If not, then she poses too great a threat to have around.

We cram into the Talberts' tight living room. The top two floors of the funeral home are the family's private space. I squeeze into a spot on the overstuffed sectional between Jessica Chang and a new girl whose name I can't remember. It's been a while since I've been up here but not much has changed except that everything is a little less shiny these days.

I notice new pastel-colored throw pillows strewn across the shag rug and the whitewashed coffee table. It seems that all that's needed to separate the living and the dead is a staircase and some home décor from Pier 1. I wonder if the spirits here actually follow the rules and stay downstairs, unlike mine, who used to show up anytime and anywhere they pleased.

There's an entire wall filled with Naomi's trophies. Some of them are from dance and cheerleading but the majority of them are social media awards. In the past few years, Naomi's empire has expanded from our tiny town to what sometimes feels like the entire online stratosphere. Between her fashion blog, *Corn-fed Cutie*, Instagram, and whatever the hell else, Naomi is a major influencer. Her social media consists mostly of her kickin' it on the farm—riding a tractor, baling hay, milking cows, and running through endless wheat fields. Usually while wearing a bikini. I'm sure Naomi, who never misses an opportunity to show off, loves every minute of the attention she gets from her fame, but the whole farm-girl thing is a stretch; I've never seen her do anything around livestock that doesn't involve a wind machine and a camera. Nevertheless, Naomi's legions of followers, which seems to include our entire town, worship her.

"Want some, Violet?" Jessica asks as she holds out a bag of almond M&M's. "If I had known we were gonna have a meeting *after* our two-hour practice, I would have totally gorged at lunch."

Jessica's parents moved here from mainland China and own the only Asian grocery store in town. Kids at school are always telling Jess how she looks just like Mulan, the same way they compare me to Jasmine from *Aladdin*. For the record, neither of us looks like either of them.

Jess has a wide, sexy space between her two front teeth and messy candy-apple-red-dyed hair that falls over her eyes and always gives her the appearance of having just come from a wild hookup. Her look is borderline edgy for Meadowdale, where shellacked mall hair and glitter eyeshadow are the norm, but as long as Jess can tame her locks with a scrunchie, she's still considered acceptable for the Squad.

I am way less indie rocker and much more generic brown girl on the cover of a college course catalog. With my big, dark eyes, jet-black hair, and round face, I have that ambiguous minority look that allows me to check multiple boxes on surveys. Even though I think I look so Indian that my picture belongs on a bag of basmati rice, I'm often mistaken for Mexican or biracial. On occasion, people want to know what casino my tribe owns. Of course, I've had my fair share of being mistaken for an "A-rab" by rednecks who usually follow that up with a slew of choice ethnic slurs. That's the thing about racists—they hardly ever get their racism right.

"You know we're always on Naomi's clock," I whisper as I grab a handful of candy. "Which includes making time for some torture."

I glance over at Madison sitting at the other end of the sofa. Her eyes are still red around the rims but she's chatting with some of the girls next to her and it seems like she's calmed down some.

"Oh, please, that puss is gonna have to grow a pair if she wants to stick around," Jessica says between mouthfuls of chocolate.

Before my freshman year in high school, I tried out for the cheer team and didn't make it. I was told I could be an alternate, which was a nice way of saying "You're not good enough," or join the Meadowdale High School dance team. I chose the latter and actually liked it.

Then when I was a sophomore, there were districtwide budget cuts and not enough money to fund both cheer and dance. So to the horror of Naomi and all of the other cheerleaders who thought they were superior, the two teams had to consolidate into a single cheer and dance squad—the poms. Officially, since our school mascot is a pioneer (neither tough nor menacing but politically correct), we're the Pioneer Poms.

These days all twelve of us girls are required to dance and cheer. The newly formed team pretty much sucks at both. The dance girls try to blame it on the cheerleaders and vice versa. Mrs. Fischer, our coach, has stopped coming to our practices, although I suspect that has more to do with Captain Naomi than the team's inabilities.

The only prize the Squad has earned is third place in a cheer competition where only three schools competed. We are ranked second-to-last in our district. Yet that doesn't stop some of the girls from acting with all the pomp and attitude that I would think would be reserved for teams that are in the national top ten.

Tomorrow is our first pep rally and football game of the new school year. It's a chance for the Squad to redeem itself after its dismal last season. Not gonna happen.

"Girls, listen up!" Collette Davis shouts. She stands still in the middle of the room with her curly blond ponytail swooshing back and forth behind her. Collette holds up a red, white, and blue hair bow similar to the kind that the Squad wears for performances. "We're going to be selling these again this year for the Meadowdale Pioneers Spirit Fest."

All of us lift our cell phones to take a photo of the bow. "OMG, the organizers still use Facebook," Collette continues. "So you can get all the details about the event there. Use your parents' account if you don't have one. But it's going on next week so I need everyone to sign up for a slot at our booth."

Collette starts to sit down, then pauses. "OMG, I almost blanked out there. Duh! We need you guys to get your moms to sew like a thousand bows per mom. They can buy all the supplies at That's Sew Crafty or Walmart. Make sure your mom mentions Pioneer Poms to get the ten percent discount."

The girls start to text the photos of the bows to their

mothers with puzzling messages like *U need to 2 make 1K 4 Pioneer Poms ASAP.*

Collette beams until she makes eye contact with me. "OMG, Violet! I totally forgot that you don't have a mom. I mean, you don't need a mom to make the bows. Your nanny can probably make them. Or, you know, someone else's mom. Maybe my mom could do it . . ."

Collette's face turns a deeper shade of red every time she says *mom.* The right thing for me to do is put the poor girl out of her misery and change the subject. But sometimes it is just so fun to watch people trip over themselves when handling this "sensitive" issue.

My dead mother accounts for many awkward moments in my life when hypercautious acquaintances assume that just the mere mention of the word *mother* or any of its delightful variations will cause me irreparable damage. But Mommy, Mama, Mom, or whatever I would have called her if I'd had a chance has been dead for fourteen of my sixteen years. I am over it.

Out of the corner of my eye, I notice Naomi trying to keep a straight face. We've always shared the same wicked sense of humor.

"Frizz," Naomi begins, invoking the nickname that she christened Collette with last season, "I'm sure that if Violet's mother were alive, she would have been honored to sew our spirit bows." Naomi winks at me. I hate myself for it, but I like being in Naomi's favor even if she is like that jerky boyfriend that you know you should quit but just can't. Not that I have much experience with boyfriends anywhere except in my elaborate fantasy life.

Collette's eyes practically pop out of her head. "OMG! I'm sure that Violet's mom would have been like the best pom mom ever. Especially because Indian people are, like, really good sewers because, you know, they have all those garment factories. And they let little poor kids work at them so they can eat. Because like there are a ton of starving people over there. Which is why I totally support India . . . Indians . . . Violet."

Ding. Ding. Ding. I hear a set of imaginary alarms ringing at the political-correctness headquarters. Collette has doubled her dipshit points by pulling out both the dead-parent card and the Indian card in the span of two minutes.

Naomi's face lights up like she's just struck gold, which secretly makes me proud. No matter how temporary being "in" with Naomi is, when she shines her light on you, it makes you feel like the most important person in the room. Naomi probably wants to take this as far as it can go, but I think we've already had enough fun at Collette's expense.

I put my hands together and bow my head solemnly in Collette's direction. "Namaste."

"OMG. Namaste, Violet," Collette gushes as she returns the gesture.

Naomi laughs and nods at me in approval. I feel a bit guilty for giving Collette crap. The girl probably meant no harm. Most people don't. That's why I usually let that race and ethnicity stuff slide right off me. But just because I pretend to be all cool about it doesn't mean that it isn't completely infuriating.

I was born in Assam, India, a tiny state in the northeast region of the country. When I was two years old, my mother died in a car crash. At the age of three, I moved to America with my father, older brother, and nanny. We lived in Texas for two years and then, over a decade ago, my family moved to Meadowdale. I've spent thirteen years in the United States, and I've visited India only a handful of times.

My connection to the "motherland" is about as strong as my connection to my actual mother.

They've both been out of the picture for practically my entire life. Yet, the same way that people expect me to mourn a person that I never knew, they expect me to claim a country that isn't mine.

Every week that I can remember in my American life, I've been asked *that* question. I can feel my blood pumping just thinking about it. People always phrase it so innocently, as though they are taking a genuine interest in me. Usually it's from a parent, maybe a mother who is surprised to see little Jenny bring a brown girl home from school. These days it's more like a mother who is surprised to see little Johnny take a brown girl to the school dance.

Where are you from? I always respond with "Here." Then they rephrase it. Sometimes they even say it slower, in case I didn't understand. *Where are you really from?*

I always understand. I am the foreigner, the other, the outsider to everyone else but me.

"Last order of business," Naomi announces, waiting until all eyes are firmly on her before proceeding. "Tessa and I have decided there's gonna be a changeup in our halftime routine."

Tessa is standing next to Naomi, and, technically, she's co-captain. However, no one actually believes that she has anything to do with whatever horrible idea is about to be thrown at us.

"No way!" Collette cries. "We've been practicing this choreography for a month now. Plus I already posted a teaser of the first twenty seconds and it's already gotten a ton of views."

"FU, Frizz. It's not a choreography change. Jessica is off the frontline," Naomi declares in her perfectly heartless way.

"What?" Jessica stands up. "I've been frontline since my freshman year!"

"That's because you used to be good," Naomi says. "But lately, you've been dancing like your legs are made out of chopsticks."

There is a collective gasp in the room for both the demotion and the racial slur. Jessica doesn't look like she is going to accept either.

"It's better than just leaving my legs open like you," Jess retorts as she glares directly at Naomi and then Tessa. "And especially you."

Tessa turns crimson from head to toe. With her raggedy hair extensions, neon-green-colored contacts, and fake tanner that makes her skin glow orange like she's radioactive, Tessa is like the cheap knockoff version of Naomi's luxury brand. Guys usually treat Tessa like a consolation prize, which might be why she's always had a reputation for doing whatever it takes to make them happy.

Still, even if Jess's comment rang true, the girl isn't really a fighter and probably doesn't deserve to be pulled into this. But that's the problem with standing too close to Naomi. There is bound to be collateral damage.

"It's temporary." Tessa looks down at the floor. "We just wanna try out something new."

"Of course, since everyone is watching the frontline," Naomi continues, completely ignoring Jessica, who is still fuming, "we need to mind the D-word."

"Dic—"

"Diversity! Not as fun as what you were about to say, Becca, but just as important." Naomi beams.

"Hello? I'm black and I'm on the frontline," Becca says, holding out her hands and then pointing to her face.

Naomi nods. "Noted. But you know that if we have only one token minority up there, people will accuse us of not really taking diversity seriously. That's why we need another one—to look like we care. So since we're moving Soy Sauce over there, we have to replace her with another flavor."

My tummy does a quick flip. There are a thousand students at Meadowdale High School. Twenty brown girls. Four Indian girls, but none of them are in the junior class with me. And three females of color on the Pioneer Poms. One is Becca, the other is Jess, and the third is . . .

"You're movin' on up, Samosa!"

I instantly cringe for a few reasons.

First, Naomi knows that I hate that nickname. When I was in elementary school, my teachers always pressured me to take part in the annual international bazaar, an event where

Meadowdale's unofficial assimilation policy was temporarily lifted and I was expected to flaunt my Indianness like I was fresh off the boat. In fifth grade, I made the mistake of bringing samosas. Amid the plethora of pierogi, brats, *pannekoeken*, and herring that most of my classmates brought in to celebrate the one drop of Polish, German, Dutch, or Swedish blood they had, the puffy brown pastries were an "exotic" delight. All would have been good if Naomi hadn't decided that I resembled a samosa and branded me with the nickname. Thankfully, the moniker didn't stick past eighth grade. Except with Naomi.

Second, Jessica is a good friend and way more into poms than I am. She'd even gone to cheer camp over the summer.

Third, people actually notice the front row, which means that I'll be out there on full display. Frontline is the opposite of blending in. A part of me has secretly wanted this—that's why I actually put some effort into poms this season—but another part of me is petrified.

Fourth, is the only reason I'm getting this promotion because of some diversity quota? Shudder. Diversity, quotas, token minorities, affirmative action—all that bullshit has haunted me my whole life.

"Keep Jess, she's better," I say, trying to sound nonchalant.

Naomi starts to respond but Jessica cuts her off. "Forget it, V. You do deserve it and I don't really care. And BTW, there's plenty of room for all three of us 'token minorities' to be on the frontline." Jessica eyes Naomi up and down. "We just gotta get rid of this white bitch."

"Really heartwarming, how you *sistas* stick together," Naomi says mockingly before turning to face the rest of the group. "Meeting over. Get out!"

The girls don't waste time gathering the duffle bags, backpacks, and purses that have been carelessly piled into a heap in the corner of the living room. A few of them congratulate me on my promotion before rushing out the door. Dancing frontline, even on a team as bad as ours, is kind of exciting.

"Violet," Tessa calls out as I am about to leave. "You really do deserve this. It's not because of that diversity stuff either. Naomi was just joking around with all of that."

Naomi shakes her head vehemently.

"Stop, Naomi." Tessa hugs me. She smells like vanilla with a faint hint of cigarette smoke. "V earned frontline because she's good."

"And because she's brown," Naomi adds wryly.

I flip Naomi off, which makes her smile. Then I exit the funeral home through the side door. A light summer breeze tickles the back of my neck as I walk into the parking lot. I check my cell. It's almost half past seven in the evening and the sun is still hanging on, lying low on the horizon.

I pop the back of my SUV, a four-year-old black Honda CR-V, the preferred car of the middle-aged divorced soccer mom. It used to be my dad's, who, as a self-absorbed, absent-minded, widowed fifty-four-year-old professor, is the farthest thing from a soccer mom there is. But he is generous and gifted me with the car on my sixteenth birthday.

I throw my poms gear and school bag into the back. As

I slam the rear door shut, a chill runs down my spine. I turn around slowly. Up in the second-story window of the house, I see the creepy intern looking at me. For a brief moment, I meet his stare. Then I drop my keys and hastily stoop down to pick them up. The blood rushes to my head. Slightly woozy, I will myself to peek up again. This time, he is gone.

I practically leap into the driver's seat. I can't stop trembling as I press the automatic locks. I steady my hands just enough to ram the key into the ignition, then drive away as fast as I can.

Three

BY THE TIME I pull up to the Fawn Ridge sign at the beginning of my subdivision, I've nearly managed to make myself believe that I didn't actually see the creepy intern. No—that isn't quite right. I acknowledge seeing him, but I am trying to convince myself that he hadn't been watching me. In the past three years, I've become very adept at denial. It is the most useful weapon in my arsenal. Without it, I will surely end up in a loony bin—or dead.

I drive along the tree-lined street leading up to my house. Meadowdale, with its charming town square, old-fashioned train depot, and locals who embody the mighty red, white, and blue that make this nation great, is straight out of *Stranger Things*. Fawn Ridge, with its community chili suppers, Sunday slow-pitch softball games, and relentlessly nosy neighbors is exactly the type of hood where ET would live.

My life, however, is a total horror flick. Or at least it was back when I was an Aiedeo. The Aiedeo are an ancient line—my line—of Assamese warrior queens. If being an Aiedeo meant I had a primarily ceremonial role that required me to wear a crown and throw a spear, I could maybe handle it. But it's so much more wack than that.

The Aiedeo started with Ananya, my great-great-multiplied-by-like-a-hundred-more-greats-grandmother. She was a queen in an ancient kingdom that ruled what is now Assam, India. I don't know much about Ananya, but from the stories that I've heard, Gram was straight-up gangsta. Ananya's husband was the maharaja but he was just a tiny footnote in her story because it was Ananya who had the real power. *Supernatural* powers.

I never got the details on everything Ananya could do, but it sounds like she was all the Avengers rolled into one. Legend has it that she single-handedly took on a battalion of Persian soldiers with her mad combat skills, poisonous arrows, and super-strength.

When Ananya was still a relatively young queen, there was a shift in the Ultimate Reality, the eternal cycle of creation and destruction, that caused all hell to break loose. Literally. War broke out between the gods and the Asuras — or, more accurately, the creators and the destroyers. Ananya used her powers to help the creators win the war, which was a good thing, because had the destroyers succeeded, we'd all be living in some dystopian nightmare under the rule of demon kings.

The gods honored Ananya by creating an entirely new position for her: an Aiedeo. Her task was to protect the world by destroying the destroyers. As if that weren't enough, the gods decided to ensure job security for Ananya's future female lineage by making us all Aiedeo too.

They also promised one female in every generation would get her own set of powers like Ananya had. However, like most Indian parents, Ananya wasn't going to give any of her progeny a trophy just for showing up, so she threw in the stipulation that an Aiedeo wouldn't be born with her powers but had to earn them.

An Aiedeo does that by going through a rigorous training that starts when she's ten and continues for the next seven years. An Aiedeo mother trains her daughter in a series of lessons designed to prepare her for various *shamas*, which are the ultimate tests of mind, body, and spirit. Every time a girl passes a *shama*, she's rewarded with a power.

My training began exactly on my tenth birthday. I kind of knew what to expect because my nanny, Dede, had been telling me about my legacy for most of my life. The Aiedeo are a highly secretive group and they rarely reveal themselves to outsiders. But apparently, when my mother was still alive, she'd told Dede everything she knew about being an Aiedeo. I sometimes wonder if that's because Laya was aware that she wouldn't be around to tell me herself.

The night I turned ten, I woke up to see a woman with long black hair just like mine sitting on my bed, and I was so excited. Not because of all the stories that Dede had regaled me with about the Aiedeo; it was never just about the *shamas* or the powers for me. What I'd held on to was that every Aiedeo girl was trained by her mother. Which meant now I was going to get Laya back. But when I turned on the light, my heart plunged. The woman saw the clear devastation on my face and smiled softly. She told me that her name was Mohini, and then she taught me how to braid my hair. First with my hands and then without my hands, just using my mind. I wasn't very good but Mohini was a patient teacher and I liked her singsong voice. She came back every night after that for an entire month until I could braid my hair with no hands all by myself.

After Mohini, more Aiedeo came to teach me. They were kind and nurturing like the TV moms on my favorite sitcoms. Except that none of them was actually my mother.

I grew up hearing stories about ancestors who could multiply themselves and assist in wars between gods and demons, so the idea that my dead mother would come see me wasn't so unbelievable. Especially because another of Ananya's rules was that there could be only one Aiedeo per generation, and both my mother and grandmother (who had died before I was even born) were gone. There was no *living* Aiedeo to teach me. Which meant that Mohini and all my teachers were *dead*. So why couldn't Laya train me herself?

About six months into my lessons, I gained the courage to ask my most recent new teacher, Bhanu, when my mother was coming. The weird thing with the Aiedeo was even back in the days when they were nice to me, I always got the sense that I wasn't supposed to ask a lot of questions. Bhanu explained that Laya was an elite Aiedeo and was needed for their most dangerous missions. She'd come to teach me only if I proved that I was good enough.

I'd grown up with a dad who was pretty much work-obsessed and rarely had time for me, so I was already used to proving my worth to get a parent's attention. I knew what I had to do if I wanted to see my mother—I needed to be the best.

I ramped up my training and slowly started to become really good. The warrior stuff was never easy and I struggled the most with that part. I'm not a natural athlete, so all that running, jumping, and fighting were not my jam. But I pushed my body as hard as I could.

Where I excelled was with the supernatural stuff. Once I learned how to focus my mind and harness my power, I found that I could do so much cool shit. Move objects, read people's thoughts; I even teleported myself to Dairy Queen a few times.

For a while, I loved being an Aiedeo. These were my ancestors and the Aiedeo was my legacy. It made me feel connected to something so much greater than myself. I'd train hard almost every night but I still had more than enough energy for school, maybe because what drove me, deep down inside, was the belief that all of this would eventually lead me to my mother.

Then, around the time that I entered seventh grade, everything changed. My Aiedeo teachers stopped being nurturing TV moms and became more like ball-breaking bitches. The *shamas* weren't just getting harder, they were getting downright scary. And it seemed that the more I gave the Aiedeo, the more they wanted from me.

I felt like they were sucking all the life out of me but I was relentless because of Laya. Although I was secretly afraid the Aiedeo would eventually break me. And they did.

I don't even remember what really happened back then, but I still feel such a wave of rage when I think about it. It was shortly after my thirteenth birthday when the Aiedeo threw me out of a moving car. Maybe it was part of a *shama*, but WTF kind of test ends with the test taker almost dying?

Miraculously, I survived, but I broke both my legs. To make matters worse, this happened on the rare occasion my father was actually in town. The moment he saw me lying there in the hospital bed, Naresh regressed back to his days as a military interrogator and started grilling me. I'd gotten good at hiding the Aiedeo stuff but I was pretty doped up on pain meds and I'm not sure what I told him. Besides, what could I really say? Whether I was pushed out or jumped out of that car, I was clearly in a dangerous place in my life. Dede tried to step in and help me but Dad didn't want to listen to anything either of us had to say. He and the hospital psychiatrist were convinced I'd tried to kill myself, so I was put on a twenty-four-hour suicide watch.

It didn't matter how often I told my father and the shrink that I hadn't tried to commit suicide; nothing I said was very effective because, honestly, I was effed any way I spun it. If I told Naresh about the Aiedeo, surely he'd lock me up in a mental institution for good. So I just kept quiet.

Dede practically lived in my hospital room and my best friend, Meryl, brought my homework assignments and loads of Little Debbie brownies every day. We'd never kept any secrets from each other. She knew everything about the Aiedeo and always believed me no matter how crazy it all sounded.

Naresh told everyone that I was in a car accident, which I guess was kind of true. To his relief, people seemed to buy it.

I think he wanted to believe it too. Meryl heard that Collette, who had an aunt that worked in the psych ward, was telling people that I'd been placed under suicide watch, but Meryl shut down Collette hard by threatening to start a rumor that she'd seen Collette making out with her cousin at the Sweethearts Dance.

The car "accident" was the first time the two parts of me—regular Violet, who was just like everyone else, and Super Violet, the secret Aiedeo—collided. I'd entered junior high the year before and I was convinced that the sole purpose of it wasn't education but so that some students could find out what made other adolescents vulnerable and then socially eviscerate them for it. Amber Baker had become a laughingstock when kids found out she'd been taking magic lessons, the kind where you pull a rabbit out of a hat. Imagine what would have happened to me if they'd discovered that I thought my dead relatives were teaching me how to shape-shift.

The consequences of being an Aiedeo were becoming too dangerous in both my inner life *and* my outer life. But I held on because of my mother.

A few of my Aiedeo teachers visited me in the hospital but I pretended to be asleep and let Dede deal with them. Laya never came. I laid there in bed with a totally busted mind, body, and soul wondering what more I could do to make my mother want me. Then one day about three weeks into my recovery, it all kind of clicked together. I was never going to be good enough for Laya to return.

There was this gaping hole that had been ripped open inside of me when Laya died. I'd thought having a mother again would mend it, but now I let it fill with all the fury and hate I had for the Aiedeo.

Those bitches had lied. They knew Laya was never coming. I was done.

I'd earned a few powers already but I was still in training and a good four years away from becoming a full-on Aiedeo. In theory, maybe the fact that I was an Aiedeo Lite would have allowed me to walk away. But from what I'd learned about my dead relatives, they did everything on their terms. What I had to do was force them to abandon me.

The night after I'd finally gotten both my casts off, I woke up to Mohini sitting on my bed just like she'd done on my very first lesson. She tried to speak to me but I was too fed up to listen. I knew what I had to do if I wanted to end this for good. My legs were still too weak for me to fight but my mind was working just fine. In fact, the forced rest had re-energized me. But this time my energy wasn't focused on joining the Aiedeo; it was turned against them.

I sat straight up in bed and let my rage fuel me. Mohini had taught me telekinesis and now I turned it back on her. I pelted her with my hairbrush, hair straightener, and blow dryer. The angrier I got, the stronger I became, and I hurled all my books at her. Then it looked like there was a cyclone in my room as everything I owned swirled around until I catapulted it into Mohini with all the force I could muster. I didn't know why she

31

didn't fight back harder but I didn't care. I just kept on hurling things at her until she finally left.

After Mohini, more Aiedeo showed up each night, and I did the same thing. Everything that they had taught me, I turned on them. After all, I'd reasoned, if I was just going to use my powers against them, the Aiedeo had no choice but to take my powers away, right? And what good was a powerless Aiedeo?

After a month of this, my plan worked. A whole day and night went by without any Aiedeo visits. I tried to open my front door without using the knob and couldn't even make it budge. I didn't have any special powers anymore.

At first, I didn't buy that it was really over. I stayed up night after night, expecting them to show. But after a few months, I started to think maybe my dead relatives were actually done with me. Months turned into years without one Aiedeo visit, and little by little, I've let my guard down.

I'm not delusional. I know the craziness that I experienced. There's a scar running down my entire right calf from the night of the car incident to remind me that that shit was real. I just didn't want anything to do with it anymore. As time went on, I found that I could choose to forget it all. It took work to make the memories fade—the bad ones and the good ones too. Eventually it all went away. Or at least enough of it that I can believe that I'm finally free.

In my new life, without the Aiedeo, I'm normal. I don't have to deal with ghosts, witches, and dead warrior queens anymore.

I'm just like everyone else, I tell myself as I pull into my driveway. And with enough denial in my arsenal, I can convince myself it's actually true.

"Dede! I've got food!" I shout as I walk into the kitchen, managing to keep my backpack over one shoulder while holding the drink carrier and BK bag.

People think I'm rich for the same reason they think Naomi is loaded. The Talberts live in a big house and have nice things, and you could probably say the same about us Choudhurys. The fact that I live in a good neighborhood, that my father works at the university, that I have a nanny, and that I travel abroad every summer seems fancy.

Rich, however, is relative. In Meadowdale, where you can still feed a family of four at a sit-down restaurant for under thirty dollars and the most expensive car in my high school's parking lot is a 2018 Mazda Miata, we sit somewhere between the middle and the higher rungs of the economic ladder. But in other parts of the world, particularly those where girls wear couture under their burqas, people consider hanging with me and my Coach wristlet slumming it.

"Bring me burger, please," my nanny yells back. "*Private Practice* starting."

I drop my backpack on the kitchen floor and head to the family room with the food. When Naresh is here, we have to eat our meals in the dining room. But when it's just Dede and me, we like to veg out in front of the TV.

My father extended his summer consulting gig in Turkey

to last the entire fall semester and now he won't be back until winter break in December. I'm pretty sure that return will be temporary and he'll be off to some other country by spring.

On most matters, my dad is quite black-and-white, but when it comes to his kid's cultural identity, he's refreshingly open. It might not have been Naresh's goal to assimilate but he has certainly made it easier for me to adapt to American life by raising me as a universal citizen.

Theoretically, universal citizenship means, in my case, that I'm neither Indian nor American. I have no ethnic, religious, cultural, or racial boundaries; I am supposed to be exposed to as many cultures as possible with no definitions or limitations. In practice, it can be simplified to this: I'm not Hindu, I eat everything—including beef—and the only language I can speak is English. (Well, unless you consider the janky-ass mix of broken English and even more broken Assamese that Dede and I speak to each other a different language, which I don't.) Naresh probably won't agree, but my interpretation of universal citizenship is that it allows me to be less Indian and more American.

"I got you the onion rings," I say as I place a Whopper with cheese on the glass coffee table in front of my nanny. "With extra mustard."

Dede smiles, which pushes her already high cheekbones up to her small hazel eyes. Her skin is the color and texture of sandpaper, and deep-set wrinkles line her face like the rings around an old tree, yet she has the speed and agility of a fit sixty-year-old woman. I've stopped trying to guess her age and Dede won't admit to anything anyway.

I plop onto the couch. My whole body aches from the hard practice and the long day.

"You miss *Grey's Anatomy* but I DVR for you." Dede pops an onion ring into her mouth.

I watch TV everywhere I can—on my phone, tablet, and laptop—but I prefer old-school-style in front of our massive flat-screen. Usually Dede, who raised me on trashy soap operas and police procedurals, is right next to me. Recently, we've become addicted to a block of Shondaland shows like *How to Get Away with Murder* and *Scandal*. It's so easy to let my mind go somewhere else with Olivia Pope's bizarre love triangles and killer wardrobe.

"What you do today?" Dede asks during a commercial break.

I shrug. I'm too tired to remember. "I don't know."

Dede smacks me on my thigh. "*Chht*, you never know! That because you keep too many secret, *swali*."

I can't help but smile at the way my nanny uses the Assamese word for "girl" to chastise me. "I don't know. School sucked. We had a long practice. And then I had to go for a meeting at Naomi's house that lasted forever," I gripe. There is something so solid about Dede that it is easy for me to regress back into a whiny child around her.

My nanny is mysteriously tight-lipped about her past but I managed to piece together a big chunk of her backstory during my last trip to India when I discovered a rather loose-lipped gatekeeper at one of my grandfather's homes who was actually old enough to remember Dede. Her real name is Purnakala Gurung and she hails from the hills of Nepal. When she was sixteen years old, she ran away from her tiny village and landed in nearby Assam, India. Most people who met the young Purnakala commented on what a rarity she was. First, she had received a formal education up through high school, which was uncommon for poor boys and, especially, poor girls back then. Second, Purnakala refused to act naive or inferior around the males she came in contact with, which was the behavior expected of females in those times. Instead, she was feisty and street-smart and unafraid to show it.

It was this unique set of qualities that caught the attention of Madhur, the wife of Assam's richest man. She observed the teenager outfox an infamous gang of hooligans in a card game and hired the girl to work for her right there on the spot. From that day, Purnakala became my mother's nanny. Laya called Purnakala by the respected title of Dede, which means "older sister," and it soon caught on as the name everyone used for her.

Dede cared for Laya until Laya was sent off to boarding school at the age of twelve. From there, what happened to Dede is a mystery that I imagine could rival the crazy plots of the trashy soap operas that we devour. Maybe Dede had a love child, was hit on the head and got amnesia, or became the lady boss of an underground crime syndicate in Assam's wild, wild east. If I had to pick, I'd choose the last option.

Wherever Dede disappeared to during what I've dubbed "the missing years," Laya eventually found her and brought her back to Assam. Laya was expecting her first child and wanted no one but her beloved Dede to be the baby's nanny.

"Talbert House of Dead." Dede cackles, exposing her

dazzling set of dentures. "Why Amricans bury dead body in ground?"

I chuckle along with Dede's high-pitched hyena laugh. Her feet, which are small enough to fit into children's shoes, barely skim the Oriental rug underneath the sofa. Everything about Dede is petite, which she expertly uses to her advantage to disarm people.

My nanny is the realest person that I know, yet in some ways everything about her is the perfect con. To anyone but me, Dede appears to be a nanny straight out of *Mary Poppins*. Her slight stature is made even more diminutive by the cotton saris that she dons, despite my ongoing pleas to her to wear American clothes. Although she did reluctantly agree to swap her sandals for a pair of white Keds in the fall and snow boots in winter.

Her frumpy-ethnic-grandma look is completed by oversize glasses that sit on the bridge of her nose and a loose bun that seems to come undone every fifteen minutes. Perhaps Dede's hair, which is black, is her only source of vanity. I only recently discovered that Mrs. Patel, Dede's bestie, mostly because she's the only other Indian woman who lives within a twenty-mile radius, has been dyeing the gray out of it once a month for the past several years.

Dede's speech is peppered with curses, off-color remarks, and salty humor. But that is the Assamese version. In public, her English consists mostly of "Do you take coupon?" and "I love Amrica."

Dede's sweet-old-lady act makes the locals treat her like a

delicate little Indian doll they purchased in a tacky souvenir shop. I'm pretty sure that's the way Dede wants them to see her.

The real Dede is far from a precious keepsake you have to handle with care. She is the savviest guru/hustler around—a cross between Mr. Miyagi and Jack Sparrow. This makes her a constant pain in my ass, but in the end, I know that Dede always has my back.

"You think burning a body and spreading its ashes somewhere random like you Indians do it is better?" I ask.

Dede scowls, which makes her look even older. "You remember that *you* Indian, Violet." Dede is not a fan of Naresh's universal citizenship and tries to shove my ethnic heritage down my throat every chance she gets. "Something happen today?" Dede continues as she leans in closer to me.

I back away. She's not an Aiedeo but my nanny has her own set of skills that include a mad sense of intuition and a wicked way of reading people. Especially me. Dede's probably picked up that something is bothering me because I'm still irked about the creepy intern. But the food coma I'm in is doing a good job of helping me forget him and I don't want to rehash it with her.

"*No.* You are not pulling that crap with me," I warn.

Dede reaches for my hand. "No crap, Violet. This about your power. What you see?"

"I see me making a call to immigration if you don't get out of my face."

"*Chht*, this not good, Violet," Dede clucks. "You are Aiedeo."

I yank my hand out of Dede's grip. My skin turns hot and

prickly just hearing their name. "Uh-uh, I am not letting you go there."

"Where I go?" Dede shrugs her shoulders. "I stay here and tell you about your mommy and whole big Aiedeo family."

Dede made a promise to my mother ages ago to do whatever it took to protect me. For her, that includes never giving up about the Aiedeo. Dede has this unshakable blind faith when it comes to them. She saw what happened to me but refuses to believe my dead relatives' motives are anything but altruistic.

Regardless of how much she pushes the Aiedeo on me, I'm not going to talk about it. Next to denial, my second-best way to handle unpleasant situations is avoidance. I pick up my cell phone from the coffee table and stand up.

"I gotta call Meryl about the lit assignment." I speed-dial my best friend. Dede lets out a loud "Hmmph" in frustration and goes back to her TV show.

I know that Dede is letting me off easy and I kiss her on the cheek before walking out of the family room.

"V, I was just about to call you."

I strain to hear Meryl over what sounds like a really bad cover version of an old-school drinking song.

"Where are you?" I ask, but then I remember it's Thursday, which is dollar-pitcher night at our local underage drinking hole, and answer my own question. "Stumpy's, of course."

"You gotta come down here." Meryl lowers her voice. "And help me hustle two frat guys out of a hundred bucks."

I chuckle. Most of us have to take crappy jobs at diners and fast-food places to earn our spending money, but Meryl makes her cash by coming up with ingenious ways to scam preppy college kids who have no business being at townie hangouts.

"What's tonight's special? Three-point shuffle or fool's pool?" I ask, referring to a couple of Meryl's classic cons.

"I'm working on a new one and I could totally use my trusted wingman. First five pitchers are on me."

"Five?" I laugh. "Unlike you, I've actually gotta show up at school tomorrow. Plus, we had a double practice and a Squad meeting that ran way over. I'm totally busted and I haven't even gotten to my homework yet."

I could practically hear Meryl's eye roll over the phone. She wasn't a big fan of the Squad or of Naomi. But she put up with it all for my sake.

"I'll massage your feet and Brain's here so he can do your school stuff," Meryl offered, referring to the ex-philosophy prof who spent most of his nights at Stumpy's getting hammered on Jack Daniel's and spouting conspiracy theories. "And I'll split my take with you. That's an easy fifty bucks at least *and* you get to hang out with me."

"That's the part that worries me. A Stumpy's night with you always means trouble."

"Satisfaction guaranteed!" Meryl laughed.

Meryl was fearless in a way that put almost everyone around her to shame. When a big, burly-ass mofo tried to mug us last summer in Chicago, Meryl kneed him in the groin and then stole *his* wallet before we ran away.

"Hey, have you heard anything about the new intern at Talbert's?" Meryl's dad is the county DA and usually knows about everything going on in town. Plus he's a friend of Jim Talbert's, so I thought it was worth a shot to ask.

"No. Why? Is he cute? Are you ready to finally move on from your six-year infatuation with Austin Coopman, V?"

My cheeks turn hot at hearing my crush's name. "Oh my God, Mer! Don't talk about me and Austin Coopman out loud in public! Someone might hear you!"

"Paranoid much? Oh, don't worry! No one here is paying attention to anything I'm saying."

I highly doubt that because Meryl causes a stir wherever she goes. She's definitely in the same elite league of hotness as Naomi but her smoke comes with a lot more dirt and grit—she's like a heroine in a Quentin Tarantino movie.

"Hey, I gotta go. Jeremy's trying to get in on my action with the college boys. Just come down for a pitcher, at least!"

"Not tonight but have fun! And call me if you need anything." I'm a little tempted to join her because it's always an adventure with Meryl but I know that I don't have the energy to keep up with her tonight. "Later!"

Before I get a chance to say "Bye," she's already hung up. I sit at my desk and reach for my Brit-lit assignment. Just talking to Meryl helps me get my mind off the Aiedeo. And much later that night, as soon as my head hits the pillow, I manage to forget all about the creepy intern.

FOUR

I WAKE UP TO THE SOUND of metal clinking. Groggily, I turn in the direction of the noise as my nostrils fill with the weirdly familiar combination of disinfectant, bleach, and wintergreen toothpaste. I open my eyes, then shut them abruptly against the glaring overhead light shining directly into my face. A flash of neon spots burns into my retinas.

"It's nice of you to visit, Violet."

The words are muffled and hard to understand. However, the voice is eerily recognizable. I begin to tremble but I don't know if it's from the fear that is rapidly setting in or from the cold air. It feels like a refrigerator in here and I realize that I have on only the T-shirt and underwear that I'd worn to bed.

"Wake up!" I shout to myself to escape this nightmare.

I squint against the light. The outline of a man with broad shoulders and a tummy as big as Santa Claus's slowly comes into focus. His face is turned away from me but I can see that he is sitting on one of those rolling stools like they use in a doctor's office. I try to sit up to get a better look but I can't move. I look down to find that I am strapped into a dentist's chair with zip ties around my chest, wrists, and ankles.

"Dr. Jen-Jenkins?" I stammer, forcing myself to say the dead dentist's name out loud.

I turn my head shakily from side to side. Somehow, I know that I am still in my bedroom but it looks like my old dentist's office. Even the jungle-theme mural that covered the walls of the clinic is now where my movie posters usually hang.

If this is a dream, it is the realest dream that I've ever had. A chill runs down my bare legs. Whatever is happening to me is as unbelievable as it is terrifying.

Suddenly, there is a faint whirring noise as the dentist chair begins to recline farther back; it stops abruptly once I am lying almost flat. I fight against the restraints but they are so tight that there isn't any room to move.

"Open wide," Dr. Jenkins commands. I know that it's him speaking but it feels like his voice is coming from inside my own head.

I shut my mouth and clench my jaw so hard that my neck muscles ache. Dr. Jenkins pries open my lips with his fat fingers and shoves his hand all the way inside. The bitter taste of the powder from the latex glove he wears rubs onto my tongue.

"Looks rotten, Violet," Dr. Jenkins says as he clamps a pair of pliers around a tooth. "We're gonna have to yank it out."

I jerk my entire body back and forth and try to scream but manage only a low moan. The razor-sharp points of the pliers begin digging into my gums and I taste my own blood.

"I'm afraid these just aren't cutting it." Dr. Jenkins laughs as he yanks the pliers out and throws them onto the floor.

His face turns cherry red but this time, I don't find it funny at all. My salty tears mix with my blood. After a minute, my cries are drowned out by the buzzing sound of a drill.

"No, no, please, Dr. Jenkins," I beg.

The dentist ignores my pleas. "Open."

This time I willingly oblige. Once Dr. Jenkins's hand is inside my mouth, I bite down hard. I feel the latex rip and then his skin open as I sink my teeth into him. Then I begin to gag. His decaying flesh tastes like a rotting pig. A disgusting liquid seeps out from the puncture that my bite has made and starts to fill my mouth. The pungent odor is so potent that I instantly feel woozy.

Dr. Jenkins withdraws his hand. "It isn't polite to bite."

I recognize the smell of formaldehyde, and it dawns on me that Dr. Jenkins is oozing the embalming fluid that was used to preserve his body. A pool of blood, spit, and embalming fluid forms at the back of my mouth and I start to choke. My throat begins to close and the air stops flowing. I buck against the chair as I try to breathe. I force myself to swallow the repulsive mix of liquids.

The only thing that stops me from vomiting or fainting is the sharp screeching noise that is rapidly getting louder. Before I know what is happening, the dentist jabs the drill into my mouth. I look up at him with my eyes wide open. The overhead light shines directly on him now and I can see Dr. Jenkins clearly. He looks just like he did earlier this afternoon at the funeral home with his face covered in thick, waxy makeup and his eyes and mouth glued shut.

"I'm afraid this is going to be a little tricky without my eyesight, Violet."

Dr. Jenkins pokes his finger around until he finds a molar located at the very back of my mouth, then he rams the drill bit through the tooth's enamel until he hits what feels like every nerve in my body. I shriek. The pain radiates in constant waves.

"Fight," I hear a faint voice call out from somewhere.

I desperately want to find where it is coming from and plead with whoever it is to help me. Nothing about this can be real but it is also not a dream.

Just as I feel myself begin to pass out, Dr. Jenkins stops drilling. Unconsciousness would surely bring some kind of relief but all of a sudden, my survival instincts kick in. I sense that I have to stay awake and endure this if I want to live. I force myself to breathe, fighting through the sheer agony that any kind of movement brings with it.

I hear the high-pitched scream of the drill again and I brace myself. He feels around my mouth but this time, just the pressure of his finger makes me jump.

"I warned you about too much sugar." Dr. Jenkins shakes his head. "I'm afraid this one is going to kill, Violet."

Then he lowers the drill bit right into the infected cavity. Every part of me, from the top of my head to the very bottoms of my feet, throbs. My body begins to spasm uncontrollably.

"Hold still," Dr. Jenkins scolds as he lifts his elbow up high and then pounds it into me.

I feel like the air has been sucked out of me. He punches me but I don't know where. There is so much pain coming from every part of my body. I gasp, then cough.

"Fight," the voice says again, but this time it is louder.

I realize it's coming from inside me and I have no choice but to listen. I don't know what is happening but I do know that only I can stop it.

I take a deep breath. My mouth is raw and pulsing. I make myself take another breath and then another until my heart rate begins to slow.

I don't hear the drill, which means that Dr. Jenkins is taking another break. This is my chance. I feel a tingle run down my spine. Harnessing all the strength I have left in me, I will myself to move. I yank my arms straight up in the air, breaking through the ties. Then I rip off the plastic tie around my chest and the ties around my ankles.

Dr. Jenkins flips on the drill and thrusts it toward my face. I knock it out of his hand and pummel him as hard as I can. He stumbles backward, then regains his balance and lunges at me. Frantically, I grab one of the dental instruments from the metal tray between us. When Dr. Jenkins is close enough, I plunge a sharp, curved hook directly into his closed left eye. He lets out a low groan. I ram it in until I hear a loud popping sound and his eyeball flies out. It lands on the floor and rolls under his stool. Embalming fluid rushes out of Dr. Jenkins's empty socket like a flood of tears.

He tries to grab me but I quickly duck out of the way. I retrieve the hook and am about to stab him again when Dr.

Jenkins suddenly disappears. The dentist chair, drill, and everything else vanishes along with him.

I stop abruptly and look around in utter confusion to see that I am back in my bedroom again. Standing in the exact spot where Dr. Jenkins was only a moment ago is a girl not much older than me. Her skin is the color of clay and her black hair is shaved close to her head.

I have never seen her but I know exactly who the girl is. She is an Aiedeo.

A rush of shock and rage pumps through me so hard that I feel as though I am going to explode. I tremble to my core.

"You bitches." I seethe as I glare at the girl.

"Violet, is that any way to speak about your family?" the girl asks in a voice that sounds much older than she looks.

She doesn't speak English and I sure as hell don't speak whatever language she is speaking, but somehow, we can understand each other. Although maybe the Aiedeo's version of Google Translate is hinky because the girl comes off speaking with an antiquated stiffness that is in stark contrast to her youthful, punkish vibe.

She's squat and compact like a bulldog. Except for the fact that she has big moon-pie eyes like me, it's hard to believe we come from the same bloodline. I don't know how many Aiedeo there are in total, but the ones I've seen all vary greatly in age, size, and coloring. If you rounded us all up, I bet we would look like that mystical rainbow of diversity that my sixth-grade health-sciences teacher, Mrs. Flores, used to go on about.

"I almost died with that Dr. Jenkins stunt!"

"Yet here you are, dearest. Alive and kicking," she says as she gives me the once-over. "I'm happy to inform you that you passed your *shama*."

"*I am not an Aiedeo!*"

The girl sneers. She's got a gold stud in her upper lip; it matches the piercings in her nose and eyebrow. "That stunt you pulled three years back by using your powers against us was clever. And we have been very patient, giving you this extended hiatus so that you could contemplate your *feelings,* as you Americans would say. But did you really think we would just let you go forever?"

"Yes! You stripped me of my powers, so I'm useless to you!"

"No, Violet, you *denied* your powers and stopped believing you had them." She takes a step closer to me. "But we never took them away. You've been in a three-year slumber and we cannot afford to wait any longer for you to wake. That's why we had to force the *shama* on you tonight."

I hear what she's saying but none of it is registering. I've had my powers this entire time? It can't be true.

The girl continues. "We need to prepare you and time is running out."

"Prepare me for what?"

"A war greater than we have ever known is coming," the girl answers. "We need the strength of all the Aiedeo to fight together and destroy the destroyers."

I shake my head vehemently. "Uh-uh. No, no, no."

The girl doesn't hear me and she keeps on going on about a

break in the Ultimate Reality and creators versus destroyers. I just want her to stop talking.

Before I even know what I'm doing, I charge at the girl as hard as I can. Her head slams back against the wall, tearing a hole in the middle of my *Breakfast Club* movie poster. Now I'm really mad. I try to punch the girl but miss.

"Do not let the anger control you, Violet," the girl says calmly. "Work through it and find the center."

My whole body tenses. That sounds like the wannabe-samurai kind of crap the Aiedeo spewed back in the day. I'm not having any of it. "Shut the hell up!"

I swing my fist but the girl catches it. "If you refuse to listen, then I will have to show you what I mean."

She grabs both my hands and stares into my eyes. Her grip is firm but not painful. I try to free myself but it's like I am locked into place. Within seconds, my calves weaken. Then my legs buckle and I fall to my knees, banging against the hardwood floor where the rug doesn't reach. I try to stand up but my entire body feels too heavy to lift and I topple over. I can't do anything but lie on the ground.

"Your fighting skills will need to improve." The girl stands over me. She's wearing a triple-stranded gold chain around her hips with tiny skulls hanging from it; it looks like it was stolen from Furiosa in *Mad Max*. She unwinds it and drops it next to my head. "Nevertheless, the Aiedeo say you earned this for your performance with the *shama* tonight."

I grunt. I grab the skull necklace and try to fling it back at the girl but I am too weak. "Screw you. I don't want anything from the Aiedeo."

"Oh, my great-great-great-great-great-granddaughter, you have no idea what is waiting for you." She laughs.

Before I can say anything else, the girl turns around and walks to the spot where the now torn poster hangs. Then she steps into the wall and disappears.

I sit on my floor in a dazed stupor. *The Aiedeo have come back for me.* The near-death *shama* they set for me with Dr. Jenkins just proves that those bitches are still shady as hell. I don't know how but I'm going to have to get rid of them. For good this time.

Lukas ducks under the leaves of the elm tree in Violet's backyard. He crouches down lower on the crooked, fragile branch that extends closest to her bedroom window and gives him a completely unobstructed view of the girl. Naresh has equipped every part of his house with some kind of elaborate security device. Even the most skilled criminal would have trouble getting anywhere close to Violet. But Naresh can't shield her from forces well beyond his imagination.

Everything about Lukas—his clothes, skin, and hair—are blue-black to match the starless sky. Everything except his eyes, which glow in the dark. Neither nature nor the neighbors, all of whom turned off their lights before going to bed, have been much help to him tonight. That's why he's had to turn his eyes into torches. But Lukas has been here for several hours, and his retinas are burning. He needs to leave or he'll surely wake up blind tomorrow.

Yet he stays.

Lukas has sat in this exact spot nearly every night for the past month watching Violet. He checks in on her during the day too but not as much as he'd like. His cover at the funeral home is turning out to be more work than he expected. Not that he minds. He's always been more comfortable with the dead than the living.

But tonight has been a revelation of sorts. He didn't know what the Aiedeo were planning when they requested he bring Dr. Jenkins's body from the morgue. Even as he watched the *shama* play out in front of his eyes, Lukas wasn't quite able to believe it. Did the Aiedeo intend it to go that far? At one point, Lukas believed that the Aiedeo were trying to kill Violet themselves. That would certainly make his job easier, though less fulfilling.

Lukas rubs his eyes. As far as Violet is concerned, from the *shama* to her destiny, the Aiedeo control everything. The sooner she grasps that, the better it will be for her and everyone around her. There is no free will in their worlds.

A light breeze rustles the leaves. Lukas still can't believe how astonishing it was to see Violet fight back in that *shama*. She's much stronger than he initially estimated. Besides, even if the *shama* was Violet against Dr. Jenkins, wasn't the real test with Jyoti? She was the Aiedeo that battled Violet at the end.

Lukas stares through the window at Violet, who is trying to crawl from the floor to the bed. Although she is moving slowly and with what looks like much pain, she isn't dead. Yet.

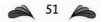

Lukas doubts the Aiedeo will return tonight. His eyes are burning so intensely that his head feels like it's on fire.

"Hey! What the hell are you doing up there!"

Lukas turns his head to see a figure standing on the street and shouting in his direction. For a second, he's stunned, but then his soldier instincts kick in and he quickly flips off his eyes. Then he leans hard against the tree until his skin, clothes, and entire body change into the exact same color as the bark so that he blends into the trunk like a chameleon.

Lukas stays perfectly still, knowing that even the slightest movement could be detected by the stranger. This is the first time in the entire month that anyone has noticed his presence. He shouldn't have kept his torch eyes on for so long.

To his relief, about a minute later, Lukas hears the stranger walking away. The chameleon technique is even more physically taxing than the torch eyes. But still, he waits another full minute to make sure he's safe before he jumps the twenty feet to the ground and lands without a sound.

That could have been a close call but, honestly, it made his adrenaline pump. Lukas looks up at Violet's bedroom window. She's earned herself another day to live, so there isn't much more to do with her.

Five

Day 2: Alive

I SCRUNCH UP MY NOSE. The greasy glob of ground beef covered in goopy tomato sauce that is posing as lasagna on my plate smells like hot garbage.

"V! I saved you a seat," Jessica shouts from the Squad's table at the center of the busy school cafeteria.

Today is Friday, which means it's game day. On game day, the cheerleaders and football players are required to eat together at the cafeteria to boost school spirit. I don't know how being forced to eat lunch in a foul-smelling, ill-lit, windowless room that resembles the mess hall in a prison movie promotes anything but antidepressant meds, but like always, I go along with whatever is expected of me.

My stomach growls. I am still spinning from last night's death match with Dr. Jenkins and that bitch Aiedeo. But no matter how distraught I am, I rarely ever skip a meal. Especially breakfast, which is my favorite. I look down at the mush on my tray and long for the PB and J that I reluctantly abandoned at home.

I deliberately avoided breakfast this morning, knowing that Dede was in the kitchen, lying in wait. I was way too shaken up to survive one of my nanny's interrogations.

"What the hell happened to you?"

I look up to see Meryl. I'm not sure what she's referring to exactly, but, like Dede, she also has a sharp radar for bull.

Meryl continues talking without waiting for me to answer. "I tried you like twenty times this morning because I lost my keys and needed you to get the spare set from my mom's." She takes a huge gulp from her McDonald's chocolate chip frappé (Meadowdale doesn't have a Starbucks). Juniors and seniors can leave campus for lunch, although they aren't allowed to bring back food from the outside. But there always seems to be a special set of rules for people like Meryl.

"My cell is dead. I forgot to charge it last night." Actually, I was too preoccupied with saving my life to even think about my phone, which is usually attached to me like an extra appendage. "Sorry I couldn't help you. But did you end up getting your keys?"

"Yeah, I sorted it all out. I was just worried when I couldn't reach you." Meryl leans in closer. "Is everything okay, V?"

I pat my hair, which is plastered with so much hairspray that it crunches like caramel popcorn when I touch it. Game day also means that we have to wear our cheerleading uniform to school—navy-blue skirt and crop top with red and white trim—plus face glitter, white sneakers, and an extra-high ponytail clipped back with a shiny bow. Since these are our new uniforms, Naomi warned us that we'd better rock them or else.

The threat is unnecessary in my case, since I'm keenly aware of the extra attention that game day brings from the entire student body and I certainly felt the pressure when I was getting ready this morning.

I don't remember sleeping but I must have nodded off for a bit. When I woke, I tried to apply a dash of my good old denial and write the whole Dr. Jenkins episode off as a nightmare. But the skull chain the Aiedeo left me lay underneath my bed like a sick souvenir from a trip that I never agreed to go on.

Even if I am a wreck, I know I can't show up on game day looking like it. I spent an extra half an hour fixing myself up so that I appeared as perky and fresh as I could, given the circumstances. I think I'm pulling it off but Meryl is always wise to my tricks. Most of them, anyway.

"Seriously, V, I was at Stumpy's till four a.m. so I know why I feel like a cat shat on me, then died in my mouth. But you were supposed to do some homework and go to bed early. Did you sleepwalk to an all-night kegger instead?"

Meryl leans against the wall, which further accentuates her long, lean body. She doesn't look like a cat did any of the things she claims. I'm pretty sure that the table of horny freshmen who are throwing all kinds of lusty stares in Meryl's direction probably would agree.

In Meadowdale, girls are supposed to be pageant-pretty, with big hair and lots of mascara. But Meryl, with her blond pixie cut and no makeup, bucks that notion like she does most of the good-girl expectations that are imposed on us. Of course, it helps that she has the sun-kissed natural gorgeousness of Blake Lively, which gives her the hot-girl pass. If she were less attractive, her rebellious behavior would land her in juvie. Instead, with her looks, that attitude just adds to her appeal.

"I didn't sleep much last night," I reply without elaborating further. I still need time to process that the Aiedeo are back in my life before I tell Meryl about it. And I don't want to talk about it here, with the entire student body around us.

Meryl's father is a bigtime DA and she prides herself on her cross-examination skills. I can tell that she definitely wants more answers.

"Okay, so you couldn't sleep and that's why you dumped at least a pound of makeup, hairspray, and glitter on yourself. Which I guess was a smart move, since these people do get easily distracted by shiny things." Meryl gestures toward the various long white tables packed with kids from all levels of the social pyramid. She stops at the Squad's table. "Especially them. They see only what you want them to see. But turning yourself into a Christmas ornament isn't going to fool me. What's up?"

"Samosa! Get over here. *Now.* We're taking group selfies." Naomi's annoyingly shrill voice carries over the blaring buzz of excited teenage chatter that fills the cafeteria.

"She still calls you Samosa? Why do you let her treat you like that?" Meryl turns in the direction of the Squad. "Suck my nuts, Naomi!"

Naomi scowls but that's all she does. She'd go ballistic if

anyone else spoke to her like that, but even she doesn't mess with Meryl.

Meryl lets out a frustrated sigh. "If I pinned you to the ground and sat on you, you'd still avoid my questions and find a way of going over there to those douchebags, wouldn't you."

"Duty calls." I punch my fist in the air. "Go, Pioneers!"

Meryl smirks. "You know that Naomi's, like, industrial-grade doucheiest of them all, right?"

"Totally aware."

"Okay, just want to make sure you haven't drunk too much of their Kool-Aid."

"Mer, something did go down last night but I just can't get into it here. Promise I'll fill you in later."

"You know I'm here. For anything."

"I know. Thanks."

"Well, glad you can handle Naomi because I definitely can't right now." Meryl rubs her forehead. "I think I'm gonna ditch the rest of the afternoon and sleep this one off somewhere."

"How very studious of you, Miss Miller."

The kid who collects the attendance sheets for the school office has a mad crush on Meryl, so he always covers for her when she ditches class.

"That's why it's junior college all the way for me, Miss Choudhury." Meryl squeezes my shoulder.

I smile back at her. Then I take a deep breath and prepare to face the Squad.

MHS has a strict dress code forbidding outfits that expose

the midsection. However, somehow Naomi was able to blatantly disobey that policy when she ordered the new cheerleading uniforms with crop tops that ended just a few inches below our chests. Like Meryl, rules don't apply to Naomi.

I take another deep breath and suck in my stomach as I position my lunch tray to partially hide my belly. Then I begin the descent into damnation.

It takes only about a minute to get from the lunch line to where everyone is sitting but it is the most excruciating minute of the school day. For those sixty seconds, it's like you're on display for every single kid to find all of your physical flaws. Guys don't ever sweat the Lunch Walk, but for us girls, it's a daily hell. Even hotties like Naomi don't escape unscathed.

I keep my head down so as to avoid eye contact as I weave through the maze of tables. Even if I don't see them, I can feel all their eyes on me. The new cheerleading uniform makes me especially vulnerable. I think I hear a few low whistles interrupted by a roar of laughter.

"Thunder thighs," a random girl calls out in a not-so-hushed voice. I ignore her and just keep on walking.

The moment I finally sit down, I'm locked into a group embrace as half a dozen cameras go off in my face.

"Pioneer Poms!" Collette shouts.

My stomach growls louder than a mama bear protecting her baby cub. I ignore Collette, stick my fork into the lasagna, and practically inhale it all in one bite. Jess is on the other side of me and I notice that both her and Collette are furiously refreshing *Heffers and Hos* over and over.

Heffers and Hos is Meadowdale's own *Gossip Girl* 3.0. It's an anonymous gossip site that posts photos and videos of MHS kids in all sorts of compromising positions. Every week, readers vote for a new Head Heffer and Honorary Ho, and those girls are relentlessly tormented until their successors are chosen.

I peek over at Jess's phone to see what's got her and Collette in such a frenzy. Collette gets excited about any kind of gossip, even if it's about people that she's never met, but Jess is usually way more blasé about such things.

"What's up?"

"Shhh, I don't want Naomi to hear," Jess hisses.

I look past her at Naomi, who is scolding the junior-varsity poms team two tables away. I can't hear what she's saying but I'm pretty sure at least two of the girls are crying.

"The princess seems occupied by the dressing-down that she's delivering to her unworthy subjects," I say in an exaggerated English accent. A string of gooey melted cheese runs down my chin and I try to catch it with my tongue. "Spill."

"OMG, Violet, maybe keep your mouth closed when you have a mound of barf in there," Collette admonishes. She leans in closer to me and Jess, then shields her lips in the most obvious way to let everyone know that she's blabbing about something she shouldn't be. "*H and H* supposedly has something scandalous on Naomi."

I heard some rumblings about Naomi gossip around third period but I've been too preoccupied with my own chaos to pay attention. "Like what?"

"Duh. We don't know yet. Could be a juicy tidbit or a dirty

pic." Collette practically squeals with delight. "That's what we're desperately trying to find out."

Jess reaches across me and pokes Collette. "Act cool, she's coming back over here."

I shrug and return to my lunch. Just as I'm about to shove another huge chunk of pasta in my mouth, Naomi snatches my plate away.

My half-empty belly fills with instant anger. "WTF?"

"Austin Coopman is staring straight at you," Naomi whispers.

"So?" I seethe as I grab for my plate unsuccessfully.

"You don't think I've forgotten, do you, V?"

I've been crushing on Austin ever since the fifth grade when he started going to my elementary school. It's a well-guarded secret that only Meryl and Naomi know. Although Naomi and I haven't discussed my infatuation with Austin for years, so it's surprising that the girl remembers or even cares. "Naomi, this isn't some Victorian novel where I'm afraid to let him see me eating. Give me back my lunch." I was pretty neutral about it before, but now I hope that whatever *H and H* has on Naomi, it's extra-salacious.

"He's walking right over here and if he's forced to witness you chowing down on this melted lard, he'll be totally turned off." Naomi looks down at my lasagna in disgust. "I've had real-life boyfriends, not just virtual ones, Violet. Trust me."

I am about to retaliate when suddenly I feel a firm hand press against my back. I turn around to see Austin smiling down at me. My stomach does a tiny flip at the sight of his lop-sided grin. We hooked up right before school started. Sort of.

"Gonna go all groupie on our resident rock star?" Jessica whispers loudly.

I'm not sure if Austin hears her but I feel my neck grow hot regardless.

"Hey, Violet, can we talk for a second?" Austin gestures to a corner far from the Squad. "In private?"

I nod and stand up. Austin grabs my hand and starts to lead me away.

"Cutie pie—"

I throw major stink-eye at Collette, which thankfully stops her from finishing her sentence. As I walk hand in hand with Austin, I can feel everyone looking at me. This time, it's a good thing.

Unlike the teen flicks that I devour, popularity is no longer exclusive to jocks and cheerleaders. At least, it isn't like that at Meadowdale High, and from what I see online, my school isn't an exception. There's still a ruthless high-school hierarchy that preys on the weak, but these days, with all the prodigies in music, sports, and anything else you can think of, teens have to do a lot more than letter in varsity to be "in." You can't merely be good at something; you have to be *exceptional* at it, like a YouTube sensation or a social media god.

Austin stays far away from the whole popularity scene, which only adds to his mystique. Although everyone thinks of him as a rocker, he's actually a classical guitarist. Playing Bach

61

and Beethoven on the acoustic guitar might not seem sexy, but practically everyone at school wants to be his number one fan. He's an exceptional kid who's already earned national recognition as one of the best young classical guitarists in the country, and his talent combined with his Jake Gyllenhaal looks make Austin the closest thing to a rock star that MHS has.

He stops when we're far enough to be out of earshot of most of the tables. I lean against the wall like Meryl did earlier, hoping it has somewhat of the same effect. Then I remember my crop top and cross my arms across my belly. Austin steps in closer to me, rests his hand in the spot next to my head, and looks at me with this hot intensity like he's Channing Tatum in *Magic Mike*.

I didn't know what to do after our hookup so I've been avoiding him. Honestly, I really don't understand how high-school hookups work. That's why my very random and quite awkward make-out sessions have taken place only when I'm far away in another country. This isn't because I'm fancy. It's just that there's this thin line at school between sexy and slut, and I still don't know where it begins and ends. Girls are supposed to dress, talk, and act like we want it, but if we're actually getting it, suddenly we're whores. Even worse is that it's not just the other students doing the name-calling. There's a vicious Parent Posse in this town that revels in gossiping about other people's children.

I haven't had enough local action to even register on the radar of the Meadowdale busybodies. Actually, I would have been fine playing celibate until I left for college, but when Austin started flirting with me at the back-to-school bash, I hit back hard. For all I knew, it was a once-in-a-lifetime opportunity.

We got to shirts off and belt buckles loosened when I kind of just panicked. I don't have a lot of experience with the mechanics of it all and I've never kicked it with someone I've been seriously crushing on. Austin is the first guy that I've really liked.

So I made up an excuse about my period (not my best lie but I had to think fast) and dashed out the door. I break into a rash just thinking about it. He's texted me a couple of times since but I kinda ghosted him.

But now, standing here with his face so close to mine that I can smell the cinnamon from the Big Red gum he's chewing, I wonder if maybe I didn't muck it up as bad as I thought.

"I was taking a walk around our hood," Austin begins. "I do that sometimes to clear my head when I get stuck with my music."

I continue to inhale his scent of cinnamon, Irish Spring, and Axe body spray. Ever since Austin's family bought a house in Fawn Ridge last year, Meryl and I have been strategizing ways for me to "bump into" him. Maybe that scheming is paying off. I hear a faint hunger moan from my belly and try to suppress it. Suddenly, nothing—even the Aiedeo—matters all that much.

"It was pretty late. I'd say about one a.m. I was going past your place."

I try to keep myself from jumping too far ahead but I can't

help it. Is he going to tell me that he realizes I'm his muse and he has to be with me? Okay, maybe I'm going a bit overboard. These days, a guy swiping right is about as big of a declaration that a girl can hope for. Although, I remind myself, Austin isn't like other boys. That's what makes him so hot.

Austin takes a deep breath. "And I saw someone sitting up way high in the elm tree outside of your bedroom and watching you through your window, Violet. I yelled at the guy—"

"Wh—" Nothing he's saying sounds like what I was expecting to hear. "What did you say?"

"Last night, V. I saw a guy watching you. He was sitting on a branch, perfectly balanced, but he wasn't holding on to anything. And this is gonna sound even crazier—I don't know what kind of high-tech infrared gear he was wearing, but his eyes were all lit up like a bat's. Before I could call the police, he just disappeared. I didn't see him climb down or anything—it was like he just vanished into thin air."

I'm jolted out of my daze. What Austin is telling me doesn't make any sense, but I cling to the words *last night*. Last night when I was fighting Dr. Jenkins and the Aiedeo. Someone saw it all. Someone else knows my secret.

"I dunno, it was so weird that maybe I don't know what I saw. Or maybe I thought it was a guy but really it was some kind of animal. I mean, it was pretty dark out."

I'm not hearing Austin anymore because my mind races with all the different possibilities. Each scenario makes the bad feeling in the pit of my stomach grow bigger and bigger. A wave of nausea rocks my body so hard that I feel woozy. There's almost nothing in my belly so I don't know what is coming up my throat, but it's moving so fast that I can't stop it from hurling out of my mouth and straight onto Austin.

Six

I ZIP UP MY HOODIE as a cool breeze rustles through the cornfield. A small crescent moon hangs low in the sky surrounded by a thousand twinkly stars. Everywhere I look, I see the tall, thin outlines of the corn stalks that are almost double my height and fifty rows deep.

My immediate vicinity is filled with high-school kids in different stages of inebriation. Apparently, almost all of them are trying to squeeze in the last possible minutes of fun before the one a.m. curfew.

I take a sip of beer out of my red plastic cup. I've been nursing it all night and now it tastes warm and bitter. Unfortunately, I don't have a curfew, which means I have no excuse to leave.

The first football game of the season is always celebrated with a cornfield kegger. A patch of corn is cut down and kegs are dragged in. Having a party in the middle of a cornfield provides protection from cops and the nosy Parent Posse, since it is almost impossible to see from the road. However, that also makes it nearly impossible to find.

The address (which is something un-GPS-compatible, like RR5 and Highway 28) and the directions (take a right at the gravel road past the Hendersons' farm, park your car near the ditch, walk twelve rows into the field, turn left @ the shed, et cetera) were posted on *Heffers and Hos* right after the football game.

I'm pretty sure that, with the debut of our new uniforms and our dismal halftime show, one of the cheerleaders will be the next Head Heffer. It might even be me.

Normally, thinking I may be singled out and ridiculed on *H and H* would make me go mental. But I'm already weighed down with so much shit—the Aiedeo, my mysterious stalker, vomiting on the love of my life—that I don't have space left in my crowded head to process anything else.

I raced out of the cafeteria too fast to see Austin's full reaction to my hurling on him. If there is anything positive about it, which there isn't, it's that at least I did it away from the other kids, especially the Squad.

"It's like Kurt's silent scream, you know?"

I'm so occupied with my own thoughts that I haven't even noticed the pudgy guy with a receding hairline and scruffy goatee standing next to me. Since these parties are usually only for high-schoolers, we need an "eternal senior" who is old enough to buy the kegs. There are a couple in the rotation but it seems that tonight, Fat Mike is the host.

"Cobain." Fat Mike gestures toward the portable Bluetooth player blaring out a depressing song that I don't recognize. "If you're into music, I'm a DJ. You should come by my place and hear me spin." Fat Mike tries to wrap his arm around my waist but I step out of the way before he can.

"Let's try to stay clear of the local child molester, shall we?" Meryl says as she leads me away. "I know you probably want to commit hara-kiri after what happened with Austin, but I hate seeing you like this, V."

I was so mortified that I had to text Meryl. However, I left out everything about the peeping Tom and the Aiedeo. That stuff is too scary for a text. We needed a face-to-face, but between school, the game, and now the kegger, I still hadn't gotten the chance to talk to Meryl alone.

"Guys! Come over here and do a keg stand!"

"In a minute, Lara!" Meryl replies.

I arch my eyebrow. Meryl dances on tables, rides electric bulls, and does pretty much everything else you'd see in a beer commercial. But I prefer watching from the sidelines.

"Guys, is your *Heffers and Hos* working?" Collette asks as she waves her cell around. "The Naomi pics were supposed to go up at midnight but I can't get any reception out here."

The whisperings earlier on in the day about *H and H* finding some scandalous shots of Naomi grew into a fury during the game. Now it seems that no one can stop talking about it.

Sexting is yet another fuzzy area for me in the sexy-versus-slutty rules. We've sat through assemblies with well-meaning counselors warning us of the repercussions of sexting since we were twelve years old. Most of the girls that I know don't send nudies casually. However, there are certain guys at school who routinely send dick pics like they're doing us a favor. No one says or does anything about that, yet it seems the minute a chick sends a nude selfie—which is usually intended for her boyfriend or a guy she likes—she ends up as that week's Honorary Ho on *H and H* or the photo is passed around in not-so-secret groups at school.

"Seriously?" Meryl takes a swig of SoCo from her flask. "I can't stand Naomi, but who cares about some photos of her in her birthday suit?"

Collette looks at Meryl like she's an alien. "Like, literally everyone cares."

Collette is right. There's always buzz surrounding any potential *H and H* post, but this time, there's a mad frenzy just because it's Naomi. There seem to be a lot of horny toads who want to see her naked. But the more malicious sentiment is that she's been up on her high horse for so long that everyone wants to watch her get knocked down. Although even for a conservative place like Meadowdale, a couple of nudies won't break Naomi's perfect image, although they do have the potential to dent it for a while.

"I heard it's not nude selfies," Jessica pipes up. "Apparently, *H and H* has something much juicier on our perfect princess."

I see the eyes of Collette and a bunch of other people who are within earshot of us light up. The claws really are out tonight.

"Like what?" Madison asks excitedly. No doubt she wants payback for what Naomi did to her yesterday at the funeral home. Her hazing is peanuts compared to what I had to go through with Dr. Jenkins, though. I get a quick taste of embalming fluid and blood in my mouth and it sends the beer in my belly swishing from side to side.

Jess shrugs. "I don't know. I just heard it's more than pics."

"Whatever it is, Naomi deserves it. She's so stuck up," Toby Wilson says as he joins our circle. "Always going to those frat parties at the college because she thinks she's too good to hang out with us high-schoolers."

All of us girls take a collective step back. Toby is a husky, hairy linebacker with clammy hands who we secretly refer to as "Sleazy Bear." This is because he always makes any excuse to give a girl a "friendly" hug so he can cop a feel of wherever his sweaty palms can reach.

"Well, I'm sure that Jim Talbert will be quick to fix it before it does any damage to Naomi's precious *Cornfed Cutie* image," Lara says snidely. "My mom works with him and she says he spends more time finding sponsorship deals for Naomi than managing his own funeral homes these days. She thinks he might even write Naomi's blog for her."

"Totally knew that," Collette says because she hates to be trumped when it comes to gossip. "Jim's like a total stage dad."

I've never heard that about Naomi's father but it doesn't surprise me. That man always has dollar signs in his eyes.

Collette's eyes gleam. "I saw Trent and Naomi arguing after the football game. And I was like, Why would he be pissed about some nudies leaking, since he's her boyfriend and she was probably sexting them to him, right? But if it's something worse and it wasn't with Trent, then—"

"Collette, everything you're saying right now is purely speculative." Meryl sighs. "We don't even know if *H and H* has something on Naomi. Or what that something may be. Or if the argument you claimed to witness between Naomi and Trent was even about any of that."

"Thanks, Judge Judy. But I'm not speculating or whatever law stuff you said. Naomi and Trent are both really good friends of mine and I just don't want to see either of them get hurt."

"Well, if you're so concerned about them, then maybe you should stop gossiping about them," I snap.

On any other night, I would relish spilling tea, especially if it concerned Naomi. But right now, I have a headache and little patience for idle high-school gossip when my problems are so much bigger.

I'm spooked out of my mind. The Aiedeo might chalk it up as another *shama,* but I could have been killed last night. And that guy in the tree probably witnessed the whole episode — who was he and what was he doing watching me in the first place?

I look around me. Standing in the middle of a gigantic field out here in the dark, surrounded by hundreds of corn rows where anything can be hiding, suddenly seems like a really stupid idea. I take another sip of my beer. Well, the alternative is to be hanging out in my bedroom by myself waiting for the Aiedeo or the peeper to come get me.

"Whatever, Violet!" Collette fumes. "I totally know about you and Austin making out at the back-to-school party at Jeb Purdum's house and I haven't said anything to anyone."

"Except that you totally blabbed to me about it," Jessica retorts.

I feel my body burn from head to toe. This is exactly why I avoid local hookups. It's impossible to keep anything on the down-low. If Collette knows about Austin and me, that means everyone knows. First, there's the whispers behind your back, then comes the trolling, and finally you're just scarlet-lettered until the next whore comes around. I'm not really sure just how much more I can take today.

"Chill, Violet. If *H and H* was gonna post something about your hookup with Austin, it would have done it by now." Collette checks her cell again. "Besides, this Naomi scandal is way bigger than you getting finger banged."

"WTF, Collette! Is that what you do for kicks? Go around secretly watching all of us?" I want to stuff her phone down her throat. "For all we know, you're the anonymous asshole behind *Heffers and Hos.*"

Collette smirks. "OMG, #FeistyGirl. Did I hit a nerve? So does that mean you *did* let Donnie Darko in your pants?"

Austin does have a kinda broody vibe going on but that doesn't make him Donnie Darko. I flip Collette off but secretly I love the reference and I'm surprised that a nitwit like her knows it.

"I'd totally do Donnie Darko." Jess winks at me. "Good going, V."

I'm trying to think of a comeback that will wipe the smug smile off Collette's face when a loud voice interrupts my thoughts.

"I seriously can't believe you dragged me here."

The words are slurred but the tone of superiority is instantly recognizable. We all turn to see Naomi emerge from the corn holding a near-empty bottle of strawberry Boone's.

"Nay-Nay, it's our senior year!" Tessa is a bit wobbly herself but not as wasted as Naomi. "This is the last time we're ever going to get the chance to go to a cornfield kegger."

"As if those two are ever going to leave this town. Tessa's gonna end up on the stripper pole at Chubby's after graduation and Naomi's bound for rehab before her senior year is even over." Jess bristles. She's obviously still pissed about her cheer demotion.

"What is Tessa wearing?" Collette whispers. "Does she think she's at a hoedown? Emphasis on *ho*."

I have to admit that Tessa does look like a second-rate rodeo hooker; she's dressed in a super-tight flannel crop top that she must have bought from the little girls' section at Farm and Fleet and a micromini jean skirt that does nothing for her hipless boyish body. Naomi, however, is rockin' a pair of vintage cowboy boots and short-shorts, although she's totally blotto. Together, they remind me of a washed-up country music duo.

Their backup band consists of the usual suspects: Trent Thorman, Naomi's long-term boyfriend and the football team's star quarterback (he's tall and chiseled, and with his farm-boy hotness, he could be the poster boy for a milk ad), and Trent's best friend, Nathan Hunter, who's a carbon copy of him down to the Hollister T-shirt and Levi's 501s. They're the type of guys that I bet a lot of cougars fantasize about.

Nate's way less wholesome than Trent and has a wild streak that's already gotten him two DUIs. While that would make most of us social lepers, Nate is the star pitcher of the baseball team. Both boys supposedly have the potential to go all the way to the pros and they're from revered farming families that have lived in Meadowdale for generations. Around here, that makes them celebrities.

The four of them form the exclusive inner circle of MHS, although Nate and Tessa aren't a couple. I vaguely remember a rumor about her giving him head in the locker room after Nate pitched a no-hitter that won us State last year. However, Nate's not the type to settle on just one girl when he has fangirls all over town. Like practically everywhere else in the world, here, boys don't have to worry about ruining their reputations for slutting around.

There's another guy with them tonight. His long, lanky frame reminds me of a scarecrow. Caleb Rainey comes from one of only two families in Meadowdale that could actually be considered rich beyond county lines. I think they own a string of manufacturing plants that make farm equipment. Caleb has mo' money than most of us so that's why he has automatic entry into the popular group, although I don't think anyone genuinely likes him. I get major mass-shooter vibes from him and avoid him as much as possible.

I wonder why he's here with those four, then I see him start to roll a joint and I get it. Nate's a massive pothead during off-season and Caleb definitely has the finances to buy him whatever he needs.

"Skanks!" Naomi shrieks as she starts stumbling toward us. "You all sucked so hard tonight."

"Does Little Miss Lush really think she can give us shit right now?" Jess hisses.

Tessa tries to grab Naomi's arm but Naomi yanks it away and continues zigzagging in our direction. It's been a while since I drank with Naomi but I remembered her being more fun.

I watch Naomi get closer, somewhat amused at her crooked walk because it's rare to see her so not in control. Although I'd heard that she'd become a sloppy drunk lately.

"Violet," someone says and I turn around. My stomach plunges. Austin is standing in front of me. What is this, my very own version of *Children of the Corn*? I have the Aiedeo and a stalker after me but Austin is still the last person I want to see. I can feel my pits filling with flop sweat.

"*Freeze!*"

I quickly turn away from Austin to see five police officers standing in the middle of the party, next to the kegs. For a few seconds, no one dares to move, then someone shouts, "Run!" and pandemonium breaks out, with drunken teens rushing in every direction.

Toby plows past us, knocking kids down like he's back on the football field. I'm paralyzed from all the commotion.

"Move!" Meryl commands as she tugs on my arm. "Your dad will kill you if you get arrested."

That's all it takes to jolt me into action. We race straight into the rows of corn. Every horror-movie instinct warns me that this isn't a smart decision. However, the worst part about a cornfield kegger is that it doesn't provide much of an exit plan.

I've spent practically my entire life around cornfields but that doesn't mean I know my way around them. The starry sky seems to have disappeared and we're trying to cut a path through the towering rows of cornstalks in utter blackness. I hold out my cell but it barely lights the hard ground beneath me.

The music from the party fades into the loud crunching noise of the cornstalks cracking under my sneakers. I can hear heavy footsteps coming fast behind me but I'm too afraid to check if they belong to kids or cops. My heart pounds in my chest.

Meadowdale is such a small town that any kind of underage-drinking bust shows up as front-page news in the *Lamoine Herald*, the local newspaper. That kind of embarrassing publicity buries kids and their families here. Even though my dad spends most of his time outside of Meadowdale, his prestigious university foundation makes him a prominent member of this community. I push myself to run faster. Bringing any kind of shame onto Naresh is grounds for boarding school or worse.

The scraggy corn stalks and the wild, spiky assortment of morning glory, water hemp, and a dozen other types of weeds that grow out here scratch up my bare legs. I really wish that I'd worn jeans instead of shorts to the party. My calves prickle like a hundred ants are crawling all over them but I try to ignore it and keep on running.

After what feels like thirty minutes but is probably only half that time, I stop. "I can't." I hunch over and gasp for air. "I'm totally lost and my legs are like jelly." We had hitched a ride to the party in the bed of some kid's pickup, but even if I had the faintest inkling of where his truck was parked, it was probably long gone. In the mass hysteria to flee the cops, neither Meryl nor I had really thought through our plan, but now we have no choice but to try to find our way out of this cornfield and home.

"We gotta keep going until we see a dirt road or a barn or something that will help show us the way back to town," Meryl whispers.

She turns around to face me but she doesn't say anything; instead, her eyes grow so big they practically take over her entire face.

"What?" I ask shakily as I also turn around. The glare of a flashlight blinds me.

"You can stop running, ladies. We've got you!" a police officer shouts as he walks toward us.

My pulse races as he comes closer.

"Run, V! My dad will get me out of this but Naresh will go totally apeshit if you're busted!"

I'm frozen, not sure what to do.

"Go!" Meryl shouts in my face.

The cop is so close that I can see the light reflecting off his badge. Just then, I feel a massive shove and realize that I'm flying through the air. Then, just as suddenly, I crash to the ground.

I lie there, too dazed to move, and see a figure standing over me with eyes lit up like a bat's. "Wh-wha—" I start, but before I can get anything else out, he's gone.

I stumble out of the cornfield and fall to my knees. The grit from the gravel road sticks to my skin. I've been walking in that endless corn maze for what seems like the entire night, but my phone battery died a while back so I can't be sure how long I was trapped in there. It's still dark and the stars are still out, so I figure it must have been only a few hours. Although it felt like an eternity.

My throat is parched and my skin is scratched and bitten. A gross taste of salt and metal mixes in my mouth from the blood, sweat, and tears I shed in my struggle to get out.

I look around. I have no idea where the hell in the boonies I've ended up. My house could be in any direction from here. Without my GPS, I don't even know which way is north. Although I prefer the open road to that claustrophobic corn hell, I make it a general rule to stay clear of the sticks in the middle of the night. Given all the rumors about KKK gatherings and Satanist cults that meet in Meadowdale's backcountry, this is definitely not a safe place for a brown girl.

I let out a frustrated cry. Being lynched or sacrificed are certainly things to avoid, but strangely, racists and devil worshipers aren't nearly as real right now as the monster with the bat eyes. The entire time that I was running in circles through the cornfield, my mind was running in its own circles with the same thought: *Is he in here or out there?* My sheer physical exhaustion only adds to my fear.

Meryl would have known what to do. I wonder if she saw

Bat Eyes push me out of the way. If not, how am I supposed to explain that to her when it makes no sense to me?

Suddenly, I see a pair of headlights flash up ahead. I drop to the ground as fast as my broken body lets me. I'm sure it's Bat Eyes coming to finish the job. I feel around, searching for a weapon. All I can find is a rock that's no bigger than my palm.

"Violet!"

I look up in confusion to see Dede stepping out of my father's SUV. She walks over to me.

"How? How did you . . ." I'm too frazzled to speak.

Dede helps me to my feet. "I put tracker in your phone when you come home before party to change clothes. I know there trouble tonight. But I lose you when battery die. So I wait for you."

Having my own version of Alfred from *Batman* following me around is usually a pain in my ass. I was furious the first time I discovered she'd tracked me. Now, though, I'm grateful.

As I crawl into the front seat, my fatigue and fear give way to relief. I'm sure that Bat Eyes is out there somewhere waiting for me. But right now, I convince myself that I am safe. My aching muscles start to relax and my heavy eyelids fall.

"Thank you," I mumble as I drift off to sleep.

Seven

Day 3: Alive

MERYL AND I sit in the bed of Old Blue, her pimped-out 1954 Ford pickup truck, sipping our McDonald's frappés. We're outside of MHS, but since Meryl somehow snagged a teacher's parking pass as soon as she was old enough to drive, we're in the admin lot. It's a little past eight a.m. and there's no one around but the two of us. It's kind of pretty here, with the sun shining down on the playing field and the cornfields that surround our school. After last night, I would be fine with never seeing another cornfield again, but that's virtually impossible when you live in Meadowdale.

"Oh my God," Meryl whispers. She takes a long sip of her drink. "The mofo Aiedeo want you back."

Chills run down my arm. I've just gotten Meryl caught up on everything that's been going on with me and it's definitely a lot for both of us to process.

"And you think that Bat Monster . . . Bat Guy—"

"I call him Bat Eyes."

Meryl nods. "Right, Bat Eyes. Do you think he has anything to do with the Aiedeo?"

"I'm confused AF about all this." I shrug. "But it can't be a coincidence that he showed up around the same time that the Aiedeo started up again."

A crisp morning breeze hits us. I'm wearing my workout T-shirt and shorts because Naomi called a surprise mandatory practice for nine a.m. Meryl pulls her soccer socks all the way up. MHS has no official soccer program, so the girls on the intramural soccer team pretty much have to do everything themselves and pay for it out of their own pockets. That means they spend a lot of time fundraising but Meryl isn't about selling candy bars or washing cars—most of her Stumpy's hustling money goes to the team. In fact, she bought their uniforms after a particularly lucrative Greek Week last year.

"I know you've always told me how shady the Aiedeo are. And I remember when you broke your legs." Meryl chews on her lip in that way she does when she doesn't want to say something because she knows she's going to piss me off.

I raise an eyebrow. "But?"

"It's a war, Violet!" Meryl says loudly. "I mean, I'm talking full-on world-destruction shit here," she says in a lower voice. "How can you *not* do anything?"

"What the hell am I supposed to do? I don't even have powers anymore!"

"But you do. You said that one Aiedeo chick who came to

your room told you that the Aiedeo never took your powers away."

"Oh, right. When she spouted that cheesy Hallmark channel bullshit about *believing* in my powers. Fine, I believe. Let's see if I can make my straw fly away." I focus on my drink straw and try to concentrate but I get frustrated after a couple of seconds. "You think I can help win a war when I can't even move a dinky straw?"

"Obviously you're out of practice. But the believing stuff might not be total bullshit." Meryl starts to chew on her lip again. "I mean, it's just that you live in this bubble where you shut out anything you don't want to deal with."

"Ha! *I* live in a bubble? That's rich, considering you just got busted by the cops at the cornfield kegger but *nothing* happened to you because your dad made it all go away. Just like he always makes it go away."

"Yeah, I know that I'm privileged AF. I'm not denying that. But isn't being an Assamese warrior queen with a shit-ton of awesome-ass powers pretty privileged too?"

"Except that my privilege comes with an almost guarantee of me being killed!"

Meryl drops her shoulders and speaks quietly. "V, what scares you more, the Aiedeo or yourself?"

"WTF, Dr. Phil."

"Do you remember what you were like when you were an Aiedeo? Even if no one else knew about it, I did, and I could *see* it in you. I mean, you didn't do any tricks, not even when I begged you to get AJ Rockman back for tripping me and breaking my arm in gym class. But there was this *confidence* in you, this inner badass bitch, because it was like you knew you were the shit."

I run my finger over the truck's metallic blue paint. I don't remember anything about what Meryl is saying. That's the thing with denial—it forces you to forget the good stuff too.

Meryl continues. "I totally get why you ditched the Aiedeo. I mean, I really do. They hurt you. I could see how furious you were with them when you were in the hospital but I also saw how it broke your heart. Especially because you never got to see your mom again. But you changed after that—"

"Yeah, I stopped being a freak!"

"No, V!" Meryl shakes her head. "You lost your confidence and you just became so afraid to go against the herd in any way. You know, to be a little different."

"Screw you, Mer!" My jaw tenses. "Look around this lily-ass town. I don't have to *be* different because I *am* different. Brown girl with the dead mom."

"I get—"

"No, you don't, damn it! In your little privileged world where you reign supreme, you choose to do your own thing, to go against the grain. You *choose* to be different." I look Meryl straight in the eye. "I don't get a choice."

"But who the hell cares what a bunch of ignorant, racist bastards in Meadowdale, Illinois, think?"

"I do! I know that sounds totally wack but I want to belong

here. Because this is all I have." I look away and blink back a tear. "I can't handle being a freak. Hell, this town can't handle my freak."

"And you think being an Aiedeo makes you a freak." Meryl laces her fingers through mine. "But all of it's on the DL, right? No one would ever have to know about you being an Aiedeo. I mean, isn't having a secret identity pretty standard superhero stuff?"

"Hmph. Maybe in make-believe. But in reality, it's too big of a risk to take. I came so close to being discovered after that speeding-car *shama*. And that was three years ago, when we were still in junior high! High school is even worse, with everyone trying to throw any shade they can on someone. God, can you imagine what *Heffers and Hos* would do if they heard I got visits from my dead relatives?"

"Got it," Meryl mumbles.

"You asked me what I'm scared of, Mer. I'm scared of all of it. The Aiedeo, Bat Eyes. I just want to survive this nightmare and go back to my normal life again." A couple tears roll down my cheeks. "Before I lose everything."

Meryl wraps her arms around me as tight as she can. "I got your back, V, and I'm sorry I'm such a privileged white bitch."

I laugh. "That's not what I said."

"It's pretty much exactly what you said." Meryl smirks as she hands me a tissue. "First things first: I'm not leaving you alone. At night, I mean. That's when it seems the Aiedeo and Bat Eyes show up. I'm sleeping over from now on."

"Okay, but how are you going to do that?" I wipe my eyes. "Didn't your dad ground you for getting busted last night?"

Meryl winks. "Please, V, you've got your powers and I've got mine. You know that I've perfected the art of sneaking out. Though it's hardly a skill these days when both my parents are too caught up in saving their second and third marriages to notice where I spend my nights."

We both stand up and jump out of the truck.

"Looks like my ride is here." Meryl chuckles as she points to a dilapidated school bus.

Clearly fundraising hasn't been so lucrative this year if that broken-down hunk of metal is supposed to take the soccer team to their away game in Peoria.

Meryl gives me a quick hug. "I'll come by after eight!"

I chuck my plastic cup in the recycling bin. It isn't fair of me to drag Meryl into all of this (although she's hardly the type to stand by and watch), but I'm relieved not to be entirely alone.

I feel my core start to tremble, followed by the muscles in my thighs and butt. My back arches against the weight of the two girls that I'm lifting up. I fight to hold on, but within seconds, the entire pyramid gives way and we all topple onto the thick blue gymnastics mat.

"Jesus!" Naomi shrieks as she lands on her ass with a loud smack. "How many times can you idiots keep messing this up?"

She stares at Becca, Lara, and me because we're the main

bases for the pyramid, but her rage seems to be directed at everyone, even the volleyball team practicing on the other side of the gym.

"What do you expect when you call a surprise mandatory practice at nine a.m. on a Saturday?" Lara whines. "We've been here for over two and a half hours and we're exhausted."

"And you know we were all out at the cornfield kegger last night and didn't get home until late." Jessica scowls. "This is crazy."

Jessica, Collette, and some of the other girls are covered in scratches, bruises, and chigger bites just like me and we are moving slower than the old people at Oak Grove Nursing Home. Seems like each of us experienced her own version of cornfield hell last night. Rumor is that a dozen tenth-graders and Fat Mike were arrested.

I take a deep breath. My body feels like it's been run over by a tractor, and my mind is even more of a mess. I'm only here because Dede went off with Mrs. Patel this morning and I didn't want to be home by myself.

Naomi stands with arms akimbo and sneers down at us. "You clumsy dicks sucked balls yesterday and now you're gonna pay for it. I don't care how much you're hurting."

"You were, like, totally smashed." Collette eyes Naomi. "How did you manage to escape the po-po?"

"Because I'm a Talbert. The cops don't mess with me," Naomi explains as if this is a basic truth.

In a way, I guess it is.

"Maybe you're not as invincible as you think." Jess grins.

"What does that mean?" Naomi asks.

"Just that when you're at the very top, the only way to go is down." Jess points her index finger at the ground.

"Is that from a fortune cookie?"

"Although I hear that you do like to go down."

"What did you just say?" Naomi barks as she steps in Jessica's face.

"Shut up," Collette whispers as she nudges Jess.

I roll my eyes. The sun had just risen when I saw that Collette had already looped me into a group-message thread all about Naomi-gate, which has apparently become a full-on obsession with most of the student body or at least the upperclassmen. With all the whispering, texting, and general hype, I'm amazed that Naomi doesn't have any clue about what's going on. Although *H and H* has yet to post anything.

I really don't care about any of it because all I can think about is Bat Eyes. I keep looking over my shoulder for him or the Aiedeo. I just put it together that he's gotta be the same guy that Austin saw spying on me in my room with what he thought were infrared glasses. Crazy chills run up and down my back.

Jess ignores Collette and glares at Naomi. "You need to step the hell back."

"Bring it, bitch," Naomi yells.

"Guys, let's take a ten-minute break and cool off," Tessa suggests. Her eyes are bloodshot and she looks scruffier than usual.

I grab my water bottle and pop a squat on the floor. Even if

I'm only here to be Naomi's punching bag, I find it comforting to hang out in the school gym.

Our gymnasium is pretty much standard-issue: basketball court, aluminum bleachers, and lots of team signage hanging everywhere. A picture of our mascot, a ruddy-faced, scowling man sporting a coonskin cap and a lumberjack beard, is painted directly on the center of the high-gloss wooden floor. His name is Boone Crockett, and these days he looks like he would blend in perfectly with the hipsters who hang out at the vegetarian café/hookah lounge near the university.

I inhale the permanent smell of sweat, leather, and shattered athletic dreams that never seems to go away despite the heavy industrial cleaners the janitors use. For decades, high-school legends were born and buried here.

Like the cafeteria, the gym is showing its age. The red, white, and blue paint is chipping off the walls, and the bleachers are wobbly. MHS doesn't have an arena or a fancy ballroom like some of the rich high schools near Chicago. This means that practically every important event, from basketball games to pep rallies to student assemblies to school dances, takes place right here. I know that I'm supposed to hate all of those things, but, honestly, there's also some good memories squished between all the terrible ones.

The gym doors burst open and a flood of varsity basketball players strut in for their preseason practice. This is their house and they always make sure to let us know it.

"Ladies! Glad you can join us," Chad Schwartz, a junior who

usually sits on the bench, calls out. "But if you really want to break a sweat, why don't you meet me out at my car in about an hour?"

In case his comment is too subtle for us to understand, Chad points to his crotch. It's no surprise that he's one of the avid dick-pic senders, and his Instagram is filled with shots of him groping unsuspecting freshman girls.

"Chad may need privacy but I don't have anything to hide. Right here is fine with me!" a gangly boy with an upsetting amount of body hair hollers as he grinds his hips back and forth.

Naomi ignores them and keeps her focus on us. "Get up. We're not leaving here until we hit that pyramid at least five times in a row—"

She's interrupted by a cacophony of bells, moos, ribbits, and meow ringtones. Like Pavlov's dogs, all the kids, including me, check their cell phones immediately. Without even thinking about it, I click on the Ho Alert from *H and H*. After a few seconds, there's a collective gasp that echoes throughout the gym. Our shocked silence is shattered by Chad.

"Holy shit! Is this real?"

"Now showing, #PrincessPorn."

"OMG! It's not pics—it's a full-on sex tape. And she's, like, doing *two* guys!" Collette announces as though we aren't all watching the exact same video of Naomi. "And neither of them looks like Trent."

I try to make out what I'm actually seeing. It's hard to

determine if either male is Naomi's boyfriend since I can't see the boys' faces; all I can see is everything from their necks down. *Everything.*

But Naomi's entire face as well as her naked body are on full display.

"Wh-what is this?" Naomi whispers as she holds out her cell phone with trembling hands. "Who did this?"

Does Naomi know that they've been building up to this? Not just in the past two days with their giddy texts and excited whispers but ever since she took the crown. For her, this ridicule might feel like it's come out of nowhere, but they've been waiting, and now they are more than ready to hurt her like she's hurt them for so many years.

"Naomi *is* always bragging that she's the master of multitasking!"

"Five-star review for your first porn, Naomi. When's the sequel? Let's say my place at eight?"

Roars of laughter pour out from every direction. I look at the others and then I turn to Naomi. I don't think she's ever been the target of such public scorn.

I stare at the clip of Naomi, which is playing on a constant loop. This goes way beyond a nudie. This is an actual video. A video of Naomi having sex is already too much for most of Meadowdale's upstanding citizens. But a video of Naomi having sex with *two* guys is going to cause an uproar from more than just the ferocious Parent Posse.

Whoever posted this isn't trying to merely knock Naomi down a few pegs. This is total destruction.

A rapid succession of abuse shoots out like bullets directly at Naomi. I hear Chad's voice the loudest, then the chorus of insults from everyone in the gym quickly merges into just one word: *slut*. They start chanting it over and over. Each time they say it, I can feel their hatred reverberate throughout the gymnasium. My ears fill with the sound. *Slut, slut, slut . . .*

Naomi is standing there, silent and shaking. Does she see the pleasure in their faces? The gleam in their eyes?

They enjoy doing this because it gives them power.

Don't ever forget this, Naomi: They like shaming you. They like making you feel like nothing. They like ripping you to pieces, just like you did when you did it to them.

I stand here with the same nauseated feeling I had when Naomi was hazing Madison at the funeral home the other day except now it's ten times worse. I know what they're doing to Naomi isn't right, but I remind myself that I'm just an extra in all this, a background player; it's not my duty to do anything. Plus I'm not entirely sure I would want to stop it because there's this part of me, a bigger part than I care to admit, that's enjoying it. I scan the faces around me and I think everyone is. Maybe Naomi doesn't deserve to be bitched out for a sex tape, but she certainly deserves it for all the other terrible crap she's pulled on everyone for so long. It feels kinda like just retribution to see her finally get some of her own hate thrown back at her.

The stunned, bewildered expression on Naomi's face is blurred by the stream of tears rolling down her cheeks. *Don't give them the satisfaction of seeing you like this,* I want to shout to her. But I say nothing. Instead, I watch as Naomi crumples to the ground and breaks down in sobs.

"I mean, can you believe that Princess Naomi has a sex tape?" Collette asks for what must be like the dozenth time tonight.

"Naomi's video is blowing up." Jess seethes as she checks the number of views on *H and H* again. "I bet that bitch is gonna score her own reality show from this."

I'm exhausted from my sleepless night and our grueling morning practice but Meryl insisted I go with her to Cool Beans, the local coffee shop. It's a pretty popular place on Saturdays, so unfortunately, Collette is here, along with half of our school. Naomi is conspicuously missing, although you could say she's here in spirit since it seems all anyone can talk about is her and the video.

"Trent and Tessa are supposedly at Naomi's consoling her. So that probably means he's not mad at her, which also probably means he's one of the guys in the tape, right? But who's the other guy? Are Trent and Naomi into doing that stuff? You know, group-sex stuff?" Collette scrunches her nose as if the milk in her latte has turned sour. "Does that make them swingers?"

"Swingers? Who seriously even uses that word? Did your mom teach you that, Collette?"

"Of course not, Meryl. We're Lutheran."

Meryl is about to counter but pauses when someone starts speaking into the mic. I turn toward the stage and see Austin sitting on a stool with his guitar. I can feel my whole face getting warm and a smile growing from ear to ear.

"A couple of the girls from soccer mentioned that Austin was playing tonight and I thought this might help get your mind off of things," Meryl says.

I start to lean back in my chair and then suddenly remember that it was only yesterday when I puked on him. "I gotta go before Austin sees me!"

"Too late. I think he's already spotted you." Meryl winks. "Just be cool and don't throw up on him. Again."

My heart seriously skips ten beats. Austin is talking to the audience but he's looking directly at me.

"Glad to see you made it here tonight." He smiles. "I'm trying something new out and I hope you like it."

Austin starts strumming his guitar, then goes into a stripped-down, acoustic version of Twenty One Pilots' "Stressed Out." I had no idea that Austin was into music post-1900s and am completely floored. Not to mention totally turned on. Judging by the serious DTF eyes that almost every girl, guy, and dog seems to be giving him, I'm not the only one. Still, every time he looks my way, I can't help but feel like he's singing only to me, although I know this sounds like something a psycho fan who ends up stabbing her favorite celebrity says. Meryl is right. Being here and listening to Austin helps drown out the noise from the Aiedeo and Bat Eyes. I close my eyes and drift away to his sexy voice.

"Violet!" I hear before feeling a pain in my side that's so sharp, I jump in my seat.

"What the—"

"You fell asleep," Meryl hisses. "I tried to wake you up but you kept nodding off. Austin finished his show and he's walking over here. Like, right now."

"And you were drooling like my grandpa when he passes out on the couch after a big lunch." Collette grimaces. "At least you didn't make a big fart storm like he does. Or did you?"

I wipe the drool away with my hand and ignore the rest of what Collette says.

"Take these," Meryl says as she sticks some mints in my mouth. "You have morning breath."

"OMG! That was sooooo amazing!" Collette gushes as she throws her arms around Austin. "You're like Ed Sheeran and Shawn Mendes wrapped into one!"

Jess and Meryl join in on giving him props. He hugs each of them while I ferociously chew my mints so that my breath won't smell like garbage by the time he gets to me.

"I loved your version of 'Stressed Out,'" I mumble as Austin pulls me in. There's no need to mention that was the only song I'd heard.

"And at least you snored to the beat for the rest of the show," Austin says in my ear.

I notice he's still holding me and I look up to see him laughing. Even though I can feel my face turn tomato red, I'm totally relieved that he's made a joke about it and I laugh along with him.

"Guess that means I'll have to give you a private concert. I think I know some ways to keep you awake."

Although I'm about to swoon like a character in a Jane Austen novel, I'm trying to find a response that's flirty and sexy but doesn't make me sound too desperate or too easy. But I don't get to say anything because the sound of glass shattering makes us all stop and turn around.

It looks like Nate Hunter, Naomi and Trent's friend, just threw a cup at Caleb Rainey.

"It was a setup, you prick!" Nate shouts, then shoves Caleb hard. Cool Beans is strictly a coffee shop but given the way Nate is swaying and slurring, he's on something much stronger than caffeine.

Caleb falls backwards. Although Caleb has a few inches on Nate, Nate has pure farm-boy strength. He jumps on Caleb and starts pounding him.

In a flash, Austin has left me and is trying to pull Nate off Caleb. I remember Austin and Nate being tight in junior high but I thought they'd drifted apart in the past couple of years. "Nate! Stop it, man! He's not worth the trouble."

Obviously, Austin feels the same way about Caleb that most of us do. It takes a couple more people to step in but eventually they're able to wrench Nate away.

"Nate's usually so fun when he's partying," Jess says in a hushed voice. "When did he become such a buzzkill?"

Collette lifts her peach-fuzz eyebrows. "I wonder what that's all about."

I shrug. It doesn't matter what the fight was about because

Collette will make up her own reasons for it. And I am way too exhausted to hear them.

"Let's go?" I ask Meryl.

Austin is busy trying to calm down Nate and it doesn't really seem like the time for flirtatious banter. Nevertheless, I'm still giddy as a schoolgirl from the way he was all into me before.

"Austin totally wants you to strum his guitar," Meryl teases as we walk out of the café and toward Old Blue. "He was so feeling you even though you fell asleep at his show!"

"I know—"

I freeze as chills run down my spine. Standing in front of Meryl's truck is a guy who's eerily familiar. I stare at his buzzed blond hair and chiseled jawline until it suddenly clicks. It's the creepy intern from the Talbert Funeral Home.

"It's the guy—the creepy intern—who works at Talbert's," I whisper.

"Who?" Meryl whips her head around. "Where is he?"

"Right there," I say. I point straight ahead but he's gone. "I swear he was standing right in front of Old Blue just now."

Meryl's brow furrows. "Okay. Maybe he was just walking by or something 'cause he's not here now." Meryl gets in the truck and reaches over to unlock my door.

"Yeah, maybe he wasn't actually standing there," I say, more to myself than her.

"You haven't told me much about him."

I half shrug. I haven't really mentioned him because with everything else that's going on, telling Meryl about a random guy who gave me the creeps seems pretty insignificant.

"I don't want to talk about the creepy intern right now." I crank up the music as we head onto Highway 51, Meadowdale's main strip. "Let's stop at the store and load up on Ben and Jerry's, then spend the rest of the night planning my next hookup with Austin."

Eight

Day 4: Alive

I SAY GOODBYE TO MY DAD and click off Skype. A crappy phone call with Naresh seems the perfect ending for a terrible week. I've barely been in school a month and he's already harping on me about midterm exams. I realize the whole strict-Indian-father-with-unrelenting-expectations-for-his-daughter is a tired cliché, but Naresh is a total Tiger Dad, straight down to the eight years of piano lessons he forced me to take.

I go to the fridge and grab a package of shrimp, a lemon, and a bushy sprig of cilantro that's straight from Dede's garden. Cooking helps me relax. It's Sunday and so far there's been no sign of the Aiedeo or Bat Eyes.

But I am still riding the wave from seeing Austin yesterday. Plus, having Meryl stay over helped me get a decent night of sleep. Even though she snores louder than a drunken bear, I'm happy that she's coming over again later tonight.

I pick up a shrimp and start to peel the shell off. I'm going to make a lemon shrimp risotto for dinner. It's funny that when

I tell people that cooking is my hobby, many of them assume I only make curries.

My phone rings and I reach over the counter for it. It's Naomi. I tense for a second, then press the red button. She's called me three times since the bitch-out in the gym and I haven't answered once.

On top of all the effed-up stuff going on with me, I bet Naomi is getting ready to wage a war. Which in some ways might turn out to be deadlier for me than the Aiedeo or Bat Eyes. I don't know what her game plan is but I'm pretty sure that right now, she's looking for allies.

I haven't been keeping up with it all but from what I've seen on the threads and social media, it's brutal. Things have really exploded into a total Naomi hate-fest. Like I predicted, it went beyond the high school, but I hadn't realized that even people who didn't live in Meadowdale would start trolling her. This is probably on account of *H and H* linking the sex video with Naomi's blog. Collette texted this afternoon to say that the tape has gone viral.

I pick up my phone and scroll through the comments on Naomi's Instagram, Twitter, Facebook, and blog. They read like the graffiti in the bathroom stalls at school except these particular messages are for Naomi alone. The comments range from typical insults (*slut, ho, whore, bitch*) to calls to action (*shut your twat; die, bitch; watch out, slut*) to creepy (*daddy's little slut; like mother, like daughter*). And there are some lifted straight out of Urban Dictionary that are just too vile to say.

I gather the shrimp shells and throw them in the garbage disposal. A wave of guilt washes over me. I know I'm heart-less for not answering her calls, but, seriously, what loyalty do I owe Naomi? There was a time that we were really close but it was ages ago. I admit that I don't hate her as much as a lot of other people apparently do, but that doesn't mean I want to ally myself with her. No one's copped to posting the video on *H and H* yet, but when Naomi finds out who it is, it's gonna be a total takedown.

I don't want to be around when that happens. I'm barely surviving high school as it is. A frightening thought comes to my mind and I stop chopping onions for a second: *What are the consequences if I'm not on Naomi's side?*

I pour some olive oil in a hot pan, then add a handful of chopped garlic. The toasty aroma wafts into the air and I inhale it.

Naomi's carefully curated social media image—or, more accurately, the image that Jim Talbert curated for her—makes her seem like the cool best friend who everyone wants to hang with. But now that she's got a sex tape, she's public enemy number one. *Slut, ho, whore, bitch.* A second wave of guilt washes over me. No one deserves that kind of cruelty. Not even Naomi.

My WhatsApp beeps to indicate that I've got a new message. I grab my phone while I stir fish stock into the rice. Speaking of the devil, it's a text from Naomi. I click to open it. At first, I think that she meant to send it to someone else, except that she used my name. I read it again and drop my stirring spoon into the pan.

I know it was you, Violet. And I'm going to kill you.

The air in my bedroom turns hot and suffocating; it's like an overheated sauna. I kick off my comforter and try to breathe. I'm annoyed that for some reason Dede turned on the heat in the middle of a summer night, but I'm too tired to get out of bed and shut it off.

A cloyingly sweet smell like rotting bananas fills my nostrils, and a hot chill runs down my body. I creep through the sludge of exhaustion until my mind starts to wake up. I hear a low, dry hiss up above me that sounds like a feral cat about to attack. Slowly, I realize I am not alone. My pulse races.

I didn't hear Meryl come in so I don't think it can be her. Has Bat Eyes come back for me? Is the Aiedeo here with another trap? I desperately want to keep my eyes shut but they fly open against my wishes. At first, I don't know what I am seeing. I blink hard.

Bright beams of moonlight shine through my windows, illuminating the silhouette of a girl. She's suspended from the ceiling *Mission: Impossible*–style except there are no ropes or wires attached to her. The girl hangs in midair like a stringless marionette. Wild, unkempt locks fall over her face and she wears nothing but a white sheet around her emaciated torso. Her bones protrude through her thin, papery skin.

The Aiedeo are certainly a diverse bunch, but I have never seen one that looks so *dead*. I am trembling so hard that my fingers are actually vibrating as I reach under my bed for the skull chain. When I find it, I try to lift the chain above my head. It's way too heavy.

I get out of bed and stand with my feet apart. Then I lift the skull chain with both hands and start to swing it around. My body eases into a rhythm. I remember when the Aiedeo taught me how to use a similar weapon back in the day.

To my uneasy surprise, the girl doesn't move, which isn't very Aiedeo of her. Those chicks always liked a good fight. Finally the girl lifts her head.

I stop midswing and stand on my tiptoes to get a better look. Nothing about her is recognizable, yet now there is no denying who it is. The skull chain drops to the ground as my body goes limp and I fall onto the bed.

My heart, which is now lodged in my throat, stops beating. I force myself to speak. "N-Naomi . . ." A hundred questions race through my head, none of which I actually want the answers to.

Naomi doesn't respond; she just widens her dry, cracked lips into a bizarre grin. I cower at the very edge of my bed. *What is this?*

I pinch myself until it hurts. Okay, I am awake. I scramble through explanations until I land on the most plausible: Naomi is playing a sick joke on me as retaliation for the bitch-out. "Naomi, I kept my mouth shut. It was Collette, Jessica, and the rest of them. Go get your payback with them."

Again, there is nothing but silence. My fear is quickly turning into annoyance. What am I doing speaking to this prop like it's actually Naomi? I can imagine her and Tessa recording this entire prank; tomorrow there'll be a YouTube video of me almost pissing my pants over a doll hanging from my ceiling. Maybe that's Naomi's revenge plan—to humiliate all of us.

"Okay, it's time to go. Fun's over, bitch." I jump up again but this time I whack at the life-size dummy as though it's a piñata.

Suddenly, there is a loud snapping sound like bones breaking. I freeze as Naomi pops each of her shoulders out of its socket and extends her arms like Gumby. She pushes me back down on my bed so hard that I bite my tongue. The sting radiates through to the back of my mouth.

Before I can move, Naomi drops down from the ceiling so that now she is floating upright directly in front of me. The right side of Naomi's skull is bashed in and her feet are backwards so that her heels are facing me. I gasp. She's even more grotesque than dead Dr. Jenkins. I try to edge back farther but I am already smashed up against the wall. But Naomi doesn't go after me. Instead, she heads in the opposite direction.

"The fun is just *starting*, bitch," Naomi whispers before she jumps out of my window.

Day 5: Alive

Meryl waits with me in MHS's parking lot until way after the school bell rings but Naomi never shows up. I know deep down inside, in a place that I'm not ready to face, that she won't. Still, I spend all morning asking our mutual friends if they've seen Naomi. They mostly reply with snarky jokes about orgies and gangbangs.

When there is still no word from Naomi at lunch, my denial starts to wane. Then the county sheriff shows up with a man dressed in a suit that is too tailored for Meadowdale and a brunette who looks like a TV cop and rumors start to fly. The only time Sheriff Hopper comes to MHS on police business is to give us his yearly scared-straight seminar that he hopes becomes a TED Talk or to oversee the biannual locker searches.

"Naomi got arrested for distributing pornography to minors," I hear Collette whisper to Becca during study hall and I whip around.

"What about Naomi?"

"Thought you were #2good2gossip, Violet." Collette rolls her eyes. "Even though it's not gossip if it's, like, a fact."

I want to rip Collette's boingy ponytail off her head but I control myself. "What's a fact? That Naomi got busted?"

If that is true, then it makes perfect sense that Naomi is absent today. Right? It might just be the case.

"Well, I don't know if she's in jail or anything, but Lara works in Principal Wagner's office and she overheard the sheriff say Naomi's name. Then she mentioned it to Colby, who she's kinda hooking up with, and his mom is like a bigtime lawyer in Springfield. Way bigger than Meryl's dad, BTW. And Colby said that since a lot of the kids who saw Naomi's sex tape were under seventeen and considered minors, she could go to prison for distributing porn to children."

I frown. I'm not sure that's how the law works; as usual, Collette's "facts" are about as reliable as a holey condom.

Becca takes a small tube of lotion from her bag and rubs it into her hands. "Girls like Naomi—" She's interrupted by the snap, crackle, and pop of our ancient PA system. "Will all students and faculty please proceed to the gymnasium immediately."

Groans and moans echo through the classroom. I wait to hear the rest of the announcement. Surely there'll be something about a special assembly with the prizewinners from the 4-H fair or a visit from the local Rotarians. They never just interrupt the school day for an impromptu get-together in the gym. The knot in the pit of my stomach grows to the size of a grapefruit.

I walk into the hallway without speaking to anyone. As I round the corner, my knees start to wobble. I step into the gym and quickly scan the place for Meryl. We're supposed to stay with our classes, but I need my best friend.

"Come on, kids! Quickly! Find a seat and sit down," Mrs. Thorpe, one of the PE teachers, shouts.

"Keep on movin'! That's right, keep on movin'!" Mr. Cox, the other PE teacher, yells at us as though he is herding cattle.

I spot Meryl on the second row of bleachers and dart toward her. The sheriff huddles with the principal and other school administrators off to the side. "There could be a million reasons why they brought us here," Meryl says as I squeeze in next to her.

I stay silent and stare straight ahead.

Meryl shoots me a worried look. "Except that Dr. Phan and Mr. Shay are up there with the cops. School counselors usually means there's a crisis."

I can hear my heart beating.

The assistant principal, who was a former army commander, steps up to the microphone. "Silence, soldiers! We need everyone's attention up here. *Right now.*" The roar in the gymnasium dulls but it's still too loud to hear anything.

"*Shut up,*" the sheriff hollers. He looks like the type of guy who spends a lot of time watching Clint Eastwood movies. The assistant principal grimaces.

"Listen up, kids. This is important," Mr. Wagner calls out. His calmer approach has the right effect and the crowd quiets down. "We have some tragic news to share with you," he continues. His face is red and splotchy, like he's been crying. "Sheriff Hopper, I'm gonna let you speak now."

The sheriff swaggers back to the microphone stand. I bite down on my lip so hard that I can taste blood.

"Children, there's no way for me to break it to y'all easy. Today, we lost one of our own."

Please don't say it, I plead over and over in my head. I grab Meryl's hand.

The sheriff clears his throat. "Naomi Talbert is dead."

Nine

I RUB MY BACK up and down against the trunk of the sycamore, letting the rough bark scratch an itch between my shoulder blades that I can't reach with my fingers. Both grassy banks of the creek (pronounced "crik" by locals) are lined with elms, maples, gingkoes, and a bunch of other trees that I don't recognize because I never paid attention in my ninth-grade botany lab. The kaleidoscope of their leaves—kiwi, emerald, moss, hunter—reflects down onto the water, giving it the appearance of a thick, murky pea soup.

The early-evening sun casts a fiery reddish-orange glow over the meadow where the cows graze. They have the same big, golden-brown eyes as me. Maybe this is the real reason why so many of my Indian relatives don't eat beef. Cows are sacred because they look like they're part of the family.

On a few previous occasions down here, I came across an adventurous heifer (as in bovine and not an overweight girl) who bravely escaped through a hole in the wire fence. Once, one of them even made it halfway across the creek's slippery rocks and fast-moving waters before a ranch hand showed up in a pickup truck to wrangle her back home.

This whole place is so damn Americana that I can imagine Huckleberry Finn and Tom Sawyer floating by on a raft. It's hardly my usual scene, especially because I am far from a nature lover, but when Meryl and I discovered it five years ago, we both thought that we'd found our own secret hiding place. We even gave it a code name: Avalon.

Avalon is tucked away about two miles into the woods, behind a cul-de-sac in Fawn Ridge where Meryl's mother lives. It isn't actually that remote, but being here always makes me feel like I'm somewhere else. And today of all days, I wish I could be anywhere else.

We lost one of our own. The sheriff's words play in a constant loop in my mind until the sound of a loud beer belch quickly flings me back to the present situation.

Just before our freshman year, Meryl and I were utterly gutted to find out that our Avalon was actually a favorite spot to hook up, get high, or both for multiple generations of Meadowdale High students. It's even rumored that the mayor lost his virginity out here. Today, it's a makeshift memorial ground for Naomi.

After the assembly, school was dismissed early. We all came out to "the Creek," which is a far less imaginative name than Avalon, but it's what this area is commonly called. Maybe not everyone, but it seems that most of the student body showed up at some point. Kids have been coming and going all day. Except

for people like me; I've been sitting out here for hours, unable to make myself leave.

I shiver. The shade is just a bit too cool now that the sun is starting to set. But I like the way the sycamore tree's low-hanging branches act like a shield, distancing me from the rest of my classmates. Meryl is sitting in the sun but she's close by, which gives me comfort.

We lost one of our own.

I look at the splotchy red faces that surround me. There's been a ton of tears all day long. Actually, *hysterical sobbing* is more accurate. At times, it feels like a competition to see who can cry the hardest. I'm not sure if I've cried at all.

Crying means acknowledging that Naomi is gone and I can't do that. I know what I saw last night. I heard the sheriff's announcement. I'm here watching them all mourn Naomi as though their best friend died. Yet I'm unable to accept any of it.

They've spent the whole day grieving. Most of them have never truly been touched by death, so I forgive them their stupidity. Death—or, rather, the dead—looms over my entire life like the branches of the sycamore tree. I grew up in its shadow and know that once it gets you, it never leaves.

"Just heard back from my dad and he says he has no info on Naomi," Meryl tells someone.

I smile to myself. I don't even need to look at Meryl to know that she's lying. There's a growing obsession among all of us about the who, what, why, and, especially, the how of Naomi's demise. Collette is working her sources like a Pulitzer Prize-winning journalist.

I overheard some of our friends pressure Meryl to ask her DA dad about Naomi and I know there is no way Meryl is actually going to do it. Both of our dads work with highly classified material. It's an unspoken rule that we never share anything we hear with civilians. Granted, my dad's field is international terrorism, which isn't nearly as juicy as the local law cases Meryl's dad deals with. Regardless, pumping her dad for inside info right now would make Meryl come off as totally amateur, which is not her style. However, the little white lie Meryl just told our friends seems a particularly befitting way to honor our dead classmate.

We lost one of our own.

"Text from Trent," Collette calls out as if it's an urgent news alert interrupting our regularly scheduled program. "He says he's too effed up about Naomi to come down here. RIP."

Collette treats this info like it's earthshattering, but considering Trent and Naomi dated for four years, it seems pretty reasonable that he's devastated. A few of the kids who smuggled down cases of Keystone Light, a beverage that Naomi called white-trash champagne, hold up their beer cans.

"And Tessa is supposedly tranquilized due to toxic shock," Collette continues.

"Toxic shock is like what happens when you leave your tampon in for too long, Collette," Becca corrects her. "You probably meant that Tessa is sedated due to shock. Seriously, get a brain, Collette."

I look over at Nate. He's the only one from their inner circle down here. I guess, as Trent's best friend, he was less close to Naomi than Trent or Tessa, but his eyes are so red that looking at them make mine burn. Then I spot Caleb a few feet away and wonder if the bloodshot eyes are because of tears or weed. I can't really see Caleb's eyes because his entire face is pretty messed up from Nate's beatdown two days ago. I'm not sure if they made up but if they did, it probably involved a lot of drugs.

"She was just so hot!" Sleazy Bear groans before chugging his beer. He's been milking all the grief out here for every hug and shady ass-grab he can get.

This is about the hundredth time today that I have heard a variation of this sentiment. There have also been dozens of well-meaning eulogies that share cherished memories of Naomi. Most people describe her as kind, generous, and full of life, which is as impossible to believe as the fact that she's actually dead. However, I'm keenly aware of the living's tendency to glorify the dead. Relatives, particularly Naresh, have canonized my mother's memory to the point where I wouldn't be surprised if they started referring to her as Saint Laya.

Naomi was a bitch. Everyone here knew it. But that doesn't make her death any less painful.

We lost one of our own.

I hurt in ways that I didn't know were possible. Like most of my classmates, I'm not sure if this clusterfuck of emotions is due to losing Naomi herself or to dealing with the fact that one of us can actually die. We've spent our entire lives listening to adults lecture us about the dangers of this and that, constantly warning us of our false sense of invincibility. And all of it had about as much effect on us as the "no sex until marriage" tweets the local Purity chapter sends out every weekend.

Invincibility is one of the few upsides of youth. We are supposed to have our entire lives ahead of us. Naomi was supposed to have hers.

"Maybe Naomi offed herself," Jessica says, then hesitates.

"We don't know anything yet," Becca snaps.

"When a healthy sixteen-year-old dies all of a sudden, you can pretty much bet it was either a car accident, misadventure, suicide, or murder." Meryl raises her right eyebrow. "Why, do you have something to confess?"

"No, Sherlock." Jessica rolls her eyes. "It's just that everyone's been making such a big deal about cyberbullying. The principal gave that totally busted lecture at the beginning of the year about MHS's zero-tolerance policy with bullying, and your dad said he'd prosecute cyberbullies to the fullest extent of the law."

My ears perk up. Just what is Jessica getting at?

Jessica continues. "And Naomi was trolled pretty hard this weekend—you know, after the sex tape. I mean, *H and H* did name her this week's ho. It's the same standard shit that happens to every heffer and ho."

My stomach churns. Slut, ho, whore, bitch. Is this really how Naomi spent her last weekend alive—surrounded by all this hate?

"Jesus." Meryl scrolls through her phone. "You call this standard? There are messages here telling Naomi to kill herself and mentioning gangbangs. This shit is depraved."

Jessica sighs. "Save the self-righteousness. We all do it and you know it. The point I was trying to make is that the cops could make a case for bullying, which this totally isn't. I mean, Naomi is—was—like an uber-troll herself. But maybe we should try to take some of this stuff off in case people start getting it twisted. Not that I was any part of it."

"The internet is anonymous, Jess," Collette chimes in. "So we're totally cool."

"I got this one, Meryl," says Becca. She turns to face Collette. "No, it's not anonymous. The police can track your IP because you're an idiot and you probably used your own phone. Seriously, you're like one of those dumbest-criminal videos, Collette."

"And for the record, we don't all do it," Meryl adds.

"Like I said, it's not my bag." Jess shrugs. "Collette was the ringleader who got everyone to troll. She even told people what to write."

"Yeah, I couldn't have thought of 'Naomi is a slut' myself if Collette hadn't come up with it," Sleazy Bear slurs as he takes another swig of his beer.

I watch with contempt as they begin pointing fingers at one another. Now it seems like everyone is playing a round of the Blame Game.

"You're all such assholes," Meryl says, seething.

"OMG," Lara shouts so loud that she gets everyone's attention.

I turn in her direction. Lara and Collette have been taking turns sharing irrelevant information all day. This breaking-news announcement is probably something as enlightening as "Naomi's parents are devastated."

"My aunt Rita works over at the coroner's office and she says that"—Lara takes a huge breath because clearly there isn't enough oxygen in her entire body to keep up with the ultra-fast pace at which she is speaking—"Naomi was murdered."

Now it's me who needs air. Suddenly, the heavy branches that surround me and the lack of light make me feel as though I'm suffocating in a tiny foxhole. I crawl out from under the sycamore as fast as I can.

"It's okay," Meryl whispers as she wraps her arms around me.

I don't know when I started to cry but now that the stored tears are flowing, it feels as though I can't stop. My body shakes uncontrollably. I lean against Meryl for support because I don't trust my legs to hold me.

"Oh God, Meryl," I sob. I force my words through the lump in my throat. "We *killed* one of our own."

Ten

A
S FAR AS I'M CONCERNED, everyone is a suspect. After we got the shocking news that Naomi was murdered, we didn't hear any more information, so I am clueless about Naomi's killer. It could be a friend, a family member, or just some random stranger.

I steady myself against the front door and eye the buttons on the keypad, trying to remember the code to unlock it.

My head is woozy from the shots of whatever liquor Brian Monaghan gave me. Once we heard that someone had killed Naomi, the unofficial memorial turned into a full-on shit-show. Everyone got wasted, everyone cried even more, and then pretty much everyone puked. I managed to avoid one out of the three. My eyes sting from all the sobbing I've done, but Meryl and I made sure we were both still standing at the end of the night.

Now all I want to do is to pass out in my bed or on the cold tile of the bathroom floor, whichever option is more convenient and makes my head stop spinning. Meryl's mother insisted she spend the night at home because, like just about every other parent in town, she's freaking out that a kid has been murdered.

I'd like to believe that Dede is just as worried about my safety although all the lights are off inside my house, which means that she's already asleep. I remember the four-digit code, punch it in, and tiptoe inside. The moment I close the door behind me, a chill runs down my spine. It's pitch-dark except for a hall light that Dede left on for me.

All of the mirrors in the house are draped in bed sheets. Dede covers all the mirrors every night because she believes that if you sleepwalk and wake up suddenly, you'll be startled by your own reflection, possibly so startled that you'll mistake the image for a ghost, which will cause you to have a heart attack and die.

It's eerie in the classic haunted-house way, and God knows that I've been teased mercilessly for it by every friend who's ever spent the night here. My pleas to Dede to stop fall on deaf ears. Of course, what makes this nightly ritual so uniquely Dede is that she uses our old sheets, so tonight, for instance, the massive front-hall mirror is covered in my worn-out My Little Pony bedding.

Rainbow Dash's and Minty's smiling faces aren't exactly on the same level of frightening as *The Others*, but a house filled with covered mirrors is creepy nonetheless.

I hold on to the banister for balance and begin climbing up the stairs. Another chill runs down my body. I try to pick up the pace but my legs aren't exactly cooperating. I focus on walking toward the lamp turned on in the upstairs hallway.

I used to psych myself out like this when I was a child. We lived in a house where the bathroom was down the hall from my bedroom, and I dreaded those midnight pee runs, convinced that something was waiting for me in the dark.

The truth is, after I turned ten, there usually was something out there. It was an Aiedeo ready to train me.

I stop suddenly. I think I see something move out of the corner of my eye. More chills radiate throughout my body. I start debating my next move. If I turn, who knows what I'll see. But if I ignore it, I won't know if something really is there. I am way too buzzed and too sleepy to think properly.

Since my personal motto is "When in trouble, lie and deny," I decide to keep on moving until I am forced to stop. This time, I can't ignore that something is definitely here with me. I hear a low, soft whistling come out of nowhere.

"Boo," Naomi says as she stares down at me from the top landing. A slow smile creeps across her face, exposing a row of small pointy teeth. "Miss me?"

I do a double take. Visits from dead people have been an all-too-common occurrence in my life. This does not make them any less terrifying. However, Naomi seems to have gone through some ghostly *Pretty Woman* makeover. She's wearing her legendary white jeans, and her lush honey-blond hair falls past her shoulders in a perfect salon blowout. The right side of her face is still bashed in, and her feet are still backwards. Plus, now she's sporting a gnarly set of sharp, crooked talons that go beyond any manicure. Naomi looks as shocking and grotesque as her previous Japanese ghoul incarnation, except now she is more like a macabre hot girl.

"No, I don't miss you," I answer. "Now get out before Dede sees you and blasts you into hell. Or is that where you're coming from?"

I am pretty sure this is straight-up liquid courage that is making me so bold but I'll take whatever I can right now.

Naomi rolls her eyes. "Why did they send me to you? Ever since I've been dead, no one can hear or see me. Except for weirdoes like you. Keeping secrets, huh, Violet?"

I strengthen my grip on the banister to keep from falling over. "Lucky me. I get the exclusive to your mean-girl wrath."

"Boo-hoo, Violet. Lucky me that I get to die and only you can see me."

I take a deep breath. "What do you mean by 'they' sent you?"

"Here's the thing about Ghost World—it's not exactly the friendliest." Her voice still has the same superior tone but it's thinner now with a slightly crooked lilt to it. It doesn't feel or sound alive anymore. "So it's not like they hosted a brunch in my honor and welcomed me in. I don't know who *they* were— they failed to introduce themselves. And my memory feels more blotto than you look. I just remember them being a bunch of frightening bitches."

"The Aiedeo." My head does a total spin. What do the Aiedeo have to do with Naomi? "My dead relatives."

Naomi raises an eyebrow, which makes the dent on the right side of her face move along with it. I look away.

"I thought that you people were all about embracing

differences—#Diversity," Naomi spits as she pulls some of her hair down to cover the gash.

I ignore her. I'm not sure how much longer I'm going to be able to stand upright and I need some answers. "Why did the Aiedeo send you to me?"

"Again, they aren't exactly the chattiest gals. You're the one who watches all those horror movies. Why do you think I'm here?"

I'd spent most of my life devouring ghost stories. Not as in Aiedeo stories, because they were just my dead relatives and didn't count. But classic ghost-story films like *The Haunting of Hill House*, *The Woman in Black*, *The Grudge*, *The Ring*, *Poltergeist*, *Paranormal Activity*—I could probably think of a couple of dozen more, but almost all of them shared a common plot device. "If you go by movie history, which I almost always do, I know it's a bit of a trope but—"

"Oh my God! I'm not asking you to nerd out like we're in some Intro to Film class, Violet! Just tell me why you think I'm here."

I take a deep breath and spit it out. "Because your soul isn't at peace."

"Why? Because I died so young?"

"Well, yeah." I nod. "And because you were murdered."

"I was *murdered*?" Her eyes turn cloudy and her shoulders slump. She isn't as assured as she was just a second ago.

"You don't remember?"

I see she's trying to stay composed but she can't. Naomi sits down on the landing and buries her face in her hands. When she speaks, her voice is shaky. "I feel like I'm at a never-ending rave. Everything is a dazed blur. The last thing I remember is Saturday in the gym."

My heart sinks. The bitch-out is Naomi's last memory alive. I go sit by her. Now that I'm closer, the stench of rotten meat fills my nostrils.

"Naomi, I'm so sorry for what happened to you. I really am. It's not fair at all." I can feel my tears begin to well up. I'm surprised I have any left in me.

"No shit it's not fair!" Naomi takes a deep breath. "Did your relatives—the Idea, Adeo, whatever—murder me?"

"The Aiedeo." I can't think of any reason why they would have done this to Naomi, but I wouldn't put anything past them. They've come close to taking *my* life and I'm supposed to be one of them. But why Naomi? I shake my head. She has very little to do with me and nothing to do with my legacy. "I don't know. They're fierce bitches, for sure, but I've never seen them kill anyone. And it just makes no sense that they would off you." I shrug. "You really don't remember anything about what happened to you?"

"As soon as I saw this"—Naomi points to her backwards feet—"I started racking my brain trying to figure out what happened, but I keep coming up blank."

"No recollection about the text you sent me on Sunday evening threatening to kill me?"

"What?" Naomi's brow furrows. "That's cray."

"And what about dropping by to see me last night?" I point to her jeans. "You weren't exactly looking so hair-metal vixen

120

and you were hanging from the ceiling but I'm pretty sure you were already dead."

"WTF? I don't remember that either. But have you always been able to do this? I mean, you can really see dead people?" Naomi's brows shoot up and her mouth drops open. Now she's the one who is afraid. I'm the freak, even to a ghost.

"Yes." After all, now that Naomi is dead, who is she gonna tell? "I don't see, like, random ghosts flying around. Just the Aiedeo. I don't know, I've spent so much time trying to forget about it that I kinda don't know what's real and what's not anymore."

Naomi nods knowingly. "We invented that game, didn't we? Lie and deny."

Lie and deny. I forgot that it wasn't just *my* motto; it had been ours back in elementary school. I glance at Naomi. I learned from the best. Or did she learn from me?

"Wait! You're a random ghost, Naomi, and I can see you," I cry out as it dawns on me. Granted, my brain is working slowly, but I can't believe it took me this long to figure it out. "You're my *shama*!"

"What?"

"*Shamas* are these tests the Aiedeo used to make me do. And the other night, they forced one with Dr. Jenkins on me. And then when it was finished, this Aiedeo showed up and spewed all the usual Aiedeo garbage, but at the end, she said that I had no idea what was waiting for me." I definitely sound like a rambling drunk right now and I can see from Naomi's annoyed expression that I'm not making much sense.

"If I'm your *shama* or whatever you call it, then what are you supposed to do with me?"

I shrug. "I don't know for sure but I'm probably supposed to help you find eternal peace or something. But it doesn't really matter because I'm not an Aiedeo and I'm not doing any more of their *shamas*."

"Then screw the Aiedeo! But what about helping me find out what happened because you can?"

"What can I do?" I hug my knees.

Naomi arches her eyebrow. "You can talk to dead people."

"What's the good in that if you've forgotten everything about what happened to you?" Then I remember the video. That was recorded before the bitch-out so maybe Naomi can recall something there that may be helpful. "What about the tape with you and the two guys? Who are they?"

I realize I could have been more tactful in bringing up the sex tape or at least not been so direct about it. For a few seconds, there is nothing but dead silence. Then I can almost hear the swoosh in the air as Naomi whips around and clasps her bony fingers around my neck. I feel the razor-sharp point of her talons on my skin, eager to slit my throat. My heart skips several beats. I don't know how we went from our heart-to-heart to Naomi seriously holding my life in her hands.

"You better figure this all out," Naomi whispers. Her mouth is black with a hot, pulsing tongue inside. She drags one of her claws across my neck like a knife. "Or I'll haunt you for every single day of your worthless life. You think just 'cause I'm dead, I'll keep your dirty little secrets? I'll make sure everyone knows

 122

about you. I'll expose you for the freak that you are. And you'll be such a miserable, lonely outcast that you'll wish you were dead like me."

All of my liquid courage evaporates. I can do nothing but silently nod. Naomi looks me straight in the eyes, and when she sees the terror in them, she seems satisfied. She unhooks her talons but I can feel them still burning into my skin. Naomi stands up slowly and I don't dare move.

Then she floats down the stairs and turns toward the hall mirror. When she is standing directly in front of it, Naomi takes a step inside and disappears.

Eleven

Day 6: Alive

THE ENTIRE SCHOOL is suffering from a collective hangover. At least, that's what it feels like to me. It isn't just the
physical effect of all the grief-drinking we did the night before.
There's more to it. It's this sense of melancholy like the Sunday-
night blues that hits me practically every week and on the first
day of school after a long break.

In order to deal with everyone's anxiety, Meadowdale High
administrators decided to host yet another miserable assembly.
It's already well into its first hour and I still can't quite determine what it's about. It seems like an unsettling mash-up of
an extended public-service announcement and an open casting
call for a really pathetic TV talent show. I checked out after
Dean Shimansky, a.k.a. MC Shuga Boi and Dena Willis, a.k.a.
Dimple$, rapped/sang "Amazing Grace."

"Holy water?" Meryl scrunches her face. "Seriously?"

Even with my head in a fog, I'm clear on one point. There's
no way I'm helping the Aiedeo or Naomi. Naomi is vicious and

I have little doubt that she'll do all the things she threatened to do. And I learned not to trust the Aiedeo a long time ago. Therefore, I need to put a stop to all of it. Like in the movies when someone refuses to pay blackmailers because then they'll always return. If I don't find a way to shut both Naomi and the Aiedeo down, they'll be after me for the rest of my life.

I'm still way more frightened than I am brave but I like how my temper is fueling my courage. Or maybe I'm still drunk. In any case, I have a plan. I need to get rid of Naomi.

"You know I haven't been to Mass since I was like eleven years old. But the last time I was at St. Joseph's, the holy water was kept in the font right where you enter the church," Meryl says.

I'd filled Meryl in on Naomi's latest visit in a quick before-school meet-up but there wasn't enough time for me to let her in on my game plan, so I was catching her up now.

"Then it's pretty easy access?"

"The trick isn't getting the holy water — it's believing that it's actually holy, Violet."

I nod. I'm putting an end to my Naomi-ghost problem old-school-style à la *The Exorcist*. Obviously, I'm not a priest. But maybe with some holy water, a wooden stake, and the discarded Ouija board stored away in the attic, I can pull off a DIY exorcism.

"V, I'll do whatever it takes, but do you really think an exorcism is going to work?"

I let out a frustrated sigh. "Got a better plan? 'Cause I don't."

"Violet, get down here now!"

My scheming is abruptly interrupted by Collette, who arranged for the Squad to perform during the assembly. "We'll talk more later." I stand up reluctantly. "Duty calls."

"Break a leg," Meryl says with a wicked little grin. I join the rest of my teammates on the gym floor.

"You need to wear this in honor of Naomi. RIP," says Collette as she pins a ribbon on my cheerleading uniform.

"Why is it blue?"

"It's not just any blue, Violet. It's Carolina blue, and it matches Naomi's eyes. My mom worked straight off of Naomi's pics to make sure she got just the right shade."

Apparently, Collette is already auditioning pretty hard for the now-vacant role of co-captain.

"Guys, I think we should say something before we begin."

I almost jump back. I didn't even notice Tessa standing among us. The girl looks like she stepped straight out of a Tim Burton flick. Her already gaunt frame is almost emaciated and her eyes pop out of her bony face like big, empty saucers. "Are you sure you should be here, Tess?" I ask with genuine concern.

She shrugs. "Probably not. I'm still hopped up on a bunch of the meds the doctors gave me. But Pioneer Poms was in Naomi's heart. She would want me up here with you guys."

I doubt that. Naomi liked poms only because she could boss all of us around and she looked way hotter in her uniform than anyone else.

Tessa does a dazed zombie walk to the microphone while

the rest of us find our places. We are going to start off with the infamous pyramid that we screwed up last Friday, much to Naomi's ire. I drop down on all fours and scan the blank faces of the crowd. Does anyone want to be here right now? It's strange to think that this gym is the last memory that Naomi has of her life.

"We'll always love you, Nay Nay," Tessa cries out. "RIP, Naomi." She wipes the tears from her eyes, then turns around to face the rest of the Squad.

Sarah McLachlan's "Angel" starts blaring through our worn-out speakers. People hold up their phones and start singing along while Collette's mother jumps up and begins taking photos. I wonder if Collette and her mom have secretly been waiting for one of us to die just so they could orchestrate this ridiculous tribute. Because clearly, they had started planning this way before yesterday.

I shake my head. The sound of the crowd singing off-key quickly fills the gym.

"Lara, your knee is wedged right in my spine," I whisper as I wriggle around, trying to find a bearable position.

"Well, I can't exactly move it with fat-ass Becca on top of me," Lara hisses. "Are you, like, one of those secret eaters? 'Cause you are crushing me!"

"Go eat a dick, Lara," Becca says, fuming.

"Shut up, guys," Jess commands.

Perhaps it's the lack of teamwork or the hangover, but I can already feel my muscles weakening. Tessa is going to be the flier today so I need to wait this out another two minutes, until she climbs to the top and Collette's mother takes enough photos. I keep my eyes focused on all the lit-candle apps swaying in the air and try to concentrate.

That's when I spot Naomi standing under the bleachers about twenty feet directly ahead. She looks furious. Her face is scrunched up in a deep scowl and her teeth are flashing like she's ready to tear me apart. I can feel her fury from here.

My arms and legs start to tremble. Did Naomi read my thoughts? Can she do that? Does she know that I'm planning to eliminate her? Is she here to get revenge?

Whatever is behind Naomi's rage, she is clearly keen on expressing it. Naomi runs out from the bleachers like the Terminator and rams straight into me. I jerk back hard.

"Stop moving, Violet," Collette snarls, "or we're all gonna fall."

I'm still trying to recover from the first hit when Naomi lands a perfectly placed kick upside my head. Then another on the other side. Even with her backwards feet, the girl can obviously inflict some damage. My neck swings all the way to the left, then back to the right. The pyramid starts to shake.

"You think you can get rid of me?" Naomi shrieks. "You think I'm gonna let you go?"

"I'm sorry!" I cry out in agony.

Naomi ignores me and twists my ponytail around her claws. She uses it to yank me forward to my feet. In one fell swoop, the entire pyramid collapses like a Jenga tower. The girls topple to the ground with a symphony of curses directed at me.

But I am too busy trying to avoid Naomi to care. Naomi punches me in the gut. Hard. I feel all the air rush out of me. Naomi winds her fist back for another hit; I duck before it can land, then I push her with all the strength I can muster. Naomi topples backwards with a chunk of my hair still in her hand.

I ignore my throbbing scalp and start running for the fire exit at the far end of the gym. It's the only door in here that leads outside. I race across the gym floor as my teammates and, no doubt, the entire school watches. I know I look crazy, but there is no time to worry about optics with a vengeful demon after me.

I push the exit door open, causing the loud, screeching alarm to sound. My car is parked in the student lot on the other side and I book toward it. I'm too afraid to look back but I can feel Naomi gaining on me.

I turn the corner and collide with what feels like a brick wall. I look up to see the creepy intern. What is he doing here? And who knew that he was so ripped underneath that drab undertaker's suit? "Move!" I shout, trying to push past the intern.

Instead, he grabs me by the elbow. Then he takes two steps forward and holds his hand up until Naomi, who is barreling toward me, stops in her tracks.

"Wait, can you see her too?"

Creepy Intern says nothing. He walks over to Naomi with me in tow and places three fingers on the side of her neck like a modified Vulcan death grip. I watch in a combination of shock and horror as Naomi drops to the ground.

"What did you do to her?" I mumble.

"It only works on new *bhoots* and it's temporary. So we don't have much time," Creepy Intern replies. "Let's go." He tightens his grip on my arm and leads me away.

Twelve

LUKAS GLANCES OVER at Violet in the passenger seat of the hearse. Normally, he wouldn't use such a blatant symbol of death to do this sort of thing, but the other Talbert vehicles were taken.

Naomi's murder is causing all kinds of chaos. He wonders if Violet's death will spark the same mayhem, then he realizes that he doesn't really care.

Violet is rambling away, as he predicted she would. He'd pegged her as a blabber. She's asking all sorts of questions about him and Naomi and talking a lot of what amounts to gibberish as far as he is concerned. There's no need to answer her at this late stage. After all, what use would it be for either of them?

Any goodwill that Violet had earned with the Aiedeo after the Dr. Jenkins *shama* was quickly erased when she continued to show how selfish and cowardly she was. The Aiedeo had finally lost their patience with her after realizing she had no intention of helping Naomi, and they agreed that she needed to be eliminated. He'd gotten the go-ahead a few hours ago. Given

Violet's recent episodes with Dr. Jenkins and Naomi, he figures she must know she's in danger. Plus, in his experience, usually even the dimmest mortals have some idea when their time is up.

The sound of his cell phone ringing jolts Lukas out of his thoughts. He clears his throat before answering. "Yes."

"Is she with you?" a sharp, clipped female voice asks. Lukas has worked with most of the Aiedeo but he doesn't recognize this voice.

"Stop," he hears Violet say in the background.

"Yes," Lukas says into his phone. His jaw muscles tense. Why is this Aiedeo calling?

"The decision to terminate has been overruled."

"Excuse me? I need you to repeat." Overruled?

"Stop," Violet says again, this time in a louder voice. Lukas continues to ignore her.

"We have decided to prolong the mission. Therefore, you must abort termination."

Lukas doesn't bother to hide the anger in his voice. "I was given specific instructions to terminate."

"Stop! Stop! Stop! Stop!" Violet shouts repeatedly. He should have gagged her. Lukas turns toward his window to try to drown Violet out.

"Yes, I am aware." The woman pauses briefly before speaking again. He can tell that she is choosing her words carefully. "However, the earlier decision to terminate has been overruled."

"By whom? Who has the authority to overrule in this matter?" Lukas barks. He knows very well that the Aiedeo have full and final say in this case.

"Maa," the woman half whispers as though she can't believe what she's saying. She waits a second before continuing. Her voice is bolder now. "Maa overruled the decision. For the time being."

"Maa?" he repeats incredulously. In all his time with the Aiedeo, he has never heard of anything like this happening.

The woman obviously isn't in the mood for further conversation. "Abort termination. Further instructions on how to proceed will be given to you shortly."

"Understood. Termination aborted."

"Stop! Stop! Stop!" Violet continues.

Lukas slams his cell against the dashboard, then pulls a hard U-turn. He looks Violet up and down. *Who is she?*

Clearly, the Aiedeo know something that they're not telling him. The hairs on the back of his neck stand up as his soldier's intuition shifts into high alert.

Lukas starts to say something to Violet when suddenly, everything freezes. From the inside to the outside, he is paralyzed. His mouth is half open and his hands continue to grip the steering wheel. He tries to move them but he can't. Nothing around him moves either. Lukas fights to make sense of what is happening but then everything goes black.

When Lukas wakes up, Violet is gone.

I can't stop babbling. I know that most of it makes no sense but I can't stop talking. Actually, the more I understand that I'm in one of those stranger-danger moments, the worse my mouth diarrhea gets.

At first, I was relieved to the point of tears of joy when I escaped Naomi. However, now I'm totally aware that I'm in a car with Creepy Intern. Not just a car—a hearse. Talk about a bad omen. And of course Creepy Intern is giving off vibes that are seriously menacing.

My palms start to get sweaty. I'm in the front seat next to him, seat belt on, doors locked, but my limbs aren't restrained in any way. If he pulled over, I could get out, but why do I get the sense that's not an option?

Creepy Intern must be Bat Eyes. A chill runs down my legs. Bat Eyes from the cornfield and from the spying on me in my bedroom. I'm willing to bet that this isn't a happy coincidence. What does he want with me? He saved me in the cornfield and he saved me from Naomi, so why do I get the distinct feeling that he's far from my hero? Perhaps because I'm riding in a hearse heading out of town. I hear my heart beating in my throat.

I sit up straighter. "Hey, uptown and everything else is the other way. This all starts to become backcountry. Where are you tryin' to go?"

Of course, my questions are only met with dead silence. This is the part in those self-defense classes that Naresh made me take where you're not supposed to try to pretend like everything is okay because you were brought up to be a nice girl. I have to acknowledge that I'm in danger. The hairs on my arms stand straight up.

I look around in a panic. The speedometer reads ninety

miles an hour. I flash back to when the Aiedeo pushed me out of that car. It was going only thirty-five, and I barely survived.

I try to calm my mind. My phone along with any other possible weapons, like my keys and the mace I carry in my backpack, are in my school locker. I wonder if I can reach over and jab my fingers into his eyes, though I doubt that'll do much damage.

Even forgetting about his magic or whatever it is, Creepy Intern is lean, muscular, and tall. I can't take him. A strange sound brings me out of my thoughts. To my utter surprise, it's a ringtone. I watch him pull out a flip phone circa late 1990s.

For some reason, when he talks into that dinosaur device, it makes him seem less frightening. I can still feel the fear in every inch of my body but I also know what I need to do.

It's still hazy but something else is coming back to me about that Aiedeo car incident. It was for a *shama*. They were trying to teach me the stop game. I never quite got how to do it and it's definitely been a while since I tried it. I take a deep breath.

"Stop," I say.

The scenery outside has changed to thick forests on both sides of the road. It looks like the kind of place where bodies are buried.

"Stop," I say again, this time louder.

I can hear him getting pissed with whoever is on the other end of the line.

"Stop! Stop! Stop!" I yell.

He continues speaking on the phone and I hear him say something about "termination aborted." This sounds like good news for me but I'm not gonna take any chances. I continue shouting, "Stop!"

All of a sudden, he slams his phone down and swerves the hearse around. There's something different about him now but I'm too far along with what I started to figure it out. It all happens in a millisecond, but for me, it's like watching it all in slow motion.

Everything *stops*. The hearse, him, even the trees. Nothing moves because it is all frozen. I have stopped time.

I can't believe I pulled it off. I know that it will wear off within minutes so I need to hurry. Just doing it sucked me dry—my head and body feel like a pile of mush. But I refuse to give up.

I gather all the strength I can muster, unclasp my seat belt, and unlock the door. As soon as I jump out of the car, I see Old Blue behind the hearse. Meryl must have followed us! I race over to the truck and climb inside. I touch her shoulder and she wakes up.

"Go!" I shout.

Meryl presses hard on the gas and we drive out of there as fast as we can.

Thirteen

"A ND CREEPY INTERN—who is also Bat Eyes—got a call and then you heard something about an abortion?" Meryl asks, then frowns because she knows that doesn't sound right but we're both too confused right now to know what all we're saying.

When Meryl ran out of the gym after me, she saw Creepy Intern put me in the hearse, so she followed us. I've been telling Meryl about everything that happened, starting with the ass-kicking Naomi gave me and ending with my escape, but just saying it out loud makes me realize how effed up this all really is.

"No. It was 'Termination aborted,'" I clarify.

"Then you stopped time." Meryl lets that hang in the air for a second so that we both can try to wrap our heads around it. "That's the shit, V."

"I know." Even though it comes from my Aiedeo training, I can't deny that making time stop is absolutely mind-blowing. Although it took so much energy to do it, it feels like my mind is literally blown.

Like so much else with the Aiedeo, I'd completely blocked out any memory of the stop game. All these years, I didn't even remember that the whole car incident was because the Aiedeo were teaching me how to freeze time. Then today, when I needed it, it came back to me, and I actually managed to pull it off. Just like that Aiedeo who came to my room said, my powers never went away.

We pull up in front of my house. I know I've got to see my nanny. Dede is my Yoda and I need her. That means I'll have to come clean about everything, and maybe she'll go ballistic. But no matter what, she'll have my back.

"Mer, you don't have to come in with me," I say as she unclasps her seat belt.

"What? No way! I'm not leaving you alone after what just happened to you."

"Dede never misses her afternoon soaps, so she's home. And I need you to go to school and do damage control. Especially with the Squad. I mean, I had a total freak-out in front of the entire student body and everyone's gotta be talking about it. You think anyone videoed me?" I chew on my lip. "*H and H* will definitely post something about it."

Meryl scowls. "Seriously? You have supernatural forces after you and this is what you're worried about?"

"I think we've already established that I have messed-up priorities. You know that looking like a freak or, to be more accurate, having my freak side exposed scares the hell out of me. Just as much as Bat Eyes or the Aiedeo." I sigh. "So can you just use your Meryl Miller swagger to smooth all of this out?"

"Whatever that means." Meryl starts up her truck. "But you know that I've got you."

"Thanks." I hug her as hard as I can. "I love you."

"I love you too."

I watch Meryl leave, then walk up the driveway. As soon as I step into my house, a feeling of safety overwhelms me. I'm crushed by the weight of everything I've just survived. My entire body aches, my nerves are fried, and my mind is in overdrive.

"Dede," I croak out in a shaky voice.

I walk into the kitchen and pour myself a glass of cold water. After I chug it and another two more down, I go to find Dede. The wall clock reads 2:46 p.m., which means she's probably too engrossed in *General Hospital* to have heard me come home.

I seriously contemplate crawling because my legs hurt so much, but instead, I half walk, half limp to the living room.

Recent events should probably have taught me to expect the unexpected. However, nothing has prepared me for what is waiting for me on my sofa. I stand there paralyzed as my stomach crashes to the ground.

Dede is sitting on one side of the couch. The TV is turned off, which is in itself is quite incredible. Sitting on the other end of the sofa, leaning against the chocolate-brown cushion, is Creepy Intern.

He stands up when he sees me and I notice he's no longer wearing his undertaker suit. Instead, he's in black jeans and a worn leather jacket that looks like it's older than Dede. How nice that he had time to change after his botched murder attempt on me.

"I'm not here to harm you." His voice is deep and assured like it was on the phone earlier but now it also has a hint of warmth that I haven't heard before. Just a very, very small hint, though, and I'm not buying it.

"Isn't that what most killers say right before they slaughter you?" My head is spinning. I honestly can't believe that after actually *freezing time* to escape Creepy Intern, he's standing in my living room. I turn to Dede. "Is this real? Do you see this monster right here?"

"It okay, Violet," Dede says in that soothing voice she hasn't used since I broke my legs. "Lukas tell me everything."

They're on a first-name basis? I want to hurl. I check Dede's eyes to see if she's been glammed or if someone's played some other kind of hypno trick. "You know this sicko bastard kidnapped me and you're trying to tell me it's all right that he's here in our house?"

Dede shakes her head. "*Mami*, sit down so Lukas can explain you everything. I make chai."

I don't know how to respond. I thought that Dede having my back at least meant that she wouldn't have a tea party with my kidnapper. I'm losing my shit really fast.

"Perhaps you should sit down, Violet," Lukas says. "We have important matters to discuss."

Maybe it's hearing him say my name or just recalling the sheer terror he put me through, but I snap. Before I even know what I'm doing, I leap across the sofa and tackle Lukas to the floor. I sit on his chest and pummel his face with my fist. I punch him over and over as blood squirts from his nose and his mouth. There is a crazed shrieking sound that pierces my ears. I look around to see where it is coming from but then realize it's me.

Lukas isn't hitting me back, which only infuriates me more. Now he's being chivalrous? *After* he kidnapped me?

I elbow Lukas in his eye. I am about to do it again when I feel Dede pull me off him. Her strength always surprises me.

I sit back against the sofa and simmer quietly. His face is a mishmash of bloody cuts and bruises; he looks like a hot boxer. I cringe. Scratch the *hot*—just because I got a few punches in doesn't mean all is forgiven. Far from it.

Lukas gets to his feet and stares down at me. "Now that you have gotten that out, let's talk about your *shama*."

I sit on a stool at my kitchen counter, my sopping hair wrapped in a towel, holding a cup of chai. Dede thinks there's nothing in the world that can't be fixed with a hot shower and tea.

However, just because I smell better doesn't mean I feel better. An entire bar of soap can't scrub away the anger I have as I see Lukas and Dede sitting together at the kitchen table. When it comes to matters concerning me, Dede doesn't get to be neutral. She is supposed to be on my side. Always.

I take a bite of my PB and J. Just chewing it hurts. Lukas passed on an ice pack for a pretty big cut that I gave him, so I did the same for the wounds that Naomi inflicted on me.

"Lukas." Even saying his name out loud pisses me off. "Let's begin with you explaining why you wanted to murder me. And don't say that wasn't what you were up to 'cause I know it was."

"From what I've observed of you in the past few weeks, Violet, usually you refuse to admit to the existence of things that are happening directly in front of you," Lukas barks. He pauses, takes a sip of his water, and forces a kind of lopsided half-grin. Unlike the rest of his body, his smile muscles aren't worked out that often. I have to admit, it almost makes him look like a person, although I still haven't figured out if he's even human.

"The Aiedeo sent me here," Lukas continues in a more even-tempered tone.

Of course my vicious relatives are behind this. "The Aiedeo want to kill me?"

"No! They not do that to you," Dede protests, but I notice that Lukas says nothing.

I'm about to press him but I get totally distracted by his eye. The cut that I just gave him seems to be fading already. "What the hell is going on with your face?" I walk over to him for a closer inspection. As I reach out to touch his eye, Lukas grabs my wrist and I jump. His lightning reflexes certainly startled me but there's something else. Before I can figure it out, he lets go. "I'm a Vida warrior."

"Vida almost like Aiedeo. They human too and they have very special power," Dede explains as she sprinkles more black pepper in her tea.

"It's a different set of abilities and we have to earn them like the Aiedeo. I can see in the dark and heal myself like you're witnessing now." Lukas traces a finger along his right eye, which, like the rest of his face, is almost back to normal. "However, unlike the Aiedeo, we're immortal."

I wonder how old he is. Sitting there in his jacket and jeans, he doesn't look that much older than me. Although he certainly doesn't seem like a teenager, unless he's a teen from the cast of *Game of Thrones* or something. He's just way more intense than any guy at my school. I think it's because he's a soldier. My father's work has put me around military men my entire life and now that he's said it, I can totally see it. I watch him out of the corner of my eye. His posture is rigid and he holds himself like he's ready for battle at any time.

"My *shama* is about Naomi, right?"

Lukas pauses for a second like he knows what he's about to say will make me flip. "They need you to find Naomi's *preta*."

"Did the Aiedeo kill Naomi? Is that why you were pretending to be an intern at the funeral home? So you could off her?"

"No, neither the Aiedeo nor I had anything to do with Naomi's death," Lukas says.

I have no reason to believe him but I do. That doesn't mean that I think the Aiedeo and he are blameless.

"Naomi's death was part of a cycle that is separate from ours. It was already in the making long before the Aiedeo came into the picture. However, when the Aiedeo learned of its inevitability, they decided to use it for your *shama*," Lukas continues.

"Instead of trying to stop it." I think of my mother's death.

"The Aiedeo do not have the ability to prevent a death that is already predetermined."

I've been fed that exact line many times before. "Except that someone prevented you from killing me. When you got the call. There was something about 'termination aborted.'" Those are about the only two words I remember from Lukas's phone conversation, but they do the trick. His face darkens slightly. "Who saved me? Because it certainly wasn't you."

"Why, I believe you saved yourself, Violet. When you stopped time."

I almost smile. The guy is as good at avoiding the truth as I am.

"You play stop game?" Dede asks, then nods. "That mean you starting remember."

I ignore Dede and keep my eyes on Lukas. He meets my gaze but now his stare goes deeper, like he's searching for something. Searching *me* for something. I know what he's doing because I can do it too. At least, I used to be able to, but now like so many of my Aiedeo powers, I've forgotten how to read people. It's not reading someone's mind, although at one time, I could do that also. Lukas is trying to read my soul—more specifically, he's trying to read my *karun*. Or so the Aiedeo call it; it refers to a person's true self. *Good luck with that,* I think, *because I've buried that so deep, it's gonna take way more than a fiery stare from across the kitchen for you to get inside of me.*

He realizes I know what he's up to and he suddenly looks away. I think he's even blushing. Only a little, because guys like him don't embarrass easily.

"How did you do it, Violet? I mean, stopping time is quite an advanced skill."

I smile coyly and shrug. "Not sure what you mean."

I see that Dede is about to say something and I give her

a look to stay quiet. She has no game when it comes to the Aiedeo. But the less they know—and that definitely goes for Lukas—the better.

Lukas realizes he's not gonna get anything more from me and shifts his focus. "Let's return to the matters at hand. Your *shama* is to find the *preta* who killed Naomi. Dede can explain what a *preta* is to you because, according to the Aiedeo, she's well versed in this area."

Dede beams like she's been given the Medal of Honor. "*Preta* is like monster inside human. It hungry soul that come from person who is selfish—he greedy. It grow and grow until it take over human. They very tricky. *Preta* hide so you no see but they out to get you."

I feel all kinds of shivers run up and down my spine. "WTF? How am I going to find this *preta* if I can't see it?"

"You have to *learn* how to see it and destroy it when you do," Lukas answers.

"Who's going to train me?"

"This isn't a traditional *shama* where you'll be trained by an Aiedeo. There's no time for that. However, I will teach you how to fight," Lukas adds.

"I just beat your ass right now, so how's that gonna help?"

Lukas snorts. "You're a terrible fighter with sloppy technique. You're lucky you even got the few punches in that you did. I didn't fight back because you simply weren't worth the effort."

I flip him off as I wonder why we're even having this

discussion. I admit, on one level, I know it would be good to help Naomi, even if she is wicked and horrible. But not if it means doing anything with the Aiedeo.

"You have until they bury Naomi's body to complete the *shama*."

"Or what?" I ask, although I already know the answer. But I want to hear Lukas say it.

"You will be eliminated."

"I told you, Dede!" I slam my fist on the counter. "Those bitches wanna kill me!"

"No, Violet, they don't," Lukas says. "You're one of them. You're their blood. And you have the potential to be the most powerful Aiedeo that ever existed."

I cock my eyebrow. "What are you talking about? There's no way! I mean, I know that whole stopping-time thing was pretty awesome, but I'm an Aiedeo Lite. I didn't even finish my training."

Lukas looks at Dede. "You haven't told her?"

"*Chht*. Violet not care when I talk about Aiedeo. Maybe she listen to you."

"Every Aiedeo earns her powers during her training. Except you already had powers when you were born. You're not like any of the Aiedeo except Ananya. She was powerful before the gods made her an Aiedeo."

I just stare back at him in shock. If this were a cartoon, I bet my mouth would hit the floor. I was powerful *before* the Aiedeo? After a few seconds of silence, I turn to Dede. "You knew this?"

"I know you always have power and I try to tell you that. But you never want to talk about it." Dede looks at me like I've just won back-to-back Olympic golds. "I didn't know you as powerful as Ananya."

I take a deep, shaky breath and repeat what Lukas said because I need to hear it again to make sense of it. "So you're saying that I'm the most . . . powerful Aiedeo?"

Lukas crosses his arms. "The complication that you present is that you don't stand up for anything—not the Aiedeo, not even for yourself. For lack of a better term, you're a lost soul, which makes you vulnerable."

"I'm sixteen. Give me a break!"

"Age isn't the issue. You know what's at stake here. Jyoti told you the war is coming and we are all preparing. The Aiedeo need you. But they also can't afford to have you out there on your own. You would be too vulnerable to the destroyers; they could easily take you and use your powers against us."

"So if I'm not with the Aiedeo, I'm against the Aiedeo."

"The Aiedeo are giving you this *shama* because they want you to be able to use all your powers to their full potential. They're not the enemy."

Right. "I did find my power when I stopped you from killing me."

"Yes! That was incredible, but that's just one of your powers. And you stopped time for only a few minutes—"

"At least five."

"Fine. Five minutes. Imagine what you could do if you could stop time for an entire day." Lukas lets out a frustrated sigh, which is about the most emotion I've seen from him.

"Everything is locked so deep inside of you. The Aiedeo are giving you the *shama* because they need to know if you'll do what it takes to unlock it."

"And if I don't, then it's—" I mime slitting my throat.

"*Mami*, please! Aiedeo try to help you!"

"No, Dede! Don't you dare try to spin this like the Aiedeo are doing me a favor! They want to use me." I'm about to say something else but I just don't see the point. Dede will always be on the Aiedeo's side. I've had enough. I slide off my stool and walk out the door.

I turn the corner a couple of blocks from my house. I don't usually go for walks but I need to get away from Lukas, Dede, Naomi, and the Aiedeo. Yet they're all that I can think about. I pass by the street where Meryl's mom lives and walk in the direction of the basketball courts. The sun is already setting and I can't believe everything that's happened today.

I think about that famous line from *The Godfather Part III*, Michael Corleone saying, "Just when I thought I was out, they pull me back in." The difference with me is that I guess I was never really out of the Aiedeo.

A faint breeze rustles through the willow tree in the Sanderson's yard. My hair is still damp and I realize I have only my tank top and shorts on. It's chilly but I don't want to go home yet.

"Hey, it's a ghost!" I hear someone call out from behind me. I wonder if Naomi is following me and I almost jump out of my skin. I feel myself trembling, then feel two strong arms around me.

"Na-Naomi," I mumble.

"You're shaking. I didn't mean to scare you," Austin says. He continues to hold me. "I was just teasing you about ghosting me 'cause you kind of disappear on me all the time. You left on Saturday without saying goodbye and you haven't returned my text."

I say a small prayer of thanks that I'm wearing a bra but I wonder if I've brushed my teeth since morning. I'm also painfully aware that my head is totally messed up right now and my stomach is tied in knots and the last time I was like this, I puked on him. A huge part of me wants to throw him off me and run away but this feels really good. He's warm and safe and doesn't have anything to do with death. I feel tears coming to my eyes and before I can stop them, I start to cry. I bury my face in Austin's chest because I am mortified and I don't want him to see me but also because I want to hide inside of him.

"I know Naomi was a friend of yours," Austin says softly as he runs his fingers through my wet hair. "It's hit us all hard."

A pebble of guilt forms in my throat. I'm crying for my own problems, not Naomi's, but if that's what Austin wants to believe, I'll go with it. "Thanks for letting me break down," I whisper after what I hope are my final sobs. I dry my eyes with the backs of my hands and look up at him. God, he's perfect. A lock of his floppy hair falls over his right eye and I'd like to reach up and brush it away but I don't trust my body right now.

"Anytime. I'm just glad you're actually talking to me."

He smiles and I want to melt. "I'm sorry. I've been . . . distracted."

He nods. "That's cool. But when you're less distracted, I'd like to hang out. Get to know you better."

"Yeah," I respond because I can't come up with anything else to say. We're standing so close that I think I hear his heartbeat but that may be mine.

I know it's coming but that doesn't make me any more prepared. He lifts my chin with his finger and dips his face closer to mine. We've kissed before but it's different this time, maybe because we're not buzzed on wine coolers and there's not a raging house party in the background. It's only him and me out here alone at the basketball courts.

I lean in and our foreheads touch. We breathe each other in. Shaky, shallow breaths. His thumb strokes my cheek and I'm dead still from excitement and fear. Austin's lips brush against mine and he kisses me.

It's a perfect movie kiss, the kind you see at the end of a romantic comedy. Except this time, I'm the girl in the movie. It doesn't make me forget everything that's going on, but for right now, I let the world around me fall away.

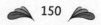

Fourteen

WAKE UP, MY LITTLE BITCH," someone sings into my ear. My eyes pop wide open and I find myself lying face to face with Naomi. She's covered in thousands of tiny maggots that have eaten through her eyes and are creeping out of every crevice in her rotting, naked body.

My heart hammers against my chest, and sweat beads form along my forehead. I jump back so fast that I fall off my bed. Just as I land on the floor, I jerk awake. Slowly, I lift my head and look around. I'm having a nightmare. Maybe.

I wait until my pulse stops racing and I can muster up enough courage to check my bed. With one eye still closed, I cautiously peek up. Waves of relief come over me. No Naomi. But my happiness quickly fades as I become aware of the cold, heavy fear that I went to bed with last night. I'm stuck in a real-life nightmare with the Aiedeo and there is no waking up from it.

After I came home from my walk, Dede was waiting to

151

teach me all about *pretas*. We fought when I refused to listen to her and we didn't speak for the rest of the night.

I totally know that the reluctant superhero is a tired storyline. After all, what asshole doesn't want to be a hero? Apparently, I am that a-hole.

But there's so much more to it than that. I stand up and check my mobile. My alarm will be going off in two minutes, so there is no point in trying to get some more sleep. I head to the bathroom.

Being an Aiedeo feels like all the different sides of me being pulled apart at once. It's my dead mother versus my absent father. My Indian versus my American. My normal versus my freak.

I flash back to my awesome make-out session with Austin last night. It was really good, but it was also more than that. It felt like for the first time ever—I fit in.

I undress and leave my clothes in a messy pile on the bathroom floor. Hooking up isn't that hard because it seems anywhere in the world that you go, there are plenty of horny guys to choose from. But having a guy actually like you for more than a night is harder to pull off. I've never dated anyone. That doesn't make me that unique; many of the other girls at my school have never had a real boyfriend. There are probably a ton of reasons why a guy won't ask me out here in Meadowdale, but I can't shake the idea that the main one is that I'm brown. I know that I risk losing my membership to the NAACP just for thinking it, but I can't pretend it doesn't cross my mind.

I remember when Jay Whitfield asked me to the homecoming dance my freshman year and then had to cancel because he said his mother didn't think we'd look good together in the pictures. I remember how Tommy Carlson told me he liked me but said he wasn't sure what his parents would do if he started dating a "black" girl. I remember Kyle Ramsey saying that I could have been hot if I were white.

All three of these boys were obviously douchebags, and I know there are a lot of very decent white boys out there, but they aren't asking me out. Neither are the small handful of nonwhite boys at my school because, quite frankly, they're busy chasing white girls.

I did what I was supposed to do each time and told Jay, Tommy, and Kyle to FO and walked away. Meryl and Jess shunned them too. But it still hurt. I wish it were the kind of hurt that I can forget. Even if I rationalize that their racism is their problem, not mine, it sticks with me deep down inside.

That doesn't mean that I think it would be easier for me if I moved back to India. I might look like everyone else there but I don't blend in. I'm an ABCD—an American-born confused *desi* (the Hindi word for Indian). Yes, I was born in India, but I left at the age of three, and it's like other Indians can sniff me out as the different one before I even open my mouth.

Whenever I go back there, I wear a pajama kurta, I eat with my hands, and I *puja* at the temple, although I don't know who it is I'm praying to exactly. My Indian relatives try to make me feel like a part of the family but I'm constantly reminded of how much of a foreigner I am. I can fake the customs and even speak the language to a point. But I'm not in on the secret codes, the mores, the rites of passage that make up their Indian identity. I'm simply not one of them.

Not to mention that I don't live in Assam. I live here in Meadowdale. I have already put in the work in this place. It's taken almost a lifetime of blood, sweat, and tears, but for the most part, I have convinced the residents of this town and, more important, my classmates and teachers that I am one of them. I've just never convinced *myself* that I'm one of them.

I step into the shower and crank the knob to as hot as it will go.

That's another reason the Aiedeo piss me off. It's all fine and dandy for them to be using their magical powers, because they aren't alone. I don't have that luxury. I am already the brown girl. I can't be the Aiedeo too.

How could it not get out in a little town like Meadowdale where some people have nothing better to do than expose others' darkest secrets and then take them down? I shudder at the memory of Naomi's bitch-out. And she was their beloved princess. I can only imagine what they'd do to an outsider like me.

Clark Kent, Bruce Wayne, and Peter Parker are too afraid to reveal their secret identities, and they are *white guys*. Am I really supposed to believe that a teenage brown girl gets outed as an ethnic Harry Potter and they'll throw me a parade? *No!* I'll be burned at the stake like those Salem witches.

That's why what happened with Austin yesterday almost feels like cruel timing. It wasn't just a hookup. Yesterday, we connected. *It was real.* I realize that doesn't mean he wants to be my boyfriend, nor do I believe that dating him would somehow give me the stamp of approval that I so crave. Even I'm not that lame.

However, it was a bite. A little taste of what it feels like to be wanted—to be accepted.

So, yes, I'm a selfish, frightened wuss because I know that I can never survive this life *and* be an Aiedeo. Now, though, the bitches have forced me back and I have no choice but to do whatever they want me to do, no matter how twisted it is. I stand under the steaming stream of water and cry. Either way, I'm dead.

I fly past the kitchen and run out the front door. I'm skipping breakfast again but it's worth it to avoid Dede. I know I'll have to face her eventually but I am just not up to it this morning.

I jump into my car and pull out of my driveway. It's especially cold this morning so I crank up the heat. I notice I have a new voicemail and play it.

"Violet Choudhury, this is Detective Alvarez. We're working on the Naomi Talbert case and we'd like to speak to you. Please give me a call. Thank you." She leaves a phone number and hangs up.

I get a little fright. I'm sure the cops are interviewing all of the people around Naomi, but still, it's unsettling. I'm running late as it is and decide I don't have the time to call the detective back now but I'll do it at lunch.

I arrive at school and race across the parking lot toward the entrance. I come to a sudden stop when I see the assistant principal standing by the front doors.

"One more tardy and it's detention for you," Mr. Kreps barks at a mousy brunette, shaking his bald head. Then he raises his hairy arm and points at a dweeby-looking freshman. "And you're gonna wind up on my three-strikes list there, soldier!"

I can't believe that with everything going on, I'm actually worried about getting a tardy. I duck as I pass by Mr. Kreps and just keep walking like everything is normal. My shoulders drop when I make it halfway down the hall without him calling me out. I race the rest of the way to my French class. The final bell rings just as I sit down at my desk.

"*Bonjour!*" Madame Morgan belts out in a slightly too sharp soprano. Rumor has it that she spends summers singing cabaret in a casino near St. Louis.

"*Bun-jor,*" a few students grumble.

While Madame begins roll call, I open my textbook and realize I've completely forgotten to finish my homework. I tap Jessica, who sits next to me. "Crud! I totally flaked on the assignment. Do you have the answers for eight, nine, and ten?"

Jessica looks at me but doesn't say anything.

"Jess, I have everything else. I just need the answers for the last three questions."

Jessica turns away. We've been copying off each other since

elementary school so it isn't like I'm asking Jessica to cross some ethical boundary. Maybe she's annoyed about something else.

"Okay, I know the Squad is probably pissed at me about yesterday but didn't Meryl explain that I was totally having a weird reaction to some medicine I took? Come on, Jess. You don't usually pitch a fit about cheer stuff," I whisper. Instead of replying, Jessica starts chatting with Beau Michaels, who sits on the other side of her.

"Seriously, Jess, you're really gonna ignore me?" I huff. "Fine. I'll just figure out the answers myself." I open my notebook angrily.

"Vee-o-let," Madame Morgan sings, using an exaggerated French accent that makes her sound like a drunken spoon from *Beauty and the Beast*.

"*Oui*," I respond as I scramble to complete my homework.

"Vee-o-let!" Madame chirps again.

"I know the old bat is blind, but is she deaf now too?" I complain under my breath. "*Oui, Madame!* I'm here!"

Madame Morgan shrugs and moves on to the next name. I'm scribbling the translation for "Henry will not eat a sandwich today. Instead, he will eat soup" in my notebook when I notice my pinkie finger. I stop writing and look down at my hands.

It's been a while since I had a proper mani-pedi but when did my nails become pointy little talons? I hold my right hand in my left and realize my skin feels frozen. No wonder I've been so cold all morning—am I coming down with the flu? I slouch low in my seat. I've been so preoccupied that I didn't even check myself out before going to school today. Just how gnarly do I look? I take out my cell phone and click on my mirror app.

"Holy shit!" I scream.

It's my face staring back at me, but it isn't. Even if it's been a rough couple of days, there is no reason for me to appear like . . . like what? I run my hand along my cheek. My eyes, my mouth, even my skin looks lifeless.

Then I gaze up at Madame Morgan. I just shouted out an obscenity in the middle of class and no one has reacted in the slightest bit. In fact, now that I think about it, has anyone made eye contact with me today?

I stand up hesitantly. My entire body shakes from both cold and fear as I walk up to the front of the classroom. I stand so close to Madame Morgan that I can see the hundreds of dandruff flakes that cover her shoulders and smell the green peppers from her breakfast omelet.

I catch my reflection in the window and stare at my full self from head to toe. I open my mouth and see my small pointy teeth. Then I wave my long Gumby arms around and stare at my hands and the talons at the ends of my fingers. I look like Naomi minus the backwards feet.

Everything inside of me stops. In fact, it is like I did the time trick again but to myself. I'm frozen in place. I recognize exactly what I am. Despite my paralysis, I can feel the loud thumping of my heart—is that my heart? Do I still have a heart? Whatever it is, I feel a rhythmic pounding.

The Aiedeo did what I was always afraid they'd do. I stand in the middle of the classroom and look down at myself and then out at the world that doesn't see me. I know exactly what I am.

I am dead.

Fifteen

Day 7: Dead

I RUN THROUGH THE FRONT DOOR of my house. Maybe I'm supposed to be invited in, or is that only vampires? I frantically race to the TV room, looking for Dede. I don't care about our fight from yesterday because that lady has several lifetimes' worth of supernatural mumbo jumbo and right about now is the perfect time to use it.

"Dede!" I yell in a panic, although it's pointless since no one can see or hear me anymore. "Dede!" I shout again out of habit.

"Hold the horse!" Dede hollers as she walks to the top of the stairs, drying her damp hair with a towel. "Where your fire?"

I am rendered temporarily speechless by Dede's mixture of idioms and the fact that she is looking directly at me.

"Y-you can see me?" I ask.

"I always see you, *mami.*"

"But I'm dead."

"I afraid this gonna happen." Dede twists her thin hair into a bun.

"You knew the Aiedeo would do this to me?"

160

"I not ever know what Aiedeo gonna do." Dede starts walking down the stairs. "You no go anywhere. We gonna talk."

A couple of minutes later and Dede is sipping her chai on the sofa, a folder next to her. My uneaten PB and J from this morning is on a plate in front of me, but I'm not hungry. Besides, isn't loss of appetite an upside to death?

"I don't know when this happened," I say. "Maybe it was last night, maybe it was this morning, but sometime in the beginning of first period, I noticed that I was dead."

Dede grunts as she takes it all in.

"Here's the thing, Deeds. I'm invisible to everyone but you. And I look like dead Naomi," I say as I hold up my tiny talons. "Except she's, like, way scarier-looking than me and kind of hotter too. Totally irritating, right?"

Of course, even in the afterworld, Naomi reigns as the hot girl and I am condemned to an eternity in the friend zone. I think about Naomi's white jeans and hope that ghosts can get hemorrhoids.

"I already know but I wonder when you gonna tell me you see Naomi." Dede smiles slyly like she is Hercule Poirot and I am the daft chambermaid that she just caught in a lie.

"Yes, I've seen Naomi. In that Naomi's wicked-ass ghost has been haunting me," I answer wryly.

Dede slaps my hand. "What I always say you, Violet? Ghost only in *Amrican* movie. Ghost not real."

"Yeah, well, Naomi felt pretty real yesterday when she was beating me up," I growl. I don't know if I can move through solid objects but now is as good a time as any to try. I stick my arm through the sofa and wave my hand from the other side. "Oh, and it looks like I can do this, which is, like, a classic ghost move."

Dede opens the folder next to her. She takes out a photo of a grotesque phantom that resembles what Naomi looked like when she was hanging from my bedroom ceiling.

I jump. "How the hell did you get that pic?"

"Mrs. Patel son help me Photoshop it." Dede cackles. She points to the image. "Naomi look like this girl in picture, right?"

"Well, yeah. I mean, the first time that Naomi came around, she definitely had a real gnarly vibe about her. Then she did a total one-eighty and now she's a babe with a big booty and princess hair. Except that she's, like, dead and evil."

Dede pushes up her glasses. "*Chht!* You need be serious, Violet! I not talk about Naomi booty. I mean, she have fingernail like knife, she wear all white, and her feet *beka.*"

"Yes, her feet are backwards, she's wearing white skinny jeans, and she's got nails so long and sharp that they're like claws. And her head is bashed in."

"Then Naomi is *bhoot.*"

"Okaaay, and a *bhoot* is basically the Indian version of a ghost or something. Right?" I ask.

"No. Read," Dede commands as she clicks on the screen of her cell phone.

"'A *bhoot* is a spirit with a lost soul,'" I read aloud. Lukas called me a lost soul yesterday, which still makes my frozen cheeks burn.

"See, *mami.* That easy." Dede beams. "*Bhoot* no scary. *Bhoot* more scared of people than people scared of *bhoot*. *Bhoot* just need your help. You always very nice with *bhoot* and they like you."

"Hold up." I raise my hand. There are so many parts of what Dede just said that make absolutely no sense. "What do you mean that I've always been very nice with *bhoots*? When have I met a *bhoot* before Naomi? You mean the Aiedeo?"

"Aiedeo not *bhoot*," Dede says. "You remember when you very little. When we live in Texas, you have friend name Sarah?"

"Yeah, Sarah Larson." I smile at the memory. "She lived next door and I played with her every day before we had to move here."

"Sarah live in house next door for over twenty year because she die there when she very little girl. Sarah was *bhoot*."

I feel chills up and down my arms. "But why didn't I notice her backwards feet?"

"Maybe you notice but you don't care because she your friend." Dede shrugs and gulps down the rest of her chai. "Remember when you have six birthday party and you kiss that boy?"

"Phineas—Finney? He was a *bhoot* too?" I ask hesitantly. Dede nods.

My face falls. The fact that my first kiss was with a dead boy is more than a bit hard to take right now. I have half a mind to go raid my father's liquor cabinet.

"You not friend with only kid *bhoot*. You also make friend with grown-up *bhoot*. One day you remember you see old lady out in rain and you bring her home and give her tea." Dede chuckles.

I grimace. "Mrs. Doherty? She was dead? How dumb was I?"

"Dumb! You not dumb because you see *bhoot*. That make you special," Dede retorts. "Like Lukas say."

"Yeah, right, I'm *special*." As far as I'm concerned, *special* is a euphemism for *freak*. But this was proof that I had these powers before my Aiedeo training began.

"*Bhoot* part easy." Dede takes a deep breath. "But there more."

I look at Dede and waves of trepidation run through me. However, I want to get the bad stuff over with, so I jump in and blurt out my questions. "Why the hell am I a *bhoot*? Is it because the Aiedeo killed me?"

Dede says nothing but takes out a stack of notebooks from her bag. They are all plain with black covers. I recognize them immediately. We used to read them together when I was a child. I called them "The Aiedeo Chronicles" because they apparently contain everything that my mother ever told Dede about the Aiedeo. I don't know how comprehensive they are because Laya couldn't have known *everything* about the Aiedeo, but they were certainly quite extensive.

My nanny opens up one of them and I feel a little quiver. They're written in Dede's small, neat handwriting, but in the margins, there are notes in flowery cursive that Laya jotted down. I smile to myself. Even now, as I glance at the pages, at the loopy *l*'s and fat *s*'s, I'm surprised that she didn't dot her *i*'s with hearts. Dede wrote everything in Assamese, which I don't read, so she always translated the stories for me. For some reason, Laya wrote her notes in English, and I read those over so often that I memorized them. But like so many other things,

I've completely forgotten about them until now. I trace over one of my mother's bubbly *j*'s.

"Yesterday, after Lukas tell us what your *shama* is, I think it sound familiar," Dede says as she closes the notebook in front of us. She mutters something to herself as she picks up another one. "I remember your mommy tell me story once about her great-great-great-*ita* . . ." Dede licks her finger and flips quickly through some pages. She smiles wide. "Here! I find."

"So what about Laya's great-great-grandmother?" I say impatiently as I tap my talons against the sofa.

Dede ignores me and reads. After a few excruciating minutes, she looks up at me. "This say that this Aiedeo—her name Suchi—she also have *shama* where she need find *preta* to help little dead boy. Aiedeo turn Suchi into *bhoot* to help her. Then, when she find *preta*, they turn her back to alive again."

"Really? She wasn't dead anymore?" I'm so happy that I lean across the couch and give Dede a huge hug. "You mean this isn't permanent? I'm just a temporary *bhoot*?"

"It say here that they turn Suchi back to alive because she complete her *shama*." Dede grimaces.

I wait for her to continue but she doesn't. "Come on, Deeds, tell me."

I see that her eyes are misty and I know it's bad. This broad doesn't get sentimental. "If Suchi no complete *shama*, then she stay *bhoot*."

"The Aiedeo are making good on their ultimatum." My hands tremble. "If I don't find the killer's *preta*, then that's it. It's over for me. I'm dead."

Dede nods and we sit together in silence. She tries to wrap her fingers around mine but it's a bit awkward with my claws, so she just strokes my hand.

After a few seconds, I speak. "But why turn me into a *bhoot*? I mean, how does that help me find a *preta*?"

"I don't know." Dede looks down at the book again and then shrugs. "And Laya say nothing about that."

"What did you say *pretas* were exactly?" I'm really trying my best to understand all this but it's difficult and the words are getting mixed up in my head.

Dede scrolls through her phone and shows me another page titled "Preta." I scan through it:

Preta is a hungry soul created by a human's vice, a human's greed—his selfish desires. His longing grows and grows until he's ravenous and the *preta* eventually possesses him entirely. *Pretas* are conniving and tricky. They hide so that you cannot see them but they are always out to get you.

I feel nauseated. I have no idea how to search for this *preta*, but, worse, I don't know how I'm going to handle it if I actually do find it.

"*Bhoot* no scary but *preta* very, very scary," Dede says as though that hasn't been made abundantly clear.

"Roger on that." I nod. "I mean, how does it work? Is a *preta* like something that possesses you? So you have no control over it?"

"No. *Bhoot* have lost soul but *preta* have evil soul. Human let soul become evil because they maybe greedy or jealous and they always want more, more, more. Never enough and always hungry. So hungry that they do anything."

"Like murder someone."

"Yes."

The wheels in my head start turning, and slowly, I begin to see a way I might pull this off. I'm not gonna kid myself here. It's still a massive long shot but I gotta do whatever it takes to make sure this *bhoot* thing isn't permanent. That doesn't mean that I'm playing nice with the Aiedeo, but I have to accept that for the time being, I'm their bitch.

This *preta* stuff is wack and I'm not even sure if I quite understand it. But if I put this *bhoot* and *preta* business aside for now, what my *shama* really boils down to is a classic whodunit. I've always loved a good mystery.

That doesn't mean I know the first thing about finding a murderer, but like everything else, pop culture has provided me with thousands of examples. From my beloved Poirot, Sherlock Holmes, and Nancy Drew to Jessica Fletcher and even Scooby-Doo. Not to mention the half a dozen Nordic-noir TV series that I binged on last winter.

So I'm gonna channel my inner Saga Norén and do some "real" detective work. It sounds absurd, since I'm far from a super-sleuth. However, I do have one pretty powerful trick up my sleeve. I can talk to the dead.

I feel Dede's eyes on me. "What you thinking, *mami?*"

My last conversation with Naomi ended pretty badly but I

have no choice—I need her if I want the Aiedeo to make me undead. "You have to help me to talk to Naomi."

I sit in front of the Ouija board, staring at the marker. From chanting to long-drawn-out rituals, Dede has tried to teach me several ways to summon the dead throughout my life. It was her way of showing me that I could talk to Laya anytime I wanted. But it never worked when it came to my mother.

Actually, I never really believed it worked at all. However, with this newfound information about me being able to see *bhoots*, I can't help but wonder if all those times I messed around with the Ouija board, there really was something supernatural going on. Like every horror film warns, I never played Ouija alone. Always with friends, mostly at slumber parties, and my only rule was that no one could bring up my mom. (It was one thing for me to try to get in touch with her on my own but I wasn't going to turn her into a parlor game.) But everyone else seemed more than happy to connect with dead relatives so we usually ended up "talking" to someone's deceased uncle or dead grandma. I always played along, but I figured that it was one of my friends pushing the marker along the board.

Now I'm hoping that maybe I was actually connecting with spirits back then because I'm desperate to speak to Naomi right this minute. Even if she claims to have no memory of her death, maybe I can help her get it back. I don't know how, but a conversation between us would be a good start.

Dede eyes the Ouija board and then me; my nanny has never been a fan of what she calls the "amateur" way of talking to the dead. I remind her that Lukas said I have to complete my *shama* before Naomi is buried, and Dede grudgingly admits that Ouija can work in a pinch when you need to find a *bhoot* in a hurry.

At least, it works if that *bhoot* actually wants to speak with you. We try to contact Naomi for nearly an hour, but the only response we get is from a recently deceased eighty-six-year-old farmer from Good Hope who's just passing through.

"Naomi don't wanna see you," Dede finally says matter-of-factly.

My *bhoot* is ghosting me. Great. Obviously, Naomi carried her knack for holding grudges to the afterlife. Although I still don't even know what it was that I did to piss her off. I feel the life being sucked out of me. Figuratively.

Lukas made it sound like it would be so easy for me to just unlock my powers but it feels like trying to walk again after being paralyzed. No matter how much I need it to happen, I just can't get anything to work. And I know I have to because there's no way I'm gonna finish my *shama* without Naomi. If she knows what's on the line for me, she'll help. Right? A tiny lump in my throat tells me not to be so sure.

"*Mami.*" Dede reaches for my hand and I think she's about to say something comforting. "*Law and Order* starting now."

I look at Dede grimly but I know not to get between her and the TV. Even the reruns. Dede clicks the remote. I hear the familiar sound of the gavel knocking and plan B comes to me.

I still have no idea if the Aiedeo turned me into a *bhoot* to help me with my *shama* or to punish me. I tend to think it's the latter, since, honestly, I don't know how being dead is a good thing. Except that I'm invisible, which means that I have access to virtually everywhere.

I watch Mr. Big interrogate a perp and realize that my life has become a surreal version of *Law & Order: Bhoot World*. I kiss my nanny on top of her head. "Dede, I gotta go."

"Where?" she asks. She doesn't turn from the TV but she does squeeze my hand.

"The police station," I say, and I walk straight through the living-room wall and out to the side lawn of my house.

My talk with Dede helped clear a few things up and made me feel loads better. Knowing that I am a temporary *bhoot* is a massive relief, to say the least. However, realizing the Aiedeo could make this my permanent gig feels like I have this bomb inside me that's ready to explode. I'm frightened as hell to find this *preta*, but dying for good is a lot more terrifying.

Sixteen

I'VE NEVER BEEN inside Meadowdale police station before, not because I didn't deserve to be here on several occasions, but because I've never been caught. Marty McClintock is the officer on duty and right now, he's sitting at his desk eating a meatball sub and playing online poker.

On the way over here, I discovered that I can't affect solid objects. For example, I could take a massive bite out of Marty's sandwich, and although I would see it, he wouldn't notice anything.

I'm pretty impressed with myself at the amount of info I've been able to gather in the hour that I've been here. I don't even think I really need to be invisible to access the files; Marty has been so focused on winning back the hundred dollars he lost at the start of the hour, anyone probably could have walked in off the street and sat down at a computer.

I scribble some notes into my pocket notebook. While I subscribe to the notion that the more I know, the better, all this new info I've gathered about Naomi's murder has only served to make this puzzle even more complex. This doesn't bode well for me, since I've got only two days before Naomi's funeral.

I rifle through the various papers one more time to make sure that I haven't missed anything.

Naomi's body was found on the playground of Grant Elementary School. Half of our high school attended Grant until sixth grade, including Naomi and me. It's located on the other side of town from the Talbert Funeral Home, which makes me wonder what she was doing there.

The official coroner's report would take weeks, but the police theorized that Naomi died from a single blow to the right side of her head. That's consistent with the way that Bhoot Naomi looks. They didn't find a weapon.

The biggest clue so far is that they'd been able to pinpoint the time of death as 7:42 p.m. on Sunday. There was actually a witness on the scene who could verify the time. His name is Carl Bixby and he's the janitor at Grant Elementary. He was after my time, so I don't know him. According to his statement, he was inside the school when he heard loud screaming. He thought he heard two voices but he couldn't make out what they were saying and he couldn't tell if they were male or female. He went outside to see what the racket was all about and that's when he saw a figure in a hooded sweatshirt kneeling over a body (later identified as Naomi) lying on the blacktop. He yelled, "What's going on out there?" and the person ran away. It was dark and raining so Carl didn't get a good look at the figure and couldn't say for certain if it was a male or a female.

Knowing when Naomi was killed is major. My belly quivers. Naomi had called me a few times on Sunday. I check my cell phone and see that the third phone call she made to me was at 6:25 p.m. I wonder if I was one of the last people she tried to get in touch with before she was killed and a feeling of guilt sucker-punches me. Why didn't I just answer? If I had, could I have prevented her murder in some way? Even if Lukas claimed that Naomi's death was already predetermined, I wonder if my neglect helped guarantee her tragic fate. If I get to go back to my life, I vow never to ignore anyone like I did Naomi.

There was also tearing and bruising around Naomi's inner thighs and genitals. Police don't believe she was sexually assaulted at the time of the murder because a preliminary examination indicates that the tearing and bruising were at least several days old.

I steady myself against the desk. Thinking about those final moments in Naomi's life stirs up a whirl of conflicting emotions. I'm angry, frustrated, and profoundly sad.

What was Naomi doing out at the Grant Elementary School playground on Sunday evening after dark? Did she know her killer or was he a random stranger? I can't help but think the only reason she would be there was if she was meeting someone. But who, and why *there*?

I mull all of this over and try to think like a detective—a TV detective. I check the weather report and verify that there was a heavy drizzle that evening, like Carl claimed. This means that the two people would have had to be shouting pretty loud for Carl to hear them inside the school. The school is in the middle of town and it's surrounded by family homes. How is it that no one else heard screaming? Unless, of course, Carl is lying and it was just him and Naomi. A shiver runs down my spine. I make a note to go check out Grant Elementary and Bixby.

I keep on reading. An interesting detail is that Naomi's purse and wallet were found with her but not her phone. What teenage girl goes anywhere without her cell? Did she lose it in the struggle? It hadn't turned up when the police searched the area. Did the killer take Naomi's phone with him, and if so, why?

I hear loud talking and whip around to see the police station doors swing open and Sheriff Hopper and two people that I recognize from the school assembly the other day walk in. For a second I duck, then I remember that I'm a *bhoot*.

I follow all three of them down the hallway. My father and Sheriff Hopper are friendly, in that Dad puts up with him because he's local law enforcement and Hopper thinks Naresh can help him get one of those crime-commentator gigs for the national news networks. Naresh might be able to do that for someone but I doubt he'd waste his contacts on helping out Sheriff Wayne Hopper.

I've probably exchanged less than twenty words with Wayne in all the time I've known him. Four years ago, when I wore my jet-black hair super-straight and almost to my waist, he commented that I made a "pretty Pocahontas."

Hopper is a total ignorant blowhard with a serious Dirty Harry complex. He's been the sheriff here for decades and it doesn't seem like he's going anywhere, especially because he's known to use his influence to help out his "favorites," most of whom are local star athletes.

I turn from Hopper to the two detectives on the other side of the desk. At least I assume they're detectives because they're dressed like cops on any generic basic-cable crime procedural. I grab the guy's badge and it says Jason Sanborn, FBI, Chicago. The woman's identification tells me she's Cameron Alvarez, FBI, Chicago. Alvarez was the detective that had wanted to ask me questions, the one I was supposed to call back.

Hopper tries to engage in some friendly chitchat but Alvarez clearly doesn't do small talk.

"We're still trying to find out who the administrators behind *Heffers and Hos* are." Alvarez turns to her partner. "Do you want to update Sheriff Hopper?"

"Right." Sanborn nods. "These kind of anonymous gossip sites have become prevalent throughout the Midwest. They seem to target small to midsize high schools. They are incredibly difficult to take down and have posed many problems for school officials and law enforcement. When they are taken down, similar sites pop up within hours."

"Sounds like a real problem," Hopper says.

Sanborn continues. "The site's administrators remain

anonymous, although we've got our best guys working on it, so we hope to find out something soon. The posts are made by local high-school kids who don't take any measures to hide their identity, but we haven't yet been able to determine who posted the video of Naomi Talbert."

"We think it might have been posted by the person who filmed it," Alvarez adds. "Judging by the angle of the camera, it might be that the subjects weren't aware that they were being taped. Which would mean that the person filming was the only one to know that a tape existed."

Sanborn pulls a photo out of the folder that Alvarez is holding. "Our techs are still analyzing the video but we were able to enhance this image of a tattoo found on the inner thigh of one of the unidentified males. Does it look familiar to you?"

I lean across the desk until I'm so close that my hair is brushing against Hopper's four o'clock shadow. I recognize the tattoo immediately because when I saw it the first time, I thought it was the stupidest thing ever. It's of our MHS mascot pioneer with a baseball thumping like a heartbeat in his chest. Everyone on the entire varsity baseball team got one when they won State last year.

Hopper squints, rubs his chin. "I think I've seen somethin' like that on a couple of the jocks."

Why is the sheriff being so cagey? I could open up a yearbook right now and point to every single one of the guys who were inked with that ridiculous image.

"To be accurate, all twelve of the varsity baseball players

sport this tattoo." Sanborn crosses his beefy arms. "Despite the fact that most of them are underage."

Hopper chuckles. "Sounds like a bad case of male bondin' to me."

"Sounds like twelve possible suspects to me," Alvarez counters.

I gulp.

"Suspects?" Hopper leans against his rolling chair. "For showin' up in some girl's sex tape?"

"An alleged sex tape is posted online on Saturday." Alvarez speaks carefully, like she's holding something back. "The female on that video is found dead on Sunday. You admitted that your team hasn't come up with any new leads. Certainly, identifying the two males in that video is a good place to start."

I snatch the folder in her hand but it doesn't contain anything but the photo. I study it to see if there are any additional clues that I can pick up, but it's just a close-up of a guy's inner thigh.

"We suggest you call in the varsity baseball team. We'll sit in on the questioning," Sanborn says. His tone is too know-it-all and you can see Hopper almost jerk his entire body forward.

"Uh-huh," Hopper says. He shoots both Alvarez and Sanborn a look saying there's no way that's happening. "This ain't the city. This is a small town and everyone's already pointin' fingers on who done what to Naomi Talbert. Anyone I even bring in on questionin' is gonna have to deal with a lot of whisperin' behind his back. So you can bet that I'm not gonna bring the entire baseball team in just 'cause some guy had sex with a pretty gal and there happened to be a camera on."

"It's not a request, Sheriff," Alvarez responds. She's clenching her fists so tightly that her knuckles are white.

"Well, as far as I'm concerned, Detective Al-va-rez," Hopper says, scowling, "you're my guest on this investigation."

Alvarez squares her shoulders and looks Hopper in the eye. "Oh, that's right. We haven't apprised you of all of the newest developments from our end. As of this morning, we've been given full mandate to take over this investigation if we see any signs of neglect or incompetence. I would say not bringing in the baseball players would be evidence of both."

You can practically see the steam blowing out of Hopper's ears. He doesn't say anything to Alvarez or Sanborn. Instead, he picks up the outdated phone on his desk and presses a button. "Marty, get the MHS varsity baseball team in here tomorrow."

The two detectives nod at Hopper smugly before taking off. I sit there on the sheriff's desk half stunned. *Holy Batman!* I try to process everything that I've just heard. I had a hunch that the sex tape might have something to do with the murder but I didn't think anyone from school was in it. Truthfully, I hadn't watched it since the first day, but I just assumed the guys were from the local college. Naomi always hung out there, and threesomes seemed on an advanced level beyond high school. But what did I know? Hopper is right. The town's gossip mill will be on fire once people find out every member of the entire varsity baseball team is being questioned. I tap my claws against Hopper's desk. I'm on a literal deadline and can't wait until tomorrow. I need to find out some answers now and I know just where to get them.

Seventeen

I cross Seth Rumley's name off my list. After going to the principal's office and getting a copy of our yearbook, I have spent practically the entire afternoon searching through the phones, backpacks, and lockers of all the varsity baseball players. Out of the twelve guys that had the tattoos, only two had graduated, so most of last year's team is still at MHS.

I slip Seth's phone back into his pocket and sit down at the empty desk next to him. He's the last guy on my list. There's a chance that maybe one of the baseball players that's now in college could be one of the guys in the video but I doubt it. I don't know what I'm looking for exactly—a note saying *I killed Naomi*, maybe—but so far, my snooping has turned up diddly-squat. Except some juicy gossip if it's really news that Marc McMillan and Tara Sullivan had sex on home base and then he posted photos of her newly enhanced size DD chest on the team's secret message group. *Prick.*

The bell rings and I walk out into the hallway with everyone else. Standing here as my classmates whiz by is weird. I usually try so hard to blend in, and now I'm actually invisible. In some ways, it's not that different. I see everyone talking, laughing, joking, flirting, whispering, and doing all the other usual high-school stuff and I feel as much of an outsider as I always do. It's just that in my current state, I don't even have to try to fit in. Nor do I need to kid myself that it's actually possible.

I see Naomi's boyfriend, Trent, walk by. Naomi and Trent were Meadowdale's very own royalty. The absurdly photogenic pair represented the very best of the white-hetero-high-school-sweethearts mythology that small towns like this feed on.

He has big, dark circles under his sky-blue eyes and his usually suntanned skin is pale. Once I started striking out with the baseball team, I widened my search to include a few more guys, and one of them is Trent.

After all, Trent had a better motive than anyone, since he probably went ballistic when he saw that sex video. Maybe he's the other guy in it, but so far, there's no news to suggest that, which means he must have been super-pissed at Naomi for cheating on him. Now that I think of it, didn't Collette mention seeing them fighting after Friday's football game? I didn't find anything interesting when I went through Trent's things but that doesn't make him innocent.

I walk by Caleb Rainey and a little shiver runs down my spine. His jaw is covered with patches of hair and I can't tell if he was drunk-shaving this morning or if he's trying to grow a beard. Either way, he looks more weaselly than usual. He takes a stack of books from his locker, and I start to go through it. After a minute or so I realize it's nothing but standard school stuff and I switch to his bookbag, which is hanging on a hook inside.

I unzip the main pocket and rifle around. Nothing unusual except for a zip-lock bag of drugs. There are a few dime bags of pot along with a couple of handfuls of loose pills. I inspect the contents more closely. Other than the weed, I don't recognize anything in here. These can't all possibly be for him and Nate.

I wonder if Caleb is a dealer. It seems a bit off since he doesn't need the money, but then, how else would he have friends? I put the baggie back. Even though the drug-sniffing dogs come out only twice a year, how arrogant do you have to be to bring drugs to school? Then I remember that the Raineys pledged a million dollars for the new football stadium and I realize Caleb clearly isn't afraid of getting caught.

He shuts his locker and the loud bang makes me jump. I stick my hand into his front pocket to grab his phone, and just being that close to his junk grosses me out. It's password-protected but I press 1-2-3-4 and it unlocks. I really can't believe how many guys use that password. I'm sure it's all the paranoia that Naresh has instilled in me about theft, but am I the only nerd who changes my passwords every three months?

I've snooped through so many phones today that I have it down to an exact science that requires only about four minutes. This time, I'm not even a minute in before I find a gallery of creep-shots. My mouth drops open. There's gotta be at least a hundred pics of girls' privates, all of which I assume were taken without their knowledge, judging by the "upskirt" angle of the photos. I start to feel sick as I scroll through them. I don't know if these are all from my school but I can feel my pulse quicken when I recognize one of the shots. I can barely make myself click on it, but I do. My cheeks flame. I've got boy shorts on underneath my cheer skirt so I'm completely covered up, but that's not the point. I feel so violated. I wasn't going commando, but that doesn't change the sense of rage, shame, and disgust that I feel.

I force myself to look through the rest of his photos to see if there's anything in there with Naomi. Could be, but I can't tell, since faces aren't what Caleb focuses on.

I want to make that sicko bastard Caleb pay for this and realize I can start by going to Cameron Alvarez. I'd taken her digits down. I spend the next few minutes using Caleb's phone to text all his photos to the detective.

I don't know if these creep-shots mean that Caleb is Naomi's killer but I certainly think his pervy ass is a prime suspect. I finish searching through his phone and am half relieved and half angry when I don't find anything more.

I make a mental note to go check out Caleb's house later to see if I can find more dirt on him. I walk down the hallway, trying to get the bitter taste of that degenerate out of my mouth, and I get happily sidetracked by seeing Austin.

He's walking in late to class and I decide to follow him.

"Sorry, Mr. P." He shrugs coolly as he hands the teacher a pink excuse note from the principal's office.

"Sit down, please, and open your textbook to page two hundred and twelve," Mr. Petrovic says.

I feel my heart race as I watch Austin saunter to his desk. I move so that I am standing directly next to him. Maybe it's a *bhoot* thing but all of a sudden, I notice that my senses feel like they're on fire. I can practically taste the remnants of the Coke he drank at lunch mixed with the piece of Big Red he's chewing on. I fantasize about all the stuff I could do to him right now while I'm invisible. It's kind of hot but also totally skeevy, especially as I flash to Caleb. Ick! I try to shake him out of my mind, at least temporarily. I've been sleuthing hard all day and deserve a perv-free moment with Austin.

Of course I'm tempted to rifle through Austin's personal belongings although I know it's shady. Even if I've spent the last several hours doing just that to other people, I really was looking for clues about Naomi's case. Yes, I uncovered some curious tidbits about a couple of the baseballers along the way, but hot gossip is not a priority with death hanging over my head. I already promised myself that I'd never mention anything I found that wasn't Naomi-related, which seems pretty fair. Except Caleb, but that's an exception that I was more than happy to make.

However, Austin isn't a baseball player and I hardly think he's the guy in the sex tape. Although I really don't know what Austin does when he's not playing the guitar. Maybe that's why I should try to find out, I tell myself. I can literally see a devil and an angel sitting on my shoulders and arguing as though I'm in a cartoon.

I hate to say it but it's not my conscience holding me back; it's fear. What if Austin has some strange obsession like our shortstop John Barnes and his furries fetish? Worse, what if I discover that Austin is crushing on someone else? I feel a pang in my chest. Our awesome movie kiss happened only yesterday but that already seems like a lifetime ago. I can still feel the vibration of him run through me, but what if I was kidding myself about our connection?

Before I can talk myself out of it, I reach down and pull Austin's cell out of his pocket. This time, I don't mind how deep I plunge my hand next to his crotch. I type in 1-2-3-4, then click on his text messages. I can hear my heart beating in my ears as I scroll through them. When I reach as far back as a month ago, a rush of relief runs through me. Girls flock all over Austin but he doesn't have a girlfriend.

I finish my investigation in exactly four minutes and happily determine that the guy is a standard horny teenage boy, but other than that, he's pretty vanilla. I'm about to return his phone to his pocket when I notice a symbol of a treble clef.

I press on it and see that it's some kind of songwriting app. I didn't know that Austin actually wrote his own music. Guilt starts to creep up again. I am just about to exit the app when I spot my name among the other song titles. I catch my breath. If a guy writes a song about you, then he's, like, totally whipped, right? Unless this is a hate ballad. What if he mentions my jiggle butt and cottage-cheese thighs?

The suspense is too much to take. I shakily click on my name. It takes me a second to process what I see. There is only one word: *exotic*. I cringe. I don't know if it's a song title but it bugs me that it's under my name.

Exotic is the word white people use to tell brown girls

they don't belong. As in, *You don't fit in with our fair-skin-light-eyes-straight-hair standard of beauty, so that makes you exotic.* I was described as exotic so often by the time I was ten that I finally looked the word up. It means "not native, different, foreign, strange." I know most of the time, people mean it as a compliment, but it never feels like one. The fact that Austin used it makes me irritated and slightly confused.

All of a sudden, I feel a strange tingly sensation run through me, like I'm being poked with a thousand different needles. At first it tickles but then the feeling intensifies. A sharp, splintering pain radiates through me as a series of cracks and crunches echo in my ears. Something is twisting my ankle bones from the inside out and it is excruciating! I look down and nearly topple over from the shock. My feet are turned backwards.

I land with a loud thud in the middle of the parking lot at the Talbert Funeral Home.

"Did you tell them to do this to me?" I scream into Lukas's face. I point down at my feet. They are grotesque, like Naomi's, with the ankles facing front. The pain is so torturous that I fall down.

Lukas looks around to see if anyone is watching, then hoists me over his shoulder and walks behind the garage. He sets me down on the grass and I sit up but I don't dare to stand on my aching feet.

"No, I did not," Lukas says. "The Aiedeo make their own decisions."

"Of course you didn't stop them!"

He crosses his arms. "No."

I glare at him in silence for a minute before I speak. "So why did those bitches do this?"

Lukas scowls. The guy is so good at making me feel like a disobedient child that I wonder if he was a strict headmaster at an English boarding school in a past life. Although immortals probably don't reincarnate.

"It's because I snooped into Austin's phone, right?" I say grudgingly. "I realize it's like a total violation of the superhero code to use my powers for my own selfish reasons, but seriously, isn't flipping my feet a bit harsh?"

"Most of what you said sounds like your usual nonsense but 'selfish reasons' does ring true." Lukas sighs. "The Aiedeo turned your feet backwards to send you one step further into being a permanent *bhoot*. It's a warning that this isn't a game."

"I know that! It's my life!" I shout.

"Violet, I'm not here to tell you what to do but I believe you should speak with Naomi," he says.

"Duh. It's not so easy since she's totally ghosted me. Know any spells I can use to get her back?"

"I don't do spells."

He lets out a noise that I think is a slight chuckle and I smile despite myself. Lukas points to an upstairs window of the Talberts' house. "Dropping in unexpectedly might work."

I follow his finger and see the outline of Naomi's back against the window. A sense of dread comes over me. I'm also not quite sure why Lukas is being nice to me. That is, if not trying to kill me qualifies as "nice." Then I remind myself that

I am already dead. That's why I have no choice but to force Naomi to talk to me.

I get up shakily and try to stand on my throbbing backwards feet. My gnarly hoofs definitely qualify as "exotic." It's good that the *bhoot* lifestyle requires very little walking because these puppies are painful. More agonizing than when Naomi forced the entire Squad to wear shimmery silver five-inch stiletto heels to our first national cheer competition. We looked like junior delegates at a stripper convention.

I turn to ask Lukas for a boost but he's already gone. I brace myself against the garage wall for balance. When I'm steady enough, I leap up and fly through a third-story window of the Talberts' house.

Eighteen

I<small>T'S A PRETTY ROUGH LANDING</small> on the hardwood floor inside Naomi's bedroom but I'm actually kind of proud of myself for managing to get up here.

"Violet?" I hear Naomi say from somewhere. "OMG. You look totally busted."

I stand up slowly on my wobbly *bhoot* feet and look for Naomi. The Talberts renovated the entire attic and turned it into a massive mega-bedroom for Naomi's thirteenth birthday. Although it was supposed to be a gift for Naomi, I bet the real beneficiaries were the Talberts and their younger son, since this effectively kept Naomi isolated from them.

"Are you blind? I'm up here."

I look up to see Naomi hanging from the ceiling like she did when she first visited me as a *bhoot*.

"I'm dead like you," I say. There is no joy at reuniting with Naomi, just queasiness. "Sort of."

"Did someone hurt you too?" Naomi asks as her face clouds with concern.

I'm touched by her display of what seems like genuine emotion. Plus, I'm surprised she hasn't thrown me out yet, so I take a seat in an overstuffed black-and-white-striped chair. "Not exactly." I prop my throbbing feet on an ottoman. I continue. "Remember the stuff we talked about with the Aiedeo, special powers and that helping you was my *shama*?"

"Powers? As in more than one? You can do more than just talk to dead people?"

I nod.

"Show me. I want to see what you've got."

I shift in my seat. I should have guessed that Naomi would egg me on. "It doesn't work like that. I can't just spark up my powers at the drop of a hat. At least, not yet."

"So you're, like, the lamest superhero ever." Naomi plops down onto her bed. "Is that why you're dead? Because the Hall of Justice decided they didn't want you around?"

"Ha-ha," I reply dryly. "I'm not a superhero. I'm a *bhoot*. You're a *bhoot* too."

"I thought I was a ghost. What's a *bhoot*?"

"Ghosts don't exist. A *bhoot* is a spirit." I falter a bit at this last part because it's awkward to tell a *bhoot* directly to her face. "A spirit with a lost soul."

Naomi stays quiet for a few seconds before speaking. "I'm still confused about the difference. But I do get the lost-soul stuff. I mean, my soul *does* feel pretty lost."

I nod. This is going smoother than I thought it would. "But I have the possibility to reverse my status back to living."

"So you're only temporarily dead? I guess I forgot to check the box for that option."

"The Aiedeo turned me into a *bhoot* so that I can help find your killer and, you know, help your soul find peace." I point to my feet. "They gave me these suckers about an hour ago to warn me that if I don't get my act together, I'm condemned to Bhoot World for eternity."

"Well, my aunt Jenny tried to make out with my boyfriend last Christmas. Guess we've got shitty relatives in common," Naomi says. "I feel your pain. I could barely stand the first day but it gets better after twenty-four hours or so. Maybe longer. When you've got eternity, you stop paying attention to time."

"Good to know, I guess."

"Aside from the fact that they killed you, the Aiedeo must really hate you, Violet." Naomi scans me up and down. "Or was it your lame idea to wear your Pioneer Poms uniform? A dead cheerleader is such a cliché."

I look down at myself and I'm completely stunned. There's been so much going on that I haven't even paid attention to what I'm wearing. I admit that I'm totally lame. Still, I can't let Naomi get away with ragging on me. I eye her skintight jeans. "It's still better than having a permanent wedgie in the afterworld."

"Touché." Naomi laughs.

"There's no doubt that the Aiedeo totally suck for making me dead. *And* for making me wear this." I pinch the roll of chub that hangs over my waist. "Check out my muffin top! It's like

191

the Aiedeo cursed me to damnation with a uniform that's two sizes too small."

Naomi cracks up and I join her. After a few seconds, we calm down enough to speak.

"But how am I supposed to trust you, Violet? I already over-heard your plan to get rid of me. An exorcism? Seriously?"

"At the time, I thought you were a sadistic spirit, so can you really blame me for being scared? You got all in my face with that haunting-me-for-the-rest-of-my-life stuff." I pause. Naomi isn't attacking me at this very moment, but that doesn't mean her viciousness isn't going to show itself at one point or another. Dead or alive, Naomi has lots of different faces, I know. "But now, it works out for both of us if we cooperate."

Naomi stays silent for a couple of seconds. "Fine. You help me and I'll help you."

"Sounds like a plan, Stan," I joke as I hold out my hand.

She takes it and we shake. I reach for my pocket notebook. "I went to the station and read your police report. Maybe some of these details might help you remember what happened the night you were killed."

I look up at Naomi and she's not listening at all. A slow, slightly devious smile breaks across her face. "Wanna see some-thing totally messed up?"

I hesitate. In the past, when Naomi asked me this, it never turned out to be something that I wanted to see. Nor was it ever really a question.

"In a second, but first, let's try to jog your memory," I say with a bunch of false enthusiasm.

"Later," Naomi says as she whizzes across the room. She stops at the doorway and then turns in my direction. "Follow me."

"Oh my God, this so messed up," I mumble.

We are standing in the Talbert Funeral Home's morgue staring at Naomi's dead corpse. The cadaver looks a lot like Bhoot Naomi except that it is naked and way stiffer with more veins sticking out.

A disturbing thought hits me. Where the hell is my real body? Have the Aiedeo stashed it somewhere? I make a mental note to ask Lukas. But now I need to put my full attention back on Naomi so I don't lose her again.

"The embalming fluid totally makes me look bloated but check out my abs." Naomi lifts the sheet to expose her six-pack. "Pretty bangin', right?"

I notice Elizabeth, Naomi's mother, watch the sheet rise.

"Wait—you can affect objects?"

Naomi nods. "It took me a few days to learn how to do it. But now I've gotten pretty good. See!" She drops the sheet, then lifts it again.

"Naomi, don't do that!" I slap her hand. "It's freaking your mom out."

Elizabeth Talbert is a long-standing MILF and the obsession of every husband over at Meadowdale Country Club, all of whom count the days to swimsuit season. Watching Liz jump off the high dive in her two-piece has become a national sport for the Viagra set.

One can see where her only daughter inherited her beauty,

but whereas Naomi is hot, Liz is more of a cool beauty. In the past few years, there's been something almost ghostly about her. Her porcelain skin appears translucent and her gaunt face looks hollow. Some of the townspeople joke that Liz turned herself into one of the corpses. She's responsible for applying the makeup on the dead bodies, and I have to admit, she has the same heavy hand with her own face. Especially the blusher, which she wears as if it were tribal war paint.

"Violet, do you see the half-empty bottle of vodka next to my mother's chair? She's too blotto to see or feel a thing. Believe me," Naomi snaps.

I watch Elizabeth swoosh the ice around in her glass, then take a big long sip. A lump forms in my throat. How did I forget about Naomi's alcoholic mother? Liz is a discreet drunk.

"Does she do this often?" I whisper even though Elizabeth can't hear us.

"Drink? You know my mom is all about consistency. She's at it every day, all day."

"I remember," I answer. "But I mean, does she sit here with your dead body a lot? Because it looks like she's been here awhile."

Naomi and I are both good at hiding things. How well you can pretend that everything is normal on the outside no matter what chaos is going on inside is what separates the amateurs from the pros. We're fierce warriors when it comes to faking it.

Lie and deny. That's our shared motto. Lie to everyone and deny to ourselves. The lump in my throat grows.

"She's been down here every day since I died," Naomi says.

"Which was Sunday evening!" I say it a bit too excitedly but I'm hoping this might shake something loose in Naomi's head. "That was two days ago. Can you remember Sunday at all, Naomi?"

But Naomi is ignoring me and glaring at her mother. "The woman is cray."

I have stopped trying to figure out why parents do the things they do but it's obvious that Elizabeth is in a great deal of pain. "Naomi, she's just lost her only daughter. Cut her some slack."

"You and your mommy issues," Naomi growls. "You've always had such a soft spot for her."

It's true that it's always easier to feel sorry for drunks when they aren't your own problem. But Naomi has downright rage for Liz and I don't think it's all because of her alcoholism.

"Hey, do you think we should wait for my mother to pass out and just do my makeup ourselves?" Naomi lifts the head of her dead body. The skin on the side of her face that is bashed in starts to slide down. "You know how my mother ends up making everyone look like a dead drag queen. And I want people to remember me as, you know—hot."

Elizabeth jumps up, kicking over her chair in the process. "Naomi? Baby, are you here? Please, please talk to me."

I race over and push Naomi away. She lets go of her head and it drops back onto the cold metal slab. "What are you doing? You're gonna give your mother a heart attack!" I scold.

"That's assuming she's got a heart," Naomi says wryly. She studies her *bhoot* fingernails, then shows them to me. "These claws are seriously out of control. I tried cutting them but it's impossible. But now that you're here, you can give me a mani-pedi."

"Naomi!" Elizabeth shrieks, then breaks down crying.

"You're being cruel."

"Back off, Violet," Naomi warns. "Lizzy didn't give a damn about me except when it helped her. Those tears will be good and dry by the time they bury me."

Then I remember. I was at a sleepover at Naomi's. It was the summer before my eighth-grade year and before Naomi went to high school. She had discovered that her mother was having an affair with a doctor up at the hospital. She swore me to secrecy. It was the last time that I ever spent the night at the Talberts'. We never talked about it again but I can see now just how much Elizabeth's transgression still hurts Naomi. She's still furious at her.

"Naomi," Mrs. Talbert calls out again.

"You're still angry at her for cheating on your father, aren't you?"

Naomi looks at me strangely and it takes her a minute to answer. "How did you—that's right, I told you at my house. Yeah, I'm still pissed . . ."

Naomi lets her voice trail off and we stand there quietly as Elizabeth continues to cry out for her daughter.

"Mrs. Talbert?"

We whip around to see Lukas walking in.

"Leave me alone, please." Elizabeth turns away from him.

"I'm sorry, ma'am, but we have a pickup and I need the

space." Lukas reaches into the jacket pocket of his undertaker suit and pulls out a tissue. "Here."

His bedside manner leaves a lot to be desired but at least he's coming off as human and even genuinely concerned. Elizabeth grabs the tissue and blows her nose. Lukas turns and now he's much more monster as he glowers at Naomi and me. He points toward the exit and mouths, *Get out*.

"Wait, can the intern see us?" Naomi asks.

I don't know how much Lukas wants Naomi to know but I really don't care. I like to piss him off. "Yup, and he can hear us. That's because Lukas isn't just an intern. He works for the Aiedeo. He kills people for them. In fact, he tried to kill me yesterday, and most likely he'll try again. Oh, and he's immortal."

"That's kinda hot."

I frown. "You did hear the part where I said he tried to kill me, right?"

"Bad boys are always more fun." Naomi winks at Lukas. "Although he discovered me cooking up a batch of fry and lorded it over me, which was a total dick move."

Fry are cigarettes dipped in embalming fluid. I have never tried them, nor would I—they supposedly mess you up bigtime. Not in a good way.

Now it makes sense. I remember how Naomi obeyed Lukas's order to leave Dr. Jenkins alone. It must have been because she didn't want to get in trouble for dealing drugs. I shake my head. Princess Naomi is a pusher? Just how many secrets is this girl hiding?

While Elizabeth strokes dead Naomi's hair in a daze, Lukas

glares at us so hard that his pupils start to dilate. Suddenly, we begin to vibrate.

"What's he doing?" Naomi asks.

"I don't know. Some Jedi mind trick. He pulled it on you at school the other day when you were chasing me."

"Really? I can't remember."

I hold up my hand toward Lukas. "We're leaving so you can stop doing whatever crazy crap you're trying to do to us."

"Yeah, we're out." Naomi checks her mobile. "Burner phone. Seems I lost my cell somewhere between living and dying. It's almost impossible to get a signal in the afterworld—"

"That was in the police report," I interrupt excitedly. "They couldn't find your phone on you, so maybe we should start there. Figuring out what happened to your phone will allow us to trace your steps that night."

"But Magnus just texted me the deets for the rave."

"Who's Magnus and what rave?"

"With the other ghosts, ghouls, spirits—*bhoots*—whatever," Naomi says, as though it is perfectly normal.

"Absolutely no way!" I yell. I point to the clock hanging on the wall. "I have to find your killer by the time they bury you, which is, like, in two days!"

"Then I suggest a little tit for tat. You scratch my back. Whatever," Naomi says in her most devious tone. "You come to the party with me and be my wingman and then I'll answer all the questions you want."

"I can't go to a party because I need to solve your murder," I protest.

Naomi eagle-eyes me from head to toe, then squishes up her face into a disapproving look. "But if we're gonna be seen together, you need a serious makeover."

Before I can object, Naomi grabs me and we are flying out the door.

Nineteen

I PULL DOWN THE ZIPPER on the jacket of my black Adidas tracksuit. Technically, it's Naomi's tracksuit, which means that the pants hug my booty so tight that I'm afraid to fart lest I rip them apart at the seams. I fought Naomi on the outfit but the fashionista insisted that the real world and the *bhoot* world are all about the badonkadonk.

Naomi also brushed my long black hair out, waxed my brows, and piled on the blusher and lip gloss. I put my (backwards) foot down and won against bronzer, which even as a *bhoot* brown girl I don't need. And I yanked off my fake eyelashes the moment she put them on because I was starting to look like a dead Kardashian. I would have loved to finish the makeover with a cool pair of kicks but footwear didn't really work with my ratchet feet. Nevertheless, I feel pretty fly.

We're back in Naomi's room and I'm letting her make me over for the rave, but the last thing that I want to do is get down to Major Lazer with a bunch of *bhoots*. I want to be home and alive and *normal* again.

Naomi stands back and looks me over from head to toe. "You look so dope! We're gonna have a blast!"

"Naomi, please, let's just go to Grant Elementary first and see if it jogs your memory. Especially because I'm pretty sure your killer isn't going to be at a rave."

Naomi crosses her arms and swings her hip out. "And how exactly are you going to find my *preta*? With your *powers*?"

I understand her skepticism. I have quite a bit of it too. It doesn't help to have a countdown to my permanent death. Of course, having Naomi with me is a bonus if she'd give me some information. I decide to take another stab at some questions.

I try to keep the desperation out of my voice. If Naomi senses weakness, she pounces. "Going back to the scene of the crime might help you remember something."

"Not if I don't have any clue about what happened." Naomi shifts her weight to her other leg. "Besides, what if this is a trick and the Aiedeo are just going to get rid of you anyway?"

As shady as the Aiedeo are, I hadn't thought of this option. "I suppose that's a possibility. But, you know, you're also getting something huge out of this too. Eternal peace, remember?"

"What does that even mean?" Naomi scoffs. "Maybe it's better to be like this and not alone. We'd be here together."

My jaw drops. "Are you kidding me? You want me to die so you'll have a permanent BFF?"

"Why do *you* get an option to live or die?" Naomi shouts. "I never got that choice!"

There it is. Naomi's other face. I can feel my blood boiling. "And what would you have us spend the rest of eternity doing?

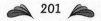

Going to raves and hooking up with random scrubs? Maybe I can video your exploits. I mean, I'm not sure if your last sex tape made it to the afterworld."

"Sex tape . . ." Naomi stares at me with a combination of rage, which I know so well from her, and hurt, a far less familiar emotion. Her voice is quiet at first, then rapidly crescendoes as she says, "Sex tape? You think me being screwed by a couple of guys when I was so trashed that I didn't even know what was going on is a sex tape? That I wanted that to happen? And that I wanted everyone to see it? My friends, my teachers, my neighbors, my parents—my little brother!"

"I didn't . . . I just thought that . . ." I don't know what to say.

"Fuck. You." Streams of tears fall down Naomi's face. "You were never my friend, Violet. And I don't care if you live or die."

I reach out for Naomi but she flies out of her bedroom window. I start to go after her when something stops me. I look down and see that my black tracksuit is now all white. I'm confused for a couple of minutes as I try to figure out what just happened and then it dawns on me. Wearing all white is another step into permanent Bhoot World.

The Aiedeo have sent me another warning. My time is running out.

Day 8: Dead

I'm at Grandma's Griddle, trying my hardest to be a detective. This is the diner where I sometimes waitress and it's not nearly as folksy as its name sounds. The apple pie comes frozen and the mashed potatoes are from a box.

Naomi hasn't answered my calls since last night. Detective Alvarez has been trying to reach me and she also stopped by my place yesterday with Sanborn. Dede covered for me with the same excuse we've been using with everybody, which is that I have a throat virus and that's why I can't see or speak with anyone.

Alvarez told Dede they wanted to ask me some questions because, according to Naomi's phone records, she'd texted me right before she died. With all the hoopla that's been going on, I seriously forgot about that threatening message from Naomi. But now I'm staring right at it: *I know it was you, Violet. And I'm going to kill you.*

Could anything sound more incriminating? It's makes it seem like Naomi and I were embroiled in a blood feud.

But I can't think about it. I've got to focus on Naomi's killer. That's why I'm at the restaurant. I texted Meryl late last night updating her on recent developments, the biggest being that I'm dead and I need to find Naomi's killer. Of course, she freaked out like I expected, and it took me a while to calm her down. This morning, she sent me a message reminding me about the power breakfast that her DA dad and some other town bigwigs have every Thursday at the Griddle. I'm crossing my fingers that they'll bring up Naomi's case.

The group sits at the large corner booth located by the picture window. I'm positive they're here not for the food but for the privacy. There are rarely any other customers at this hour. In fact, the only time Grandma's is ever busy is on game days, and that's only if every other place in town is packed.

The group consists of Stan Stevens, the mayor; Joanie Gilbert, head of the city council; Leslie Adams, county treasurer; Sheriff Wayne Hopper; and Dan Miller, the district attorney and Meryl's dad. These are the people responsible for the way politics, law, and commerce are handled in Meadowdale. I'm not quite sure in what way, but I know in our tiny town bubble, these guys are at the center of it all. Usually they're joined by Jim Talbert, who is conspicuously absent from today's meeting.

I'm sitting between Dan and Joanie. Good old-fashioned eavesdropping seems like it's the heart of detective work. Veronica Mars makes a habit of it.

They've been droning on about fishing licenses to the point where I want to stick my face in the lake of maple syrup that the sheriff poured over his pancakes and drown myself. I've waited on them a couple of times. I usually don't pay attention to anything they say.

Once I overheard Joanie make a racist joke using the N-word. Maybe the rest of them were uncomfortable but no one said anything. They just laughed along. Even Dan.

I never told Meryl about it. I'm not sure why, since Meryl is far from a daddy's girl.

"The Talbert case is turning into a shit-show," Mayor Stevens says through a mouthful of Denver omelet. "We have to get it under control. Now."

My ears perk up and I look at the mayor.

"Stan, I'm doin' all I can," says Sheriff Hopper. "We got all our guys on it. It's our top priority."

"Naomi was Meadowdale royalty." The mayor pours creamer into his coffee. "Well, at least until that goddamn sex tape showed up. What a shame."

"Sex tape?" Dan frowns.

Dan Miller is the shining star of this crew and pretty much any room he walks into. It's rumored that he's on the fast track to becoming state's attorney but Meryl told me what her dad really wants is to be governor. He's got the instincts of a shark, which will probably take him as far as he wants to go.

"Well, surely you've seen it?" Joanie exclaims. "'Cause just about everyone else has. Back in my day, a girl kept her legs shut. Or at least knew better than to record it. I mean, that video was triple-X pornographic!"

"Joanie, a seventeen-year-old girl was murdered. Have some respect. It's a heartbreaking tragedy," Leslie Adams says shakily.

"Of course it is! God bless the Talbert family. I don't think there's a single person who doesn't feel their pain. That's why we're desperate for Wayne and his team to solve this case, so we can all start healing." Joanie presses her hand to her heart.

Ever since I heard Joanie tell that racist joke, I have fantasies where I take her down in front of the entire town. Seriously, even without knowing what a fake she is, does anyone really buy her "concerned for the community" act?

Dan clears his throat. "What I meant is that by calling it a sex tape, you're implying that it was something that Naomi was complicit in. Wayne, I understand that those two FBI detectives from Chicago—Alvarez and Sanborn—were in to see you yesterday."

"They were. They want to link this tape with the murder just like you're suggestin'." Hopper arches his eyebrows as though the notion is pure poppycock. "Actually makin' me bring in the entire baseball team 'cause of a simple tattoo."

Mayor Stevens and Joanie exchange looks that I can't quite read.

"I forgot they visited you twice yesterday. I want to discuss what happened on their second round to your offices, right before they came to see me." Dan speaks to the sheriff like he's a teenager caught shoplifting. "They gave me the same information they gave you and I want to know what your office is going to do about it."

The sheriff lets out a long-drawn-out sigh. "For Christ's sake. The FBI is tentatively saying that they identified the two boys in that sex tape. But my team still has to confirm it."

My heart starts to pound harder.

"You know who they are?" Leslie asks. "Why hasn't anyone told me?"

"Because we haven't made an official statement, but you can't stop the busybodies from spreading their fake news."

"What do you mean by fake, Wayne?" Dan shakes his head. "This is not tentative or speculative. The FBI *confirmed* the identity of the two males in the video."

Now my heart is pounding so hard that I can hear it.

"Just hold on a minute before we start jumpin' to all kinds of places we don't need to go. I don't see how this sex tape necessarily relates to my murder investigation." Sheriff Hopper picks a piece of gristle out of his teeth with a toothpick.

I want to reach across the table and shove the entire pack of toothpicks down his throat.

Dan sets his coffee mug down and glares at the sheriff. "A girl is raped. The day after the video is leaked, she's murdered, and you don't think there could be a connection?"

Rape. My stomach churns.

"Rape! Listen, it's no surprise that Jim and Liz are comin' up with these cockamamie stories. They acted like Naomi walked on water or somethin.' And hell, everyone knows what a pretty penny Jim was makin' off his daughter's influencer business. But don't tell me you're buyin' it, Dan." Joanie scoops up a piece of grapefruit and pops it into her mouth. I hope it's rotten and full of worms.

"I've seen it hundreds of times before. Especially over there at the college." Hopper sits back against the booth and kicks his leg out into the aisle. "A pretty young girl gets inebriated. She has sex. Sometimes it's with multiple partners like they show in those rap videos. The girl finally sobers up, and of course, she's full of regret and shame. So then she cries rape."

"Cries rape? What you're describing is a backward, outdated way to treat sexual assault. You're putting all the suspicion on the female." Dan pauses for a second. "I have a teenage daughter that we all know is hell on wheels. But if she ever tells me that someone hurt her, I'd back her up without question. Doesn't matter how much she had to drink."

I want to stand up and applaud. Maybe Dan isn't so bad. In this clan of ignorant bastards, at least, he seems enlightened.

"Well, that's the point, Dan. If your daughter *told* you." Joanie purses her thin lips. "But Naomi didn't claim rape. It's her parents who are saying it."

"Because Naomi can't! Her parents have to be her advocates," Leslie counters.

Except that's what Naomi *told* me just yesterday. She didn't use the word *rape*, but that's what she described. And I was the ignorant one who referred to it as a sex tape, like Hopper and Joanie are doing now.

"We don't need to sit here and debate whether she was raped because there's a video that shows us exactly what happened. And I never heard her say stop," the sheriff retorts.

I really don't know what to think but I do realize now that we all blamed Naomi and didn't even question what we saw.

"That was a one-minute clip. We have no idea what happened before or after. I have to admit, in a court of law, it would be difficult to prove intoxication based solely on a video." Dan runs his hand through his neatly trimmed blond hair. "But she doesn't need to shout 'Stop' or 'No' for it to be nonconsensual sexual activity. We've all seen the recording and you can't say beyond a reasonable doubt that Naomi was coherent. To put it to you in simple terms, Sheriff—having sex with someone who is too inebriated to know what's happening is a crime."

"Listen, son, I've been doin' this since you were fourteen and walkin' beans in the summer for thirty cents an hour and still knew your place." Hopper glowers at Dan. "There's two sides to every story."

"Well, I hope you're open to listening to both of them because it sounds like you've made up your mind," Leslie says. "I understand that the medical report said that Naomi had heavy tearing and bruising in her private areas."

I read the same thing. The police concluded it was older bruising that hadn't occurred when Naomi was murdered. They dismissed it just like I did. Surely it can be used as evidence for her rape? I want to ask Dan but I remember that I'm invisible.

"Pfft! That can be from anyone. You can't make me believe that Naomi and Trent were waiting for marriage," Joanie scoffs. "According to my niece Collette, Naomi had a few guys on the side."

My knuckles are clenched so tightly that they start to ache. Of course Collette and her gossip would find its way in here somehow.

"Which is exactly my point, Joanie!" The mayor takes a bite of his toast. He hasn't spoken for most of the conversation and it looks like the others have no idea what he's talking about.

"You plumb lost me, Stan." Hopper shrugs.

"It's one thing when there's a crime up at the college. They're mostly out-of-towners down here from the suburbs. *Outsiders*," Mayor Stevens clarifies. "But a rape scandal on top of a murder involving a popular local girl and two of our beloved student athletes—that would be devastating to our community. That's

why we need this all to be resolved with as little collateral damage as possible."

"And I certainly shouldn't have to remind anyone here how generous Shawn Rainey has been to all of our campaigns." Joanie smiles. "He's already spoken to me about making a sizable contribution to our civic-center project."

A set of chills run down my spine confirming what my mind had already suspected. Maybe not consciously, but hearing Caleb Rainey is one of the boys in the video doesn't come as a surprise. Although knowing it doesn't make it any less sickening. He's a predator, which could also make him the *preta*.

"And what are Nathan Hunter's parents buying our town to ensure that their son's innocence is not questioned?" Dan asks, barely concealing the disgust in his voice.

My body instantly turns to Jell-O as I try to comprehend what I've just heard. I have to grip the edge of the table to keep myself from sliding off the seat. *Nathan Hunter?* Trent's best friend and Naomi's good friend? Nate is cocky and used to getting what he wants, which isn't that different from a lot of the guys in Meadowdale. But a rapist? I would puke but there's nothing inside of me.

"The Hunters are part of the backbone of this town. They've been a proud farming family for sixteen generations," Hopper says, as though this alone clears Nate of any wrongdoing. "They don't need to prove nothin'. I've known Nate since he was in his mama's belly and I can tell you all those Hunter boys come from good stock."

Hearing the way Hopper is talking about Nate, it's clear that he hero-worships him just like we all do. That's why we trust him. That was why Naomi trusted him.

"I don't have to tell you all just how important Nathan is to our community," the mayor adds. "He's going to bring home the national trophy for our Pioneers baseball this year and he's all but guaranteed a scholarship to a Division One university next fall."

"So are you suggesting that we ignore the possibility that these boys committed a violent crime because one has a rich daddy and the other has a golden pitching arm?" Leslie asks tersely.

"We need to protect our own, damn it!" Joanie cries. "The Talberts are from one of those hoity-toity Chicago suburbs. These boys were born and raised right here."

Protect our own. Those words ring in my ears. Immigrant families like mine are perpetual outsiders. I guess that also extends to families like the Talberts when they're forced to go against the pack.

"Oh, come off it, Joanie!" Leslie's cheeks turn red with anger. "The Talberts have lived here for years and they've been an important part of this community. Naomi was beloved by many. She was like our very own princess and I know my two little girls wanted to be just like her."

Hopper jumps right in. "Settle down now, ladies. No need to get all worked about this. We need to keep our emotions in check here."

I half expect the next line out of the sheriff's mouth to be something about PMS or how fragile the weaker sex is.

"Naomi was an angel. God bless her soul," Mayor Stevens says, sounding about as authentic as his combover looks. "Wayne, I won't tell you how to do your job, but you need to at least consider those boys as suspects in the murder. It would look bad if townsfolk thought you were taking sides. But as far as rape, just from the rumblings that I've heard, the town is already pretty divided about that. We all know the Talberts lost nearly half their bookings after that sex video came out. And now with them being so vocal about all this rape hubbub, they're getting more cancellations due to the deep loyalties that lie with the Raineys and the Hunters. I think it would be in everyone's best interest to help the Talberts rethink pressing rape charges."

"I tried talkin' some sense into Jim last night but he's just downright stubborn about it."

Jim Talbert is a shrewd man. I can't see him being easily swayed by the likes of Wayne Hopper.

Dan raises his hand. "Stop! I don't want to hear this, Wayne. I'm not going to break the law."

"No one is asking you to, Dan," the mayor says. "I'm thinking about the Talberts here too. They've just lost their daughter, their business is in trouble, and now they want to suffer through a rape trial? I'm sure with a little pressure—"

"What kind of pressure, Stan?" Leslie pushes her plate away.

"Maybe *pressure* is the wrong word. Perhaps we should just get the Talberts to look at the whole picture." Joanie leans forward. "We all agree that Naomi's death was a tragedy. But I don't see any reason to add more heartbreak by accusing two boys of something that there is no way to prove they did. It's he said/she said and the she is dead. I know it sounds cold to put it this way, but Naomi has no future. And those boys do. A rape accusation could ruin their lives. If things get worse and they actually end up goin' to trial for this, then they're as good as dead themselves. What's the point of putting them, their families, and this town through all that?"

I spit into Joanie's bowl of oatmeal, then swish it around using the dirty talon of my middle finger. To me, she's the worst kind of racist, bigot, misogynist—whatever you want to label her—because she genuinely believes that what she does is for the greater good. That is, the greater good that fits her narrow white and morally right standards.

"How about for the sake of justice, Joanie?" Dan asks dryly. He doesn't suffer fools and he's arrogant enough to show it.

"Justice? Don't forget that I've known you since the sandbox and you're not foolin' anyone with this Atticus Finch routine." Joanie smirks. "Everyone here knows the governor has been sniffin' around Naomi's murder and that sex tape. That's what's got you so interested in this case."

Dan shoots Joanie a look that could break ice. "The governor is interested in this case for several reasons and it's my intention to cooperate with him as much as I can. That's why I'm supporting the two FBI detectives' request to turn over the case to them. You'll get the paperwork before lunch, Wayne."

"What?" Mayor Stevens jumps in his seat. "This is the first I've heard of this!"

"Don't look at me. I didn't know about it till this very moment," Hopper bellows.

"That's because it's the governor and the FBI," Dan says. "They don't need to fill you boys in on anything and they certainly don't have to ask your permission. All they needed was for Wayne and his team to prove themselves incompetent, and they did that with flying colors."

The three men sit and stare at each other without saying a word. I wonder which one of them will be the first to pull out his manhood and measure it.

"Uhhh . . . you guys want anything else?" my stoner boss Zak asks as he strolls up to the table. His eyes are red and glassy. Eight a.m. might be too early for most people to smoke up but Zak loves a good wake-and-bake.

I wave my hands to shoo him away. This show is damn good and Zak is like an unwanted commercial break.

"Just the check," Dan replies as he turns on his million-dollar smile.

"Got it right here." Zak places the bill in front of Dan, which I can clearly see irritates Hopper.

"When the FBI wants your full cooperation, what do you plan to tell them?" Joanie demands as soon as Zak walks away.

I feel a slight quiver at the back of my neck. She's definitely angry but I also hear genuine fear in her tone.

"The truth, Joanie," Dan answers coolly.

"I'd step carefully," the sheriff says, doing his best Dirty Harry impression. "Once the feds start lookin' into town business, Lord knows what skeletons they might dig up."

Dan pulls out his wallet. "Wayne, why don't you save your empty threats for the teenyboppers and anyone else dumb enough to believe that there's actually any authority behind that badge? Us big boys will handle the real work."

"We're all on the same side here."

"Clearly we're not, Joanie," Leslie barks. "We might have colluded in the past on petty town matters, but to cover up a rape—"

"Alleged!" the sheriff slams his fist down on the table. His MHS State Football Championship ring clinks against his coffee mug. "I'm truly sorry the girl was killed. No one deserves to go that young. But don't try to make this into somethin' it's just not. Those boys did the same thing any red-blooded males would do when a pretty young gal throws herself at 'em. We're just so lost with our political correctness, racial sensitivity, and sexual-harassment hogwash that we're tryin' to turn everyone into a criminal these days."

"Wayne, sometimes I really wish I were recording you," Dan says as he stands up and looks down on the rest of them. "Because you are such a dumb son of a bitch, I know you'd go viral in an instant."

I practically want to throw my arms around Meryl's dad right now. I always thought she was more like her mother but it looks like her dad's got quite a bit of badass in him as well.

"I've had just about all I can take myself," Leslie declares as she joins Dan.

"Think you're bulletproof just 'cause you got the governor's ear, Mr. DA?" Hopper sneers.

"Nope. I just know that if I go down, I'm taking you all with me." Dan smiles smugly. He walks to the door then turns around. "One more thing: We don't need to keep up with these breakfasts anymore. As far as I'm concerned, our business together is done."

I watch Dan and Leslie leave Grandma's. Judging by the expressions on Joanie's, Stan's, and Wayne's faces, their business together is far from over. Who knew these guys are like a Hicksville *House of Cards?* Now I have to figure out if Naomi is a mere guest star in all this drama or the lead.

I feel my insides grow weak when I think of Naomi. She was raped and she doesn't even know who did it. But I do.

Stan, Joanie, and Wayne continue to discuss Dan and the FBI, but I'm too caught up in thinking about Naomi to listen. Plus they're not really saying anything that they haven't already said. Except that Hopper's using a lot more expletives now.

I wait until they leave to get up. I was going to go to the police station next but there's a more pressing matter at hand. I have to find Naomi.

Twenty

I PICK UP A PASTEL THROW PILLOW. It's hard to believe that it's only been a week since I was sitting here in the Talberts' living room with Naomi and the rest of the Squad.

I came back here after Grandma's Griddle hoping to find Naomi, although I didn't think I would, and I was right. I look around the room for what feels like the hundredth time today. I've been sitting here for a long while knowing that with every minute that goes by, the clock ticktocks toward my permanent death. I check my cell. It's already past three p.m., which means I have twenty-one hours left until Naomi's funeral, yet I can't make myself leave this damn living room.

Nothing has changed in here since last week except now it doesn't feel like there's a separation between the downstairs and the upstairs anymore. Death lives here too.

I don't need to look at the video ever again. I knew the first time that I watched it that those images would never leave me. Yet there was so much that I didn't actually see. *Lie and deny.*

Those are the blinders that have kept me alive. Now they will kill me.

I guess it's kinda ironic that I can see *bhoots* because I've closed my eyes to just about everything else. Or maybe it's that my eyes are open but I see what I want to see. Isn't that how life is supposed to be these days? Perfectly curated images so that anyone can be exactly who she pretends to be?

Naomi was curated into the ultimate hot girl. It was hard to know how much of that was her doing and how big a role her father played in it. From the bikini pics to the Daisy Dukes and thong shots, it wasn't clothes that Naomi was selling. It was sexual fantasy. She had hundreds of thousands of followers out there as well as right here in Meadowdale.

I would have traded anything to have guys want me the way they did Naomi. I can hear my high-school guidance counselor chime in right now about everyone being beautiful in their own way. *Yeah, right.*

Yet Naomi more than any of us must have understood that the point of being a sexual fantasy wasn't the sex, it was the fantasy. A scarlet wave of shame runs over me. I watched that clip along with everyone else and I saw exactly what I wanted to see. It wasn't evidence of a rape. It was evidence of Naomi's imperfection.

The Naomi Talbert that we all knew died that day in the gym. She was no longer the goddess, the princess, or the good girl. Naomi was a slut.

That's when everything gets confusing for me again. There's this line us girls teeter on between *slut* and *not slut*. I don't really know where that boundary is. I just know you are supposed to get as near to the edge as possible but never cross over. In a town like Meadowdale, if you step over it, you aren't allowed to come back. Yet it seems that no matter what we do, we somehow end up crossing that line.

Girls are sluts for having sex. Maybe not the girls with official boyfriends, but even then, everyone knows they're doing it and people gossip about them.

Girls are sluts for liking sex. Boys are allowed to talk about sex 24/7 and we're supposed to take an active interest in the conversation. But if a girl ever comes off hornier than a guy, she's branded a slut for life. Just for liking it.

Girls are sluts. This is kinda what it all boils down to. It feels like for everything we do or don't do, we're judged. By everyone, including each other.

I slut-shamed Naomi. My first transgression wasn't mistaking that clip as a voluntary sex tape; it was condemning Naomi for having a tape at all.

My heart aches. My next transgression is the mistake I've been making for longer than I care to admit: I see only what I want to see.

I look around the living room once again and my heart sinks at my realization. This is why I've spent so long here. I probably already knew it even if my brain didn't register it, but I recognize the light blue sectional and the gingham wallpaper. They're in the background of the video.

Naomi was raped right here.

I tremble with rage. I can hear the countdown to my death,

but screw the Aiedeo—this isn't just about them anymore. For the first time in this entire nightmare, I know exactly what I have to do.

"What am I doing here?" Naomi barks.

I open my eyes with suppressed excitement. To my utter amazement, my trick has worked this time. Even though I had to go at it solo since Dede is eating dinner at her favorite Chinese buffet with Mrs. Patel.

Naomi is standing in the middle of my bedroom. I set down the Ouija board and smile at her. I've been searching for her everywhere and can't even begin to explain how relieved I am that I was actually able to summon her. Only problem is that, although I can bring her here, I don't know how to make her stay.

"Just hear me out, please."

"Oh, so is this one of your powers? To have me come at your command? Wanted to show off a bit, huh?" Naomi says wryly. "I'm not interested in anything you have to say."

Naomi starts to fade.

I grab her arm. "I'm sorry! I'm a self-righteous, judge-y bitch! I totally effed up and I will do whatever it takes to make it up to you."

"Are you just saying all of this because you need me to save your ass?" Naomi eyes me suspiciously.

"Honestly, no." I'm really not thinking of myself right now but that doesn't mean that my own life doesn't matter to me. "I was wrong."

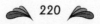

"You were. If that's all, then I'm out."

"No, wait." I continue to hold on to her. "I wanted to apologize and I need to talk to you . . . about the video."

"I should have known this was a trap! I don't want to discuss it."

I didn't think she would. *Lie and deny.* It might have helped us at one time but now it's going to end up damning us both to our own personal hells.

"I get that. But I think the only way we're both gonna get through whatever it is that we're in is if we start seeing things for what they are. Problem is, I don't think we know how to do that. I sure as shit don't. That's why I need you to do it with me."

Naomi stares at me. "Why?"

"I think that video is connected to your murder."

"I told you that I was trashed. I don't remember what happened."

"I can help fill in some of the holes, and together we might be able to figure it out. If you want. This isn't about eternal peace. It's just about the truth." *Truth.* The idea is so foreign to me that it almost feels strange to say the word.

Naomi nods while looking me up and down for a bit like she's assessing my offer. "Fine. But I'm only going along with this because my feet are killing me from dancing for the last two days and I need to rest them." Naomi sits on the other side of the bed. The tension between us is awkward and I don't know what to say but I know that I have to say something or Naomi will leave.

"Okay, let's start with what you do remember."

Naomi sits with her arms crossed in front of her. "That's the thing. It's all so hazy. I don't even know for sure who the two guys were except that I think one of them might have been Nate." She says this like she's trying to sound casual.

"I was at Grandma's this morning to see if I could get any info on your murder investigation. You know that usual group that meets there every Thursday?"

"Yeah, the mayor and my dad and a few others."

"Except that your dad wasn't there today. Anyway, Sheriff Hopper said they'd identified the boys in the video." I take a deep breath before saying their names. "It was Caleb and Nate."

Naomi's entire body freezes. It feels like an eternity before she speaks again. "Caleb . . . and Nate."

Her voice is full of emotion now. I can't tell if she's asking a question or letting it sink in. "I'm sorry, Naomi. I know this has gotta be so hard to hear."

We sit in silence again. When Naomi resumes talking, she sounds like she's somewhere else. "It was the Saturday before our first game. My parents and little brother went up to Naperville to visit my grandparents. I stayed home because we had those double practices scheduled all weekend. That evening, I decided to have some people over. Not a rager, because everyone always watches everything I do. If I had a kegger the entire town would gossip about it the next day. But I decided to invite just a few people over. I texted you, remember? I knew you probably wouldn't come because you're always with Meryl and she and I hate each other."

222

"That sounds about right. But why was Caleb there? He's not part of the usual crew."

"Nate hangs out with him all the time these days because Caleb supplies the drugs."

She's being surprisingly candid but everything about her, from the neutral expression on her face to her rigid body language, looks detached. "Drugs are the only way Caleb has any friends. Actually, Trent's been worried about Nate lately. He's been getting into some pretty hard shit, apparently. I was worried too because Nate was my friend." Naomi's eyes glaze over.

"He was mine too. We were all fooled by him." I want to rip Nate to pieces. Caleb is no better, but Nate's betrayal stings more.

"There were about twelve of us in total. People were coming and going because, remember, that was the night of the college's bonfire?"

I nod. The university kicks off the school year with a cookout that is supposed to be family-friendly but always ends up being the perfect opportunity for college guys to hook up with high-schoolers. Meryl and I after-partied at the Phi Epsilon house that night.

"Who all showed up beside Nate and Caleb?" Saying their names makes me sick.

"Of course Trent and Tessa were there. Plus Jess, Collette, Lara, Becca, and a few of Trent's football crew. Some people brought beer but I knew where my mother hid her stash of vodka so we had plenty of booze."

"Absolutely no judgment here—I promise—but did you drink a lot?"

"Yeah, I guess, but not really a lot for me. You know how we always joke about how I inherited my mother's tolerance?"

"Liz is definitely a power drinker," I quip.

"Right. But that night, it hit me so fast and so weird. I guess now, knowing what we know, Caleb or Nate probably put something in my drink." Naomi leans against the headboard.

"Sounds highly probable." I clench my fists. That would mean that those bastards planned it.

"How could I have been so stupid? Drugged at my own party?" Naomi grits her teeth.

My heart sinks. "I'll say this as many times as I have to until you believe it. None of this was your fault."

"Keep on repeating it because I'm nowhere near buying it." Naomi draws a shaky breath.

"I will." I hate Caleb and Nate so much. "You said Trent was at your house."

"For a while, but we got into a fight that night. That's not so unusual these days. Or I guess it wasn't so unusual." Naomi bites her lip. "I loved him, Violet. I really did. But it was so much pressure."

I only knew them as MHS's very own version of a celebrity power couple. Everything on the outside looked so glam. I never really gave much thought to how it felt to be them.

"You know how we really got together?" Naomi asks rhetorically. "I mean, not that cutesy tale we tell everyone about meeting on my first hayride."

I'm surprised by her forthrightness now. I think she's been holding all of this Trent stuff in for so long that it must be a relief for her to finally let it out.

"What's the real story, then?"

"It was the summer before my freshman year and my dad said"—Naomi lowers her voice and does her Jim Talbert impression—"'Sweetie, you're starting high school and you're going to be dating more seriously now. You might as well be smart about it. Your best option is either Trent Thorman or Nate Hunter. They're good boys with bright futures and they come from solid families.'"

"Are you for real? Your dad picked out your boyfriend for you?" I know all about demanding fathers. Naresh has quite high expectations for me and always makes sure to let me know when I fail to meet them. But even he doesn't go that far.

"And I thought it was only you Indians that had the arranged marriages."

"One of my favorite stereotypes." I grin. "But why did he narrow it down to Nate and Trent specifically?"

"If you're going to survive being a Talbert, you have to know how to read between the lines when Jimbo gives you one of his 'suggestions.' The Thormans and the Hunters are the two biggest farm families in Meadowdale. An alliance with them was good for business. It wasn't really a hard sell for me because I'd been crushing on Trent from the first time I met him."

I notice there's a glimmer in Naomi's eyes when she talks, like she's remembering a happy time in her life.

"Trent was cute and fun. We genuinely did fall for each

225

other. But then everyone around us started making such a big deal about us. Not just the kids at school but, like, all the adults. Parents, teachers, people at church and around town. I liked the attention initially because, you know, he was my first boyfriend. It all felt so grown up."

I prop myself up against a pillow. "So when did it change?"

"It wasn't like there was this one big moment or anything. It was much more gradual than that. But there we were, only fourteen years old, and people would talk about us getting married one day and having children together!" Naomi's eyes grow big. "It felt like my whole life had already been planned out for me."

"Team Edward." I smile. Practically every girl I knew went crazy for the Twilight series back in junior high. Naomi loved Jacob and I was a die-hard Edward fan. Naomi always teased me that among the many challenging aspects of being with a vampire, the worst was that you were stuck with him for life or longer.

"I forgot about that, but yes, I guess you could say I had my very own vampire." Naomi chuckles. "I know we played up that whole high-school-sweethearts crap ourselves. I mean, we did have our own couple name. Taomi. Totally obnoxious, right?"

I cringe. "I forgot about that, or maybe I blocked it out on purpose."

"I don't blame you." Naomi turns serious again. "I felt like we had become so much bigger than just two kids with a crush. It made me feel like I was trapped in that relationship for the rest of my life because I'd be disappointing all these people if we ever broke up. Especially my dad."

I'm floored. I never realized what it truly meant to be Naomi Talbert.

"You said that night that you guys fought. What about?"

Naomi shrugs. "Who knows? Looking at it now, I guess we were sort of junior versions of my parents because we fought about everything. I think once we actually got to know each other, Trent and I realized that we were pretty different people."

I don't know Trent very well but I'd also wondered how they fit together. Like everyone else, I bought into the sweethearts façade, although I wasn't gullible enough to believe it was as perfect as Naomi's social media posts made it out to be. Trent is like a good ol' boy and Naomi is a total big-city cat.

"What happened after Trent left?"

"This is where it starts to get hazy. Trent pretty much stormed out. I think it had something to do with me finding out he was cheating on me with that sophomore Missy Garrett."

Naomi is remarkably blasé about it but I do a double take. "Wait. You found out he was cheating on you? Were you this calm about it that night?"

Naomi's face falls. "I knew Trent cheated from time to time and he knew I cheated on him too. But I only hooked up with college guys and boys I met on spring break in Cabo. I didn't suspect anything about Missy until that night."

"Was there something specific that tipped you off?"

"I'm not sure." Naomi frowns. "Maybe I saw something on Trent's phone. I admit that I checked it from time to time, but he was usually quite discreet."

"Got it," I say gently. She's really letting it all hang out here and I don't want her to feel any kind of judgment from me. Even if the whole idea of Trent and Naomi having an open relationship blows me away. I didn't even know that was something people did in high school.

Naomi traces the paisley pattern on my bedspread with her finger. "I can remember being pissed off that he was doing it with someone at MHS. Especially because what if Collette and her big mouth found out? Then everyone would know about it. I think that was probably what Trent and I fought about."

Naomi sticks her tongue between her teeth. I haven't seen her do that since we were little. She seems to be thinking about something, so I wait patiently until she's ready to talk more.

"After Trent left, I remember now that I started hitting on Nate. Hard. I knew he'd always liked me but he was Trent's best friend so I never went there. But that night, I did. I think it was payback for Trent being with Missy." Her cheeks turn red. "Oh God, Violet! I started it with Nate."

"None of this was your fault."

Naomi buries her face in her hands and there's another long silence. When Naomi speaks again, I can see that she's gone back to that other place. "I see these flashes of stuff but it's all disjointed. I have this image of kissing Nate. Tessa was there and she tried to stop me. We told each other everything so she knew all about Trent and me. We were in the kitchen and she said something about it not being right because Nate was Trent's BF but I said I didn't care. Maybe I tried to use the Missy thing as justification, I don't know. But Tess was really mad and we argued. She left. Or maybe I kicked her out? Then I was back on the couch. My head—I was so dizzy and everything was so blurry . . ."

Naomi stops speaking and I wait for her to resume.

When Naomi continues, her voice sounds smaller. "I heard talking but I couldn't make out the words. By then it was like I was fading in and out. I felt hands moving all over me. Fingers pressing into my hips. I knew it was happening to me but it didn't feel like me anymore. I was screaming and punching and kicking but it was all going on in the inside because on the outside, I was paralyzed. Then everything just went blank."

Naomi stares out the window. I notice that I've been holding my breath and gulp in a big mouthful of air.

"I woke up the next morning on the couch wearing one of my T-shirts." Naomi's eyes were back on me. "I remembered the party and fighting with Trent. I had a flash of kissing Nate but I didn't think much of it. Tess filled me in on our argument but she'd been pretty drunk so she wasn't quite clear on the details herself and we just laughed it off. And that was it. I thought it was a pretty standard night."

I think back to the coroner's observation of tearing and bruising. There's no easy way to bring it up but I gotta ask. "Did you have any physical signs the next day? Your medical report said there was tearing and bruising."

"Yeah, now that you say it, I remember feeling kinda sore." Naomi fidgets a bit. "But Trent and I used to get pretty rowdy, so I didn't notice much."

"So then you didn't know what happened until you saw the video the following week?" I ask.

"I watched my rape on *Heffers and Hos*," Naomi whispers.

I close my eyes. The guilt I feel for being there, for watching, for judging, sinks in. "Watching that video was the last memory you have of being alive, right?"

Naomi nods.

"It makes sense that seeing it like that would trigger the trauma that you suppressed."

Naomi nods again but I can tell she isn't listening. "When I look at my life, it's divided in two forever now. Before and after that night. It doesn't matter that I'm dead because what they did to me changed everything all the way down to my spirit. Wherever I go after this, I'll carry it with me. I hate them more for that than anything else."

Naomi covers her face with one of my pillows. I move forward and hug her as tightly as I can. Neither of us wants to talk anymore. It's been enough truth for now. Naomi buries her head in my shoulder and together we cry.

Twenty-One

Day 9: Dead

BRIGHT RAYS OF SUNSHINE cascade through the windows and the birds chirp merrily outside, warning me that this is my judgment day. My stomach flips.

Once our tears dried, Naomi and I spent the rest of the night "detectiving." I study the makeshift murder board spread across my bedroom wall. Caleb's and Nathan's photos are pinned to the center since they are the two main suspects. If Naomi had stayed alive long enough to tell her side of the story, maybe it wouldn't have been enough to prove rape in a court of law, but the boys would have faced a trial in the court of public opinion. That threat alone might have been enough to make one or both of them want to silence Naomi for good.

Caleb's beady eyes stare back at me and I have no problem condemning him as the killer. This is much more about my prejudices than the truth, because I don't have a single shred of actual proof against him. I just hate him. But I know that's not enough.

I shift to Nathan and it's almost the opposite feeling. After everything that Naomi told me last night, I know he's a rapist. Yet I still can't help but see my friend. My clear bias stops me from imagining Nate as the *preta* even though he's as much of a criminal as Caleb.

Trent's and Missy's photos are also on the board although even I have to admit their motives are shakier. I understand the power of a jealous-lover storyline and they are definitely shady, but how many high-school love triangles end up in blood?

We can also include just about anyone Naomi has ever met as well as random strangers up on that murder board because I really have no clue who the killer is. The only thing that I've proven is that I suck as a detective.

"Okay," I say. I hear the crackle and see the heat rise off Naomi's hair as she runs my straightener through it. How can good hair be anywhere near a priority right now? But I guess someone like Naomi, someone whose looks have been scrutinized for so many years, probably doesn't know how to step out if she's anything less than perfect. Even though she's dead and invisible. "Let's run through what we know."

Naomi sighs. "We've gone over this like a dozen times already."

"Humor me and let's make it a dozen and one," I say. "According to the police report, you were murdered on Sunday evening on the blacktop of Grant Elementary School. It took one blow from a blunt-force object. We don't know what it was. It was raining that evening and our only witness saw a person in a hoodie running away from the scene. Police say that I was the last person you called before you were killed."

I get a pang of guilt and fright at saying the last two lines. I never made it to Grant Elementary to check out the witness's statement. Likewise, the fact that I must still be high on the detectives' list of suspects scares me out of my mind.

"Which means that you could have been the person to show up at Grant and off me." Naomi mimes bashing the side of her head that is now smashed in.

I shake my head vehemently. "No, because I was here at my house all night. Dede can alibi me. Even though we have to admit that I could have climbed out the window. But if that—"

"Chill, Violet. I was just ragging on you. Please don't bore me again with all the reasons why you didn't kill me."

I stop midway through what I am saying and frown. Naomi seems incredibly nonchalant, considering what today is for both of us. "Well, can you at least finish going through the trolls?"

We've been desperately trying to figure out why she called me in the first place and sent that text but we're not having much luck.

"I can. But it's not exactly easy to read that I'm a cum dumpster or a jiz bank over and over," Naomi says as she scrolls through my tablet. I asked her to go through all the comments posted on her social media after the video came out just to see if something might jog her memory. To my somewhat surprise, she agreed, but I know it's gotta be difficult to relive all of this in such glaring detail.

"Got it. Sorry to have to rush you but it's already seven twenty-five," I say as I look at my cell phone anxiously. I've got less than five hours before Naomi's funeral to find the *preta*.

I try to do something with my fidgety fingers and pick up a hairbrush. Then I put it back down on my dresser because I'm way too nervous to care about how I look. Plus, I'm a *bhoot*, so it's not like anyone who matters can see me.

"OMG! I think I got something here," Naomi exclaims as she shellacs another coat of pink gloss over her dry, cracked lips.

I look at her excitedly. "From the comments?"

"Remember the other day in the morgue with my mom when you mentioned the affair she had?" Naomi taps her talons on the tablet. "I was weirded out for a second because I forgot that I told you."

I nod and prompt her to keep on talking.

"This comment here," Naomi continues. "It was posted on Sunday afternoon and I have a slight memory of thinking you wrote it."

I bend down to read it. *Like mother, like daughter.* I'm confused. "I don't get it."

"Even now, it just stands out to me because everything else is like brutal but pretty standard. Whore, slut. Someone even called me a jezebel—thanks, Grandpa." Naomi smirks. "But this feels personal. To call out my mom like this makes me think it's about the affair."

I vaguely recall Naomi telling me about her mother's cheating, but I don't remember much about the moment other than that it was at her place.

"But you texted me that you were going to kill me."

"Right, slight exaggeration, but I must have been super-pissed. I mean, I'm pissed now just looking at it. Like I said, it felt so personal, like someone really wanted to hurt me. I probably connected that comment with whoever posted the video. As in, this is the person who really hates me. I can't be sure because my memory is still pretty shaky but I must have thought you were the one trying to sabotage me." Naomi looks down.

"I wasn't. I could never do something like that," I say quietly.

Naomi nods. "I know that now."

We stand together with this pained silence between us for a couple of seconds before Naomi breaks it.

"Ready?" she asks as she puts on one more round of lip gloss.

In a few hours, our eternal futures will be determined for us. There is no way that I'm ready for that.

"Hell no," I answer for both of us.

We look at each other then we transport ourselves out of my bedroom.

Less than five minutes later, we're standing in front of our high school. We could have gone anywhere but both Naomi and I have a gut feeling that her killer's *preta* lies here. Neither of us has been very good about trusting our instincts but we don't have too much else to go on.

Students are standing in groups around the parking lot. This is where we all usually meet up in the mornings. I notice most of them are dressed in black and am reminded that they are all going to Naomi's funeral. She sees it too and her earlier casual attitude shifts to a more somber mood.

The magnitude of it all is sinking in. I squeeze Naomi's hand and she squeezes mine back. "Violet!" I hear someone say but it feels like it was sent telepathically.

I look around a bit confused and see Lukas waiting by the front doors.

"You and your hottie hitman got some last-minute business?" Naomi teases as she gives Lukas her best "F-me" eyes.

I realize this is her way of coping and I don't stop her. Whatever she needs to get through this.

"Glad you can still manage to flirt despite damnation looming over us. But just chill here for a second," I say, forcing myself into the same jokey mood for Naomi's sake.

I walk over to Lukas. My stomach does a small flip and I'm not sure if that's because the sight of Lukas is usually a bad omen or because I find it oddly comforting to see him. "What up, Grim Reaper?"

"Sorry, wrong guy," Lukas replies. "I came here to tell you that the Aiedeo are pleased with you for your work yesterday."

"They're commending me for crying with Naomi all night?"

"I think you're aware that it was more than that. They'd like to reward you."

"Awesome. Tell 'em to turn me back."

Lukas shakes his head. "No, you still have to complete your *shama*. But you'll see what they have for you inside."

"Those gals really like their surprises, don't they?"

"Empathy. It's one of your most powerful tools as a fighter," Lukas says.

"Gotcha," I say, although I don't really know what he means. But I have no patience for riddles right now. I stand there for a second. I'm not sure what to do next so I decide it's best to turn around and walk back to Naomi. I guess now that I think about it, empathy was what got Naomi to open up to me last night.

"Wipe that goofy grin off your face," Naomi commands. "We've got work to do, Samos—"

To my amazement, Naomi stops herself.

"You really hate it when I call you that, don't you?"

"Yup," I answer.

"Fine, I won't do it anymore, but you could have said something earlier. It's okay to stand up for yourself, you know."

"You're right." I shrug. "Stop calling me Samosa, racist hag."

Naomi grins, and if this were one of those buddy flicks, we would probably high-five each other right now. But it isn't.

I take a deep breath and march through the front door. I only stop when I hear a loud thud, like when a bird smacks against a window.

"I can't get in!" Naomi shouts.

I scramble back and fling open the door. Naomi tries to walk through but she bounces backwards like there is an invisible shield stopping her.

Lukas steps in front of Naomi. "This is *your* shama, Violet. You either fail or succeed on your own."

Panic and fear rush through me.

"Screw you!" Naomi shrieks as she tries to push Lukas aside, to no avail.

I want to give a massive middle-finger salute to the Aiedeo and call, *Game over*, but I know that I have to continue. My life and Naomi's soul are at stake here.

"I got you, Naomi!" I shout, sounding way more confident than I feel.

I turn around and immediately freeze. My blood turns to ice as sweat begins to trickle down my forehead. I could swear that my heart stops except the sound of my pulse bangs against my ears.

Up until this moment, I've had a reference for everything that has happened to me, no matter how bizarre. The scene unfolding before me definitely belongs in some horror flick or sci-fi fantasy, but I've never seen anything like it.

"This is real," I mumble to myself for what seems like the millionth time in the past week.

Everything at my school looks like it always has except that now, everyone is hairless, skinless, and, more disturbing, faceless. Hollow sockets appear where their eyes, noses, and mouths are supposed to be. Their skin is peeled away like horrific burn victims, leaving their flesh, tendons, bones, and organs exposed.

I have no way of distinguishing them. There are no white girls, black girls, or brown girls anymore. Just me and a bunch of . . . what are they? My stomach churns around and around. They are abominable. The sight of them makes me want to hurl and run at the same time, but I can't do either.

I hear a bloodcurdling scream and it takes me a moment to recognize it's coming from me. The sound of bones cracking echoes through the school hallway as the beasts snap their stiff necks in my direction. They all start to move toward me, stumbling and teetering like a drunken flash mob. I dive for the door but I can see through its window that Lukas is standing on the other side, holding it closed. Naomi, my only ally, is nowhere to be seen.

"This is your reward. Figure out how to use it and it will be a major advantage," Lukas says in his irritatingly calm voice.

I lift my leg up high and kick the glass, right where Lukas's face is. Neither he nor the door budges. Reward? Only sickos like him and the Aiedeo could think this Stanley Kubrick nightmare is any kind of prize.

In the reflection of the window, I can see the horde closing in. They're faster now. I try to run but they stop me. Their hungry moans and groans fill my ears. Now that they are so near, I can see the thick, murky sludge of blood that pumps through their organs and their snake-like intestines.

My skin crawls as they grope and grab me all over. They pull at me from every direction. A rank smell of diseased, rotting flesh mixes with the aroma of fresh, tender meat. Some of them are alive and some of them are not. I hear their rattled breathing as they tear at me in a rabid frenzy.

I'm probably supposed to feel pain but I don't. Perhaps the fear has numbed me. There are just too many of them to fight. My eyelids grow too heavy to hold open and I feel myself sinking to the floor. The last thing I see before my eyes close is a pair of sharp teeth.

"Find the *karun* and you will find the *preta*."

I can't see my grandmother but I recognize the Indian Mrs. Butterworth sound of her voice. I call out to her in Assamese. "Ita?"

I wait for a response but there's none; instead, I feel a chubby hand slam against my cheek. The sting wakes me up. I blink my eyes and see that there's no grandma next to me.

However, the scene at my school is still wack. The skinless creatures are roaming about as though this is just another day at school. I guess that's better than them tearing me apart.

I inspect myself and find I have no cuts, bruises, or even scratches. I study the monsters closer and realize it's actually an absurdly normal scene. They're carrying textbooks around and chatting with one another, though I don't hear the conversation.

Did my fear trick me into believing that they were harming me earlier? I don't have any visible wounds. The idea that it might have been a hallucination gives me more courage. I walk nearby one of them standing next to its locker.

Karun. I remember what Ita said in my short dream. *Karun* is a person's true self.

I look around, and suddenly, it all begins to click together. These are my friends, classmates, and teachers. They're stripped of all the distinguishing physical characteristics that I use to identify them and, to be honest, judge them. Now, only their insides are visible. Not just their organs and blood but deeper than that, all the way to their *karuns*.

I get why the Aiedeo gave me this as a reward. Right now, everything is out here in plain sight. No one and nothing can hide from me. Especially a *preta*. But that's only if I can read the *karuns*, which I haven't done in ages. Even if my *shama* is all about testing my skills, no matter how rusty, reading *karuns* is difficult as hell. That, I do remember.

I walk down the hallway and flash back to my Aiedeo lessons. Reading *karuns* is like mind-reading but way more intense. I try to recall what the Aiedeo taught me but the technique is pretty vague right now.

I take a deep breath and continue walking. Repulsion runs through me. I want to look away from them because they are so grotesque, but I force myself to keep my eyes on them.

I realize that I'm somewhere in the midst of my third lap around the school when the horror begins to fade. I stop next to one of them leaning against the wall and a sharp, stinging energy pulsates through my entire body. I look at the large crowd gathered in the hallway, and a massive wave of shame hits me so hard that I have to steady myself against a locker.

There's a scramble of voices buzzing sharply in my ear like a radio that's between stations but I can't make out most of the words. I try to focus harder but all I hear is *Freak. Freak. Freak.* Over and over.

I follow the sound into a classroom and step inside. *Freak. Freak. Freak.* Another gigantic wave of emotion rushes through me, but this time, it's fear.

I stand there confused, trying to figure out what's going on, when the crackle from the overhead intercom startles me back to now. The school secretary clears her throat and announces that Naomi's funeral service will be held at the cemetery; there'll be a reception for the guests at the Talbert Funeral Home afterward.

The clock on the wall reads 12:30 p.m. My heart plunges. Naomi's funeral will start in thirty minutes.

They all pour into the hallway in droves and I cannot escape them. *Freak. Freak. Freak.* I am terrified that they will hurt me again yet I am paralyzed to stop it. Feelings of shame followed by fear continue to slam against me like I'm in a violent sea storm. My body trembles from the weight of the emotions. *Freak* is all I can hear in my ears, in my head, inside of me. I taste the saltiness of my tears before I realize that I'm crying and try to prepare myself for their assaults. They surround me. I raise my arms in defense.

They know who I really am, I shout to myself.

Freak. Freak. Freak. I hear it so loud that it hurts my ears. I try to see how many of them are saying it when everything stops. I realize that they're not even looking at me. None of them notice me at all.

Freak. Freak. Freak. I cover my ears because I feel like my brain is going to explode. Then suddenly, I feel *it.* It's a *karun* with layers and layers of heat radiating off it. Its rage is terrifying. It knocks into me so hard that I actually topple over. I'm afraid its overwhelming hunger will swallow me whole right here, and I stay down on the ground. I found the *preta.*

I lift my head cautiously. Even though I'm already on the ground, I feel like I've been slammed down again. I can actually see the *preta* now. It has sallow, mummified skin, emaciated limbs that are twice as long as its thin frame, and a mouth no bigger than a coin. It's like a poltergeist and phantasm combined into one, and its appearance sends shock waves of chills down my spine.

My inclination is to stay right where I am but I know that I can't. I will myself to my feet and begin to follow the *preta*. The *preta* moves fast, darting from spot to spot so that it's just out of my reach.

It moves outside. The minute I step into the fresh air, my entire body breathes a sigh of relief. For a second, I place my head against the brick exterior of the building and let it cool me while I collect myself.

I see that practically the entire school is gathered in the parking lot, preparing to go to Naomi's funeral service at the cemetery. The *preta* is among them. My every instinct warns me not to go any farther but this is my last chance. I have to do this or I will die.

I chase the *preta* into the cemetery. Everyone else has changed back to normal and it is the only skinless human out here with me. It looks like the other beasts that I just faced except that its limbs are more mangled and twisted like wild vines of ivy. I know that it must have seen me but it has not looked at me once.

Out of the corner of my eye, I see a crowd of people sitting in folded chairs. Meryl and Dede are in the back row but neither of them turns when I run by. It seems that not even my nanny can see me now.

I keep on running and my eyes fall on Naomi's dead body lying in the casket. I've already seen her dead body in the morgue, but that doesn't compare to seeing it here. At her funeral. The reverend is giving a eulogy and everyone is crying. I feel like I've been punched in the chest and I look around for Bhoot Naomi but she isn't here.

It can't be too long before they lower the body into the ground. My heartbeat falls in sync with the rapid ticktock of the clock that I can hear in my head.

I notice the *preta* crouching behind a gravestone. Does that big-ass monster really think it can hide from me? I race to where it is, unsure of what I'm supposed to do if I catch it.

To my surprise, I'm fast on the *preta*'s heels when it suddenly transforms in front of my very eyes. It's long, narrow frame turns into a hulking, massive man's body ripped with muscles so tight that the veins pop out. The head takes on the shape of a lion with a mane made of a thousand vigilant eyes. It bares its long fangs and needle-sharp claws.

I cower. It's here to destroy me.

It's worse than any nightmare but the almost painful buzzing in my brain reminds me that I am fully awake. My heart hammers in my ears and my muscles tense.

The bright sun shining up above retreats and blackness covers us. I blink my eyes to adjust to the darkness but I can no longer see it. I can only hear the faint sound of its paws slinking in the grass around me. It is stalking me like prey.

I am sure it can smell my terror, which oozes from every pore. Then I feel a gust of wind and I know that the beast is charging toward me.

I have always hated nature shows but Dede loves them. It's the only TV that we ever argue over. Now I mentally race through all the animal specials and remember something vague about lions charging straight at you because they are unable to change their direction. I pray this includes half-lion, half-human beasts as well.

When it is close enough that I can see a faint silhouette, I jump out of its path and onto the ground. My hand rushes to my heart when I realize that it missed me. I catch my breath before jumping up and starting to run.

"Violet! They've forbidden me to fight along with you," Lukas shouts as he appears out of nowhere. He grabs my arm and places something in my hand. "Take this."

I look down. I don't really know how useful the skull chain is, considering I was never given even basic instructions on how to use it. However, I decide to hold on to it since I have no other weapons and no idea how I am going to survive this battle.

Suddenly, I feel the beast pounce on me and throw me to the ground. The weight of its body bears down on my chest. I feel my lungs cave in and I struggle to breathe. I try to raise my head but it slaps me down with its large paw. Its claw rips through the side of my face and I cry out in pain.

I sputter and cough as the *preta* continues to choke me. I can now see it in its full glory and it is heinous, part man and part beast. Its white fangs gleam in the dark.

Terror like I have never experienced rushes through me, paralyzing me from head to toe.

I feel the beast's razor-sharp teeth bite down on my throat and hear the loud pop of my skin as it's sliced open. Waves of excruciating agony radiate through my body and settle somewhere deep inside of me. I tremble from the shock and pain.

The creature plunges its talons into my belly and rips it apart. It is ravenous, just like *pretas* are supposed to be. I can feel the life drain out of me. Images flash through my mind. The Aiedeo. Tears of rage roll down my cheeks. I hate them with every last breath left in me. The Aiedeo are quickly replaced with thoughts of Naresh, Meryl, and Dede. I hear the fading sound of my heartbeat. I don't know where the hell Naresh is but Meryl and Dede are only steps away. I think of Naomi lying in that casket and I remember that this isn't just about me. The thought sends a rush of adrenaline through me.

I feel the creature bite down on my liver. I try to push the horror of what's happening to me aside and I fight to wrap my fingers around the skull chain, which is lying beside what I believe is my half-eaten stomach. The beast looks up at me with its face and mane soaked in my blood. I want to turn my head away from it but then I decide not to. If these are going to be my last seconds on earth, then I am going to look straight into my killer's eyes. Fuck fear. I've been afraid all my damn life, and clearly, it isn't working for me.

My heart beats louder. *I am alive.* Barely, but I am and I decide that chow time is over. I muster the strength that I didn't know was in me and manage to lift the skull chain with my right arm. To my own awe, I begin to swing it in the air. First, it starts to buzz, then it gradually rattles until it flies around in my hand with an energy that I have never seen. I don't know if the force is going from me to the skull chain or from the skull chain to me, but whatever the case, I'm strong.

Before the beast can do anything about it, I wrap the skull chain around its neck and pull as hard as I can. My muscles feel like they're shredding apart because I'm tugging so hard. The jaws of the beast stop moving and it looks at me again. I tighten the chain until its eyes pop out of its head and roll onto me. Its belly, which is now bloated and bulging with my flesh, convulses and spasms. It opens its mouth and regurgitates all over me. A large chunk of my liver falls next to my head. The sour, putrid smell makes me gag but I don't stop.

I pull tighter and tighter until I have no more power left in me. My body goes limp. I try to hold on but I feel my grip loosen. I hear the faint moans of the beast, and my heart plunges into a deep, dark abyss. Its breathing is labored but it is still breathing. That means the *preta* is alive and I am not. They won. I drop the skull chain and let go.

Twenty-Two

L UKAS SHUDDERS AT THE SIGHT of the dead beast on the ground. In all of his centuries of fighting, he's never seen a *preta* so savage. He lays Violet's limp body across his lap and rests her head against his chest. The guests at Naomi's funeral don't notice him, but in any case, he looks like he is merely sitting under a tree to get away from the unusually bright afternoon sun.

Lukas sees Dede's face grow pale. She wasn't able to see the battle but now she can plainly see her girl's mangled body. Dede starts to get up from her seat but Lukas raises his hand to stop her. She scowls but stays put.

Meryl can't see Violet at all, but apparently that doesn't matter. She's halfway out of her chair and looks like she's about to charge at Lukas but Dede yanks her back down.

Lukas takes off his suit jacket and uses it to cover Violet's torso. That monster literally ate her alive. He forced himself to watch the entire battle even though he couldn't step in. Lukas almost gave up hope sometime between the throat-slitting and the liver-eating, then was surprised to realize that he actually believed in her. Slightly.

He'll probably receive a reprimand and perhaps even a permanent note in his file for helping her out with that skull chain but he's never been good about following the rules. Besides, Violet earned the weapon from the Aiedeo, so all he did was give her what was rightfully hers.

Lukas picks a blade of grass. He knows the Aiedeo are desperate but what were they thinking, sending a *preta* that vicious to an amateur? Lukas looks down at the girl. Even if Violet obviously isn't really an amateur at all.

Perhaps the Aiedeo are so pushed that they can't afford to have limits anymore. All Lukas knows is that all these family, ancestor, and legacy matters are way too complicated for his pay grade. He's looking forward to a much-needed hiatus from the Aiedeo and to getting Violet off his hands completely.

Lukas takes out his cell phone and checks the time. It's been nearly a half an hour and the Aiedeo still have not contacted him. He looks over at Naomi's funeral and sees that it's close to the end. For Naomi, certainly. But what about Violet?

Lukas sighs and leans against the tree. Patience is a trait that has been trained into him; it doesn't come to him naturally. However, he realizes that right now, he can do nothing but wait.

"They won," I hear myself murmur, although I barely recognize my weak voice. "They won."

I look up and blink my eyes repeatedly because it's hard to

believe what I'm seeing. It's Lukas. He stares back at me with a surprised expression that quickly changes to what I think is relief. I realize he's even smiling when it dawns on me that I'm sprawled across his lap, and I want to jump up because I don't know what the hell is going on. But I can't move at all.

"No, *you* won, Violet," Lukas whispers. "Your *shama* is complete and the Aiedeo are satisfied."

"I'm going to live?" I croak out. My throat is parched and my entire body feels like it's been ripped into pieces. I flash back to the *preta* eating my liver and I feel sick.

Lukas nods his head.

"I can't be alive if you're smiling."

"Apparently, today is a day for miracles or whatever you think is responsible for the fact that the worst fighter that I've ever witnessed managed to destroy the worst *preta* that I've ever seen." It's a major backhanded compliment that makes me want to punch him. Except that I can't lift my arms.

"The Aiedeo are in the process of returning you to the living. They've informed me that you'll be rid of your *bhoot* body in a half an hour or so. You sustained some very serious injuries in your battle with the *preta* and they must attend to those in order to assure a smooth transition back to your human form without any complications."

I don't pay attention to most of what he's saying because all I can think of is that I destroyed that mofo *preta*! "I gave that beast a serious beatdown, right?" I beam. I can already feel my voice growing stronger and louder. "Slayed it."

"An exaggeration, as usual. Although it was your first *preta*, so I understand the excitement." Lukas grins and arches an eye-brow. He's still reserved but he doesn't seem to hate me as much as usual at this moment. "But try taking twenty at a time like I've done."

I roll my eyes and continue to gloat. Then I remember what this is all about and I feel a lump in my throat. "Who is the *preta*? I mean, who did it belong to? Who killed Naomi?"

"You're about to find out the answer along with everyone else." Lukas points to the crowd at Naomi's funeral.

I lift my head slowly. Just as the coffin is being lowered into the ground, a cacophony of phones start to ring.

"You'd think they'd turn their cells on silent for a funeral."

"This wasn't their doing," Lukas says as he angles his phone so I can see the screen.

"How did you get a text message from Naomi?"

There's an audible series of gasps, whispers, and cries from the crowd and I assume all the funeral guests received the same message. Lukas opens the text and presses the link inside of it. A video comes on the screen. I squint to see it better. It's shot at nighttime and it's hard to make out what's going on. Then slowly, a swing set and a slide come into focus.

"It's Grant Elementary School," I say under my breath.

My pulse starts to race. Suddenly, Naomi's *bhoot* is standing right in front of me. I push Lukas's phone out of my face and sit upright.

"Wh-what's happening?" Naomi asks in a shaky voice.

"I'll show you." This isn't about my *shama* or my Aiedeo powers. I don't have to struggle to do this. In fact, it feels so natural that I ease into it quickly. A shot of the Grant Elementary School playground projects in my palms. I start to see it all like a movie, except that instead of watching this, I am in it. It's not mind-reading, channeling, or even finding anyone's *karun*. Instead, I've been pulled inside the scene and I can *feel* it. And I can help Naomi feel it too.

Naomi recoils at the image. "You're going to show me what happened, aren't you?"

I reach out for her. "You're not alone. I'm here with you."

Naomi nods hesitantly.

It's dark and wet outside and I can feel the humidity in the air stick to my skin. The blacktop glistens from the rain shower that fell earlier in the evening.

After seeing that video of herself on H and H yesterday, it's like her entire world went to hell and she doesn't know what to feel anymore.

"Hey, I know you need to talk but I gotta get back before my parents find out I'm not in my room. They're really pissed off about the party."

Naomi would have preferred to phone Tessa but Tessa's parents had found out about her going to the cornfield kegger. They'd grounded her for two weeks and taken away her computer privileges and her cell. Tessa was always getting in trouble for something, but luckily, the girls still had the secret walkie-talkies they'd bought together when they were nine. If one of them needed the other, she could radio and they'd meet up at their usual spot here at Grant Elementary School.

"I won't take long, Tess. Just that I gotta vent."

Tessa slides her hood back and reties her messy, mangy hair extensions into a ponytail. "What's up?"

"I was reading all the stuff those trolls wrote about me in the comments section of my blog. I think Collette had a hand in some of the particularly nasty stuff but there was one that stuck out—"

"Nay Nay! I told you not to look at any of that crap. It'll just mess with your head. People are so cruel. And we'll make sure Collette pays."

Naomi nods. "Forget about Collette for right now. The comment I'm talking about, it was posted this morning but I didn't notice it until later. It says 'Like mother, like daughter.'"

Tessa gives her a confused expression.

"I know at first it doesn't seem like a big deal," Naomi continues. "Except then I started thinking about it and out of all the trash that everyone has written about me, it's the only comment that's personal. The reason it hit me is that no one knows about my mom's affair—"

"I don't think they're talking about your mom screwing that doctor specifically. It's a pretty general remark."

Naomi is too caught up in her own thoughts to pay much attention to what Tessa is saying. "I think whoever wrote that was the one who posted that video on H and H. They want to take me down."

"Really?" Tessa's eyes grow wide. "Who do you think it is?"

"Violet Choudhury."

Tessa stands there for a moment before breaking out into loud laughter. "What?"

Naomi is so sure that whoever wrote that comment is responsible for the video that Tessa's dismissive attitude really irritates her. "I just tried calling and texting her but she's ghosting me. Violet does have the brains to pull this off."

"But, like, none of the brawn. She's a scared little mouse who would never have the courage to come after you. Even if she wanted to."

Naomi mulls over what Tessa just said. She's right about Violet being an unlikely suspect, not just because she's a chicken shit but also because Naomi thought they were friends. Or at least, Violet doesn't hate her as much as she knows a lot of other people do. She's about to say something when she spots Tessa eyeing her. Goose bumps run down her legs. There's something about her right now that just doesn't feel right. Naomi can barely find the words. "You're the only other person I told . . ."

Tessa arches her eyebrows and juts out her hip in the same way Naomi always does. Naomi never noticed it before but now that she does, it totally creeps her out. Tessa is like her shadow.

"You couldn't figure it out because you can never give me credit for anything. You don't think that I can pull something like this off. Instead, you wanted to blame it on little loser Violet."

Naomi feels like someone's just stomped on her chest. "Why?"

She knew she could be wicked but never to Tessa. They're sisters and they don't hurt each other like this. For the first time, she sees Tessa for the fake that she is and her hurt quickly turns to rage. But the artificiality goes way beyond just looks. Tessa is always the "nice" one although she's been just as much a part of their mean-girl schemes as Naomi and she's reaped the benefits as well. Without waiting for Tessa to answer, she lays into her.

"I made you! Without me, you'd be wearing ninety-nine-cent dresses from the Salvation Army. I paid for our spring breaks with my modeling money just so you could see something else besides this hell hole. I even made you co-captain of the Squad even though you have a flat ass and no rhythm. No guy would even look at you twice if you weren't best friends with me. And this is how you repay me?"

"Repay you for what?" Tessa yells back. "For the hand-me-downs you make sure everyone knows were yours first? The trips to Cabo where I spend most of the week holding your hair back as you puke? Sloppy seconds you throw my way because you can't stand the idea of any guy liking me over you? And for making me your all-around little bitch, stuck in your shadow, always second best, because you haven't wanted to share the spotlight for one damn moment of our eight glorious years as best friends? Did it ever occur to you that people might genuinely like me because I don't have to step all over them to make myself feel better the way you do?"

"Like you? They feel sorry for you because without me, you'd be nothing but poor white trash."

A slow smile crosses Tessa's face. "And without me covering up all your secrets, everyone would know you're nothing but a drunken slut who screws anything that moves the moment you cross the county line. You're a whore. Like mother, like daughter."

Naomi clutches her gut. It isn't just the words, it's the hate behind them. That's why at this very moment, she knows. It was Tessa recording her that night.

"You were the one that put that video up on Heffers and Hos." Naomi's voice is trembling along with the rest of her body. "You recorded my rape."

"Rape? Is that how you're spinning it?" Tessa crosses her arms in front of her. "I just finally showed everyone what a regular weekend with Naomi Talbert was really like. It's not the Barbie life you sell on Instagram."

"I was trashed. I didn't even know what had happened until I saw it on H and H."

"I admit that you did seem a bit more out of it than usual. I think Caleb improvised a little with some drugs. We hadn't discussed that part."

Naomi feels nauseated. "You told Caleb and Nate to do that to me?"

"Now who's being the dumb one?" Tessa rolls her eyes. "I didn't give them specific instructions. In fact, I didn't say anything to Caleb. He was just a happy coincidence. You're the one who always tells me that every guy is into you. Nate was no exception. So I just outed Trent and Missy's cheating, which I knew would piss you off. Then I told Nate to make out with you. I thought I was going to record you guys kissing on the couch. I had no idea when I snuck back up with my cell phone, there'd be a threesome right there in the Talbert living room. It was so juicy I decided to hold on to it until the first football game for maximum exposure."

"Why?" Naomi whispers, trying to fight back the tears. "Because you were jealous of me?"

"Yes, if you want the easy answer. But mostly because I hate you. Not just because you have everything handed to you on a plate. I mean, that does really piss me off. But because you get away with everything! Everyone thinks you are so perfect and here I know what you really are. I'm just as sick of Princess Naomi as everyone else but I can actually do something about it. I can bring her down."

"Is that why you're admitting everything? Because you think that I've fallen so low there's no redemption?"

Tessa bobs her ponytail like an excited puppy. "Pretty much. This is Meadowdale. Once a slut with a sex tape, always a slut with a sex tape."

"Here's what you never seemed to understand about storytelling." Naomi smirks. "People love a good comeback. And they love a villain even more." Naomi holds her cell up.

"What the f—you recorded this?"

"Payback is a bitch, bitch."

There's a light drizzle that is getting heavier now and Naomi turns to leave. There's nothing much more to say to Tessa. She stays cool on the outside because she knows how to do that but her insides feel like they've been ripped out.

There's never been a breakup that has hurt this much; the bitch-out in the gym didn't compare. She knows her heart is broken and it will never heal.

Naomi struggles to keep her composure and doesn't even notice Tessa charging at her with full force. She knocks her down on the blacktop and Naomi's mobile tumbles to the ground. Tessa pins Naomi.

"Tessa! Stop!" Naomi shrieks.

But it isn't just Tessa. Naomi sees it lurking inside her best friend. It's a monster. The preta gives Tessa the strength to pick up the large rock next to her. She holds it over her head.

"No, Tessa!" Naomi cries out as she turns her head quickly. Fear pulses through her entire body.

Before Naomi can stop it, the rock lands on the side of her face. It takes only one blow to crush her skull in. Tessa lifts the stone to strike her again but a man comes running out of the school building. "What's all that noise?" the stranger calls out. "What's going on out there?"

Before he can get any closer, Tessa grabs Naomi's phone from the ground and, still holding the rock, races away. Blood gushes out of Naomi's head and onto the blacktop. The man crouches down next to her but it is already too late. Naomi Talbert is dead.

I turn and find that Bhoot Naomi is gone. Across from me at the funeral, Tessa stands up, but before she can escape, Alvarez and Sanborn grab her. I watch as the *preta* beast beside Tessa shrinks until it disintegrates into thin air.

There are about a hundred different emotions running through me and even more questions flying around in my head. I blurt out the first one that I can manage to ask. "How did Naomi send the message with the recording if Tessa had her phone?"

"Don't ever underestimate what the Aiedeo can do, Violet. That's a rule to live by," Lukas says. "The Aiedeo retrieved the phone from Tessa's possession and sent the video."

"Wait, what? The Aiedeo knew Tessa was Naomi's *preta?*"

"It was your *shama*, not theirs."

I shake my head. "Shady bitches."

Suddenly, I feel this enormous energy being sucked out of me. I jerk back and forward. Then I freeze for a second as I see my *bhoot* standing outside of my body. I don't know why but I want to reach out to it but before I can, it disappears.

"Now that you've been fully reinstated to human," Lukas says evenly, as though what we just witnessed were an everyday occurrence (it might be for him, but I'm temporarily stunned), "I need to attend to my other tasks."

I want to say something but I can't really form the words. But I guess it doesn't matter to Lukas because he turns around and leaves.

I slowly start to stand up when I'm suddenly wrapped in hugs and covered with kisses.

"*Mami!*" Dede cries out.

"I've been so scared. If anything ever happened to you—" Meryl's voice cracks.

My face is drenched and I don't know if it's their tears or mine. "I'm okay," I whisper.

In the distance, at the far end of the cemetery, I see Lukas lead Bhoot Naomi away.

Twenty-Three

L UKAS PULLS THE CAR into the Talbert Funeral Home parking lot. I finally let go of Dede and Meryl and let Lukas bring me here because there's one more thing that I need to do. The guests from Naomi's funeral will soon be arriving for a small reception, but right now, most of them are still at the cemetery trying to figure out what just happened.

I'm continuing to collect info, but from what I gather, the funeral guests didn't receive the full movie that I got; they heard a lengthy audio recording of Naomi's death. I don't know how the Aiedeo managed to pull it off, and despite me plying Lukas with questions during our entire fifteen-minute car ride, he's been tight-lipped as usual. I overheard Naomi's parents and the police speculating that the message was sent from someone who secretly knew what Tessa had done and wanted to do the right thing. It sounded totally lame but how else are people going to explain a text from a dead girl? And I sure as hell am not going to bring up the Aiedeo's involvement.

As I turn to open the car door, Lukas grabs my arm. A jolt

of electricity runs through me and makes me jump. I look up at him quizzically. "What?"

He doesn't say anything at first. I realize that his hand is still touching me and I don't move. "You did really well, Violet."

There's not a hint of sarcasm in his voice and I'm taken aback by the sheer genuineness of his words. I don't know how to respond except to thank him. I think back to the skull chain he threw me earlier and I actually mean it. "Thanks for sticking your neck out for me with that beast."

He nods. "The weapon definitely helped but I think you're more powerful than you give yourself credit for."

"Probably. But I'm just so damned happy to be alive that I don't want to think about any of that right now." I beam with way more cheer than I think I've ever had. Even more than when I'm actually cheering.

"Great," Lukas says wryly. "One more thing, Violet. Could you try to act a bit more somber, given this is Naomi's funeral reception you're about to walk into?"

I realize that I'm totally cheesing it and screw my face up into what I think is a mournful expression. "Is this better?"

I see Lukas's eyes brighten although the rest of him is deadpan. "Absolutely not."

I laugh and he does too. We're like that for a couple of seconds before Lukas becomes serious again and I feel him let go of my arm. "You should go see Naomi now. Like I said, keep it brief."

I nod although I don't plan on obeying him. This is one

goodbye that I'm not going to rush. Lukas opens his car door and I walk into the house.

Despite what he said about being somber, I'm actually whistling like one of the Seven Dwarfs as I walk up the stairs to Naomi's bedroom. I'm back, baby! Alive and kicking! I strut inside, feeling every bit the hero who just gave Naomi eternal peace, then pause. She's sitting on her bed with her face in her hands.

"My best friend murdered me," Naomi says, looking up at me. Her eyes are red and puffy, like she's been crying for years.

"Yeah." I heave a deep sigh and plop down on the bed next to her.

In the story that I created about Naomi, I believed she was invincible. That nothing could bring her down. Seeing her now, I realize how wrong I was.

Tessa, Nate, Trent, and even her parents were the people that Naomi trusted the most in her life and they all betrayed her in one way or another. While the rest of us—her classmates, the townspeople, and her other sycophants—helped twist the knife in farther.

A massive load of guilt drops onto my shoulders. I've been on such a high from destroying the *preta* that I didn't even stop to consider the impact that discovering its identity would have on Naomi. *Tessa.* I still can't believe it. I realize it must have been difficult to be Naomi's BF—bitch forever—but I really believed what they had was real. As genuine as what Meryl and I have.

But that's the thing with stories. It all depends on who's

telling them. I only knew Naomi's side and I never bothered to learn Tessa's.

I try to think of something comforting to say and I can't. But I don't have to because Naomi apparently has a lot to say.

"Don't try to tell me it's not my fault because that doesn't fly for this," Naomi snaps. "The only person that I think I truly ever loved killed me. She might have had a *preta* inside of her but it's not all on Tessa."

She's right. Everything that Tessa said about the way that Naomi treated her was true. But I let myself believe that Tessa loved Naomi so much that she didn't care that she was always in her shadow. Like most everyone else, I had no idea about the amount of hate that was growing there in the darkness with her. Tessa fooled us all.

That's the part that eats at me the most. I could have seen what Tessa was becoming and I didn't need my Aiedeo powers to do it. After all, I'd known Tessa longer than Naomi and I was there at that first sleepover when they solidified their friendship. Yet, like most of us, I paid attention only to Naomi and ignored Tessa.

This doesn't exonerate Tessa, nor does it justify murder. But like Naomi said, it wasn't all on her. "It's on all of us."

"But mostly me. I was such a horrible person," Naomi says, more to herself than me. "Don't try to say otherwise either."

I don't. "You were terrible."

Naomi looks at me and she's not mad. Instead, her eyes are soft as though she's relieved to hear the truth.

"I don't know when I stopped being me and I started being her," Naomi says as she points to a photo on her nightstand of her in full Naomi Talbert splendor. "If I was ever me at all."

I nod toward the pic. "From what you've told me, it doesn't sound like you had much of a choice in whether you wanted to be that Naomi Talbert. Your parents pushed you pretty hard, and so did everyone else."

"Yeah . . ." Her voice trails off. After a couple of seconds, she picks up where she left off. "There was definitely a lot of pressure. Especially as everything just got bigger and bigger with my blog, with Trent, with my life. I was just so *scared*."

"Of what?"

She shrugs. "Of all of it. Of everyone finding out that the real me was just a freaky nobody."

"No way," I exclaim, because this part I just can't buy. "Naomi Talbert is the ultimate insider who decides who the freaks are."

"Exactly. Naomi Talbert bullies everyone around her so that no one notices what an outsider she really is."

I shake my head. I've been the one who doesn't belong my entire life and it almost makes me angry for Naomi to suggest that she could even come close to knowing how that feels. I grab the framed photo of her from her nightstand and shake it in front of her face. She looks like the goddamn American dream with her perfect white skin, light hair, and bright eyes standing next to Trent, her real-life Ken doll. "You don't know shit about what you're saying. There's nothing freaky about you."

"No, there's nothing freaky about *her*," Naomi shouts as she points to the picture. "That girl lives in perpetual fear and so she hides everything. That Naomi Talbert is as manufactured as—" Naomi stops herself.

"Go on. That Naomi Talbert is as manufactured as?" I ask but the anger stirring inside my belly already tells me the answer.

"Violet Choudhury."

I spring off the bed. "Screw you. We're nothing alike."

There's so much rage filling up the room that if either of us says or does anything, we're gonna explode. I walk to the window and watch a puffy white cloud roll by. After several steely minutes, Naomi speaks. Her voice is calm.

"I'm not going to pretend to understand everything you're dealing with, Violet, but I have some clue. We're both scared and we lie and deny our way through it all."

She takes a long deep breath and I think about how both Naomi and Tessa said I was a coward. Maybe that wasn't their exact word but it was their sentiment and it stung like hell.

"The difference is that I'm a mean girl. I can even say that, sometimes, I enjoy the power that being a mean girl gives me. In fact, I'm such an uber-mean girl that my best friend killed me."

I turn around and face Naomi again.

"I could have also been the funny girl. The smart girl. The artsy girl. But I was too afraid to show them anything else but the mean girl." Naomi's voice breaks and she looks away. "And now I'm dead and that's all I'll be remembered as."

The fury I felt a few minutes ago melts into a pool of heartache. I stare at Naomi's slumped shoulders and her splotchy face and I realize that she's never looked as human to me as she does now. My lips tremble.

There is so much to Naomi that I will never get a chance to know. None of us will. She's probably shown more to me than most. Not just over the last few days, but in those early years, and even in small glimpses later on. I just chose to forget them in my quest to tell myself the story that I wanted to believe about her. We all had a hand in building Naomi and tearing her down.

"It's time to leave," Lukas says as he walks into the room.

There's an overwhelming sadness that follows his words and I notice that the calm in Naomi starts to crack.

"I'm not ready."

I don't see the proverbial light at the end of the tunnel like they show in the movies, but nevertheless, isn't she supposed to feel some kind of happiness at this part? But if I were Naomi, I wouldn't be thrilled about walking off into eternity when my life here was cut so tragically short either. Hell, I was almost permanently dead like Naomi just a couple of hours ago, and I let a beast practically ravage me just so I could become undead. I think fast.

"Don't take her now, Lukas." I try to sound confident but it comes out whiny. I push my shoulders back and sit up straight. "Let Naomi stay for a bit longer, and when she's ready, you can come back for her."

Naomi crosses her arms. "That works."

"Do you really believe that I have the power to make that decision?" Lukas says in an exasperated tone that sounds like a stressed-out dad talking to his two twitty teenagers. "It simply doesn't function in that manner. Dead is dead."

"Except for Violet," Naomi blurts out and I don't blame her for the resentment in her tone. "It's not fair."

"No."

The guilt on my shoulders grows heavier. Maybe Naomi would have stayed a mean girl or maybe she wouldn't. We'd never know because Naomi wasn't going to get what I got today—a second chance.

Lukas places a firm hand on Naomi's back. "We need to leave."

Naomi and I stare at each other. We both know we can continue to argue with Lukas but we're not a team anymore. Our destinies are no longer entwined and now we have to go our separate ways. Even though we technically won, it doesn't feel like a victory.

"Don't die, Violet." Naomi grabs my hand. "Because it sucks."

"I love you." I know at one time that I did and I realize now that I still do.

"Ditto, Molly."

I smile at the reference to *Ghost*. We stand together for a few more minutes until tears run down Naomi's face so hard that they stain her cheeks. Neither of us says anything else to each other as Lukas leads her away.

He's standing with his shoulders back and he looks every bit the professional but there's a tenderness to the way that he handles her that I didn't know he was capable of. Naomi leans her entire body into him and he supports her fully.

They walk through the window and continue on a straight path through the clouds. As I watch Naomi, I feel that hole inside of me—the one that started with my mother's death—rip wide open. It's raw and it pulsates from somewhere so deep that the pain reverberates through me. I see the last swish of Naomi's long, honey-colored locks in the distance and then I collapse to the ground.

Twenty-Four

Day 11: Alive

I STARE AT THE MURDER BOARD on my wall. At the center, under *Victim*, there's a photo of Naomi from our school trip to Six Flags last year. She's eating a massive stick of pink cotton candy and laughing because most of it is stuck in her hair and on her face. I didn't think the pic looked murder-board appropriate but she insisted that I use it.

Under *Suspects*, we've got photos of Nate, Caleb, and even Trent, but there's no Tessa. Neither Naomi nor I imagined that she was a possibility. It didn't even occur to either one of us that Tessa was capable of killing anyone, let alone her best friend. Even now, after seeing it all unfold, I can't quite believe it.

Dede brought me home from Naomi's house on Friday and I climbed into my bed. I haven't gotten out since. All the shades are drawn in my room so I don't really know if it's morning or night except that I can hear those damn cheery birds outside my window.

Dede leaves trays of food by my door but I haven't touched them; Meryl stopped by but I turned her away. Not because I'm angry with either of them specifically but because I'm furious with the entire world and beyond. Sleep is my only reprieve from the mishmash of emotions that I can't allow myself to feel right now.

The next time I wake up, it's to the sound of a cow's moo. At first, I think it's a part of my dream, but then I realize it's coming from my phone. I rub my eyes and check my mobile. It's Sunday morning, which means that I've been sleeping on and off for the last thirty-six hours or so. Still, I feel completely depleted.

I click on the message before realizing that it leads me straight to *Heffers and Hos*. An image of Tessa under the head-line "Mad Cow" appears. This is a special segment on *H and H* that usually showcases psycho girlfriends. My body trembles as I watch the video of the last minutes of Naomi's life on that playground. It's right next to a constant loop of what I now understand *H and H* refers to as the "rape tape."

H and H is mocking all of it—the rape, the murder, every-thing. Apparently, the cops still haven't found a way to take the site down. Which means that all of this has been turned into a joke. And Naomi is the punch line.

The gaping hole inside of me hurts more than ever. I can't bear the pain and so I retreat back to my bed, pull the covers over my head, and try to make it all go away.

Freak. Freak. Freak. Their chanting fills my ears. I sit up straight in bed. I'm wide awake now but I relive that moment in school with the skinless humans as though it is a nightmare. I'm mired in fear, shame, and hate. Beads of sweat form along my forehead and I take a huge gulp of water from the glass on my bedside table.

Those skinless humans are freaks. They're also my classmates and some of them are my friends. With their outer costumes—skin color, eyes, hair—all I see are our differences. But that day, we were all the same. Freaks drowning in our collective river of pain.

I start to tremble. Sitting here in the pitch-darkness of my room, I feel so alone. Yet I know that beyond these walls, I'm not. *Not if I don't want to be.*

What had Lukas said? That empathy is one of my most powerful tools as a fighter.

Naomi was killed for reasons beyond her control. But the girl lacked any sort of empathy for others and herself. So do I. *Lie and deny.* I can try to say that Naomi and I are different people, but she called me out on it. We're not. We're both manufactured. I am Naomi.

So what is it that I want? I mean, I was given a second chance. Am I really going to piss that away by continuing to be blind to everything that's happening around me? I walked through my school hallways and I felt *them.* There was no denying it. I could recognize their fear, their shame, and their hate because I've been trapped in it for as long as I can remember.

I just thought I was the only one. Like Naomi did. Now I know that I am not alone. I feel the rage run through my veins and it fuels me. I am so angry.

I turn on the lamp on my nightstand and grab my phone. I hold it in front of my face, open the camera, and press the Record button. I pay no attention to the fact that my teeth are yellow and my hair is a big, messy ball on top of my head.

Before I begin, I don't really know what I'm going to say, but it's okay. I can feel someone else guiding me. My last conversation with Naomi plays fresh in my mind. Once the red light goes on, I start to speak. My voice is quiet, and at first, it doesn't even sound like it's coming from me.

"Naomi Talbert was a mean girl. A mean girl is a caricature. She's a one-dimensional stereotype who doesn't exist outside of fiction. But Naomi had colors, curves, corners, and even cobwebs because she was *real*. Somewhere underneath Princess Naomi, my friend did exist. She just spent her entire life too afraid to show it."

I take a long, deep breath.

"I'm scared too and I know I'm not alone. We're all so afraid of showing our true selves that we turn on each other any chance we get. We slut-shame, body-shame. Shame, shame, shame. It's killing all of us, bit by bit, and I don't want to die."

I hear my voice quiver and start to shut off the camera but then I decide to continue. "I'm a freak. I tried to hide it but now I know I can't. And I don't want to."

I press the Stop button and upload the video onto *Heffers and Hos*. Then I lie back down in bed. The giant, gaping hole continues to pulse and ache inside of me. I close my eyes and let myself collapse under the weight of it all.

Day 12: Alive

I slump down behind my desk. It's Tuesday morning, first period. I didn't want to come to school but Dede threatened me by saying that she would bring Naresh back home if I didn't get out of bed, so I reluctantly took a shower, brushed my teeth, and put on some almost-clean clothes. Meryl was so sure that I was just going to sneak back to bed (which was exactly what I was going to do) that she insisted on driving me here.

"Hey, Violet!" Emma Lammas, a senior who has never paid attention to me, calls out. "Welcome back, *chica!*"

I haven't been counting but this is, like, the ninth friendly greeting I've gotten already and I've been here less than fifteen minutes. It's true that if you added up the dead days and my absence yesterday, I've been gone for four entire school days, but that is hardly cause for all the friendliness.

Mr. Helm turns the television to the in-school channel, WMHS. Morning announcements are always a bore to listen to. I take out my French binder. I'm way behind in all of my subjects.

I open my textbook and stare down blankly at the page. I can't stop thinking about Naomi.

On my way to homeroom this morning, I walked past Naomi's old locker. It's still decorated with photos, ribbons, and messages like *RIP* and *We miss you.* A part of me wants to believe that it is all phony and my classmates have moved on. That may be somewhat true but it isn't the entire picture. Even if all of us are going on with our usual daily routines, there's this cloud of sadness that seems to hang over us. I realize that I'm not the only person here suffering from the loss of Naomi, and knowing that somehow makes me feel a little better.

Plus, I haven't heard from the Aiedeo since Naomi's funeral, which also helps to raise my spirits. I know they aren't gone for good but I'm happy for the rest.

"Violet Choudhury."

I hear the school news anchor say my name but I have no idea what it's connected to. Suddenly, the class erupts in cheers.

"Way to go, V!" Jess shouts.

"Congrats!" a bunch of other people yell.

"You have no idea what just happened, do you, Violet?" Austin smiles.

I feel butterflies flutter around in my stomach. I ghosted him again, but from the way he's looking at me, I don't think he minds. I think about our last kiss and my face turns pink.

Austin reaches out and caresses my cheek. "Your humility is so hot."

At least he didn't say I was exotic. I know that I need to call him out for that, but that means I have to cop to snooping through his phone. I reason that it doesn't have to be right at this exact moment. I mean, he's touching my face!

"Oh my God, Violet! Why aren't you jumping for joy?" Jess leans across her desk. "You're the first junior to be nominated for homecoming queen in, like, twenty years!"

"What?"

"We voted on homecoming-queen nominations yesterday when you were still sick. Which is even cooler, because you weren't out there begging for votes like some of those desperate seniors." Jess points to two girls sitting in the front of the class. "But apparently, enough people wrote your name in that you're now officially on the ballot for homecoming queen, which you know is usually only for senior girls!"

"Why?" I wonder if I'm being punked.

"Because of that kick-ass freak video you posted on *Heffers and Hos*," Austin chimes in. "You were awesome with all that colors, curves, corners, and cobwebs stuff!"

I gulp. I completely forgot about that tape until this very moment. It *was* pretty ballsy. Especially for MHS, and particularly for me. "People watched that?"

"It's gone viral," Jess says. "You're like our very own Beyoncé."

Austin lowers his voice and says, "It was a really powerful way to honor Naomi."

I blink back my tears and Austin squeezes my hand. I don't know what to make of all the homecoming stuff but for the first time in a while, I don't feel like I'm dead inside. I don't know how long that will last, but for now, at least, I want to hold on to it.

"You're sure you don't want to celebrate with me at Stumpy's, homecoming queen?"

I laugh and shake my head. "Mer, it's just a nomination. And I promise I will celebrate with you, but not tonight. I've got way too much homework to catch up on from all the days that I missed."

"Lame. School sucks and you suck." Meryl stops rummaging through my closet and turns to face me. "I hate all that royalty bullshit, but this is a *big deal*. Because you got it being yourself. I'm so proud of the way you let your freak flag fly," Meryl says, then goes back to rummaging through my closet.

I lift an eyebrow. "Both you and I know that I've got a whole lot more freak than that."

"It's a start."

"I don't know what it is, but I have to admit that today felt good. I mean, of course there were some haters. But overall, kids and even some teachers were really supportive of what I said in that video."

I still couldn't quite believe just how many people came up and thanked me. Their encouragement gives me courage to stand behind my words. I think my head is actually kind of swelling from the attention. That doesn't mean that I'm not wrestling with my usual tendency to stay silent and hide. However, for the moment, at least, I feel like I actually matter.

"I heard Austin wants to write a song about you." Meryl grabs my phone from my hand. "Just what I thought. You're not skipping Stumpy's because of homework—you're totally spending it sexting your bae! Actually, why aren't you guys just booty-calling? I mean, he lives down the street."

"He's stuck babysitting his little brother and sister, so the booty call is gonna have to wait for another night." I throw a pillow at her. "And don't call him my bae! Especially in front of him."

Meryl plops down on the bed next to me. "It just feels good to see you happy again."

I nod and rest my head on her shoulder. "It's been a wild ride."

"But you survived." We sit there in silence for a second before Meryl holds out a set of bangles. "Can I borrow these?"

I take one of them from her. "Where did you find them? They're from Assam. I didn't even know I had them anymore."

"Oh, then they're way too nice for Stumpy's," Meryl says as she stands up and carefully places them in my jewelry box.

"No. You can totally have them!"

"They're yours." Meryl shuts the jewelry box. "But maybe take better care of them because I found them on the floor of your closet and they look kinda special."

I thought I lost these bangles years ago and I'm a little confused on how they just turned up.

"Come out if you change your mind." Meryl opens my bedroom door. "Later."

After spending a little bit of time studying and a lot more time chatting with Austin, I finally go to bed feeling loads better than when I'd left for school this morning. That night, for the first time in I don't know how long, I actually have a good dream and not a nightmare.

Tucked deep in the foothills of the Himalayas lies my kingdom, mighty Assam. Majestic river valleys loop through rolling blue hills like the bamboo baskets the tribal women weave along

the banks of the Brahmaputra River. I throw my chappals off and bury my feet in the cold sand, then get up and run through the dark red poppies that grow everywhere.

The hot Indian sun burns down on me before she takes her afternoon nap. While she sleeps, buckets of rain pour from the dark, angry sky, washing away the filth from the city streets near the river.

Drenched from head to toe, I run to my room, dripping water onto the cold marble floor. I quickly change out of my wet clothes and into a warm, dry kurta. My long hair is sopping and curly. I wrap it up in a towel before heading to the balcony. There I sit in an oversize bamboo chair, watching the rain.

My house rests on top of a giant hill, surrounded by the thick, lush minty greens of the jungle. Monkeys greet us on our porch some mornings, but those are the only animals the armed guards allow in.

When I was little, my mother took me for walks in the jungle. We ignored the uniformed men following close behind, their guns ready to shoot any beast that threatened to harm us. We pretended we were explorers as we ran through the tall plants, searching for gold. In our knapsacks we carried magnifying glasses, a book for identifying the flora, and bananas in case we encountered an elephant that let us feed him.

A loud crack of lightning shatters the sky and I tuck my feet up underneath me. I hear a lion roar as he ushers the *other animals to safety. I know this is just my active imagination teasing me, but I play along.*

My game is interrupted when a servant places a cup of chai in front of me. A bloom of cardamom and cloves lingers in the air. I suck on the cinnamon stick floating in the cup before taking a long, delicious sip. The steaming, hot liquid tastes sweet as it slides down my throat, warming me from the inside.

My mother turns the corner, scolding me as she approaches. She throws a blanket over me and tucks me into the chair, insisting that otherwise I'll catch a cold. As she dips her head near me, I smell jasmine and cilantro. Her brow furrows as she continues to chastise me for coming home soaked and barefoot. I try to look sorry but I know she isn't really angry. She's never really angry.

Her scowl turns into a smile and I smile back. She is beautiful standing in front of me wearing a white sari. Her hair is black like mine. She wears it to her shoulders with light bangs that frame her oval face.

Mine is slightly rounder and my cheeks are chubbier. Our skin is caramel velvet, like the chai, without a scar, pimple, or wrinkle. When we talk, which is often, we both gesture wildly as though we're Italian rather than Indian. And when we laugh, the green speckles in our big brown eyes dance. We get many compliments on our eyes, though secretly our lips are our favorite features—lush and pink, the bottom lip a bit plumper than the top.

Neither of us would ever pass up a plate of potatoes or a

basket of lucci. And we hate all sports except tennis. She is me and I am her. We are not alike or identical. We are one . . .

My name is Violet Choudhury. I descend from an ancient royal heritage. Since the days when India was the enchanted playground of gods and maharajas, the women in my family were queens — Aiedeo. The men in my family, many of them kings themselves, added wealth and prestige to our name with their courage and honor. But it was my female ancestors who were powerful.

Thousands of years ago, the first of our line, Ananya, stepped onto the golden pathway that would forever bind our destinies. Her blood, fused with the blood of my mother, my grandmother, and the generations of women between us, runs through me. Their power is my inheritance.

"Not since Ananya has anyone else been so powerful," they whisper when they think I cannot hear.

I reach out to my mother. My fingers skim the top of her hand before it all goes away — the tea, the balcony, the rain. Her. Everything disappears. Only I am left.

I wake up refreshed, renewed, and ready. I have never dreamed of my mother before and I don't know if I ever will again. But I do know that last night, she was with me. And if that's all I'll ever get of Laya, then I'll settle for that. For now, I have to put my pain aside and do what I need to do.

The Aiedeo is not about my mother. It's not about my duty or my responsibility or even about my legacy. It's about me.

I am an Aiedeo. From now on, *I* get to decide what that means because I've spent too long letting others tell me who I am. I don't know what those bitches have planned for me, and that scares me shitless. But I will no longer allow my fear to keep me from claiming my power.

Epilogue

O KAY, SO I GOT IT. *Exotic* is not cool." Austin's lips skim mine and I taste his cinnamon gum.

"Thanks for letting me school you." I smile.

Luckily, I didn't have to confess to snooping through Austin's phone when I was a *bhoot* to have this very necessary conversation. He actually complimented me on my exotic hair, which gave me the perfect opportunity to talk to him about it.

"You can school me anytime, Miss Choudhury," Austin says as he swoops me up in one those movie kisses that I love.

After a few more seconds, we finally unlock. "So I'll see you tonight?" I ask. "Meryl says your friend better be hot because she's skipping dollar-pitcher night at Stumpy's to go out with us."

Convincing Meryl to go out on a double date with me, Austin, and his buddy who was visiting from out of town was harder than any *shama* I've ever had to do.

"He's waxing his back hair just for her," Austin jokes, and he heads down the street we both live on.

I laugh and turn the other way to walk home. Inside the

house, I'm about to call out for Dede when I remember that she and Mrs. Patel are shopping. My stomach grumbles. I drop my stuff and go into the kitchen.

A witchy-looking woman with a long, sinewy frame and wild white hair that flies all around her is stirring something putrid in a big black pot on my stove. She turns to face me. I stare. Her skin is so black it's like the light has been sucked out of it. My pulse races. I instantly know that she's not of this world. I am so over being a Bhoot Buster that I don't bother to hide my disgust.

"This is a no-*bhoot* zone. Get out," I shout in what I hope sounds like a menacing voice.

"*Bhoot?*" The woman cackles. She starts creeping toward me.

"Stay back!" I holler.

"You know nothing, Little One." She sneers as she runs a bony, crooked finger down the side of my face. Her touch feels like a hundred spiders crawling all over me and I shiver. I feel chills down my spine.

"Who the hell are you?" I ask, realizing I sound a lot braver than I feel.

The woman opens her mouth, exposing her black tongue and tiny rotten teeth. I want to run away but I'm frozen in this spot. I watch her mouth getting bigger and bigger by the second. Her tongue turns into dozens of writhing snakes. They lash out and coil themselves around my body and jerk me closer, so close that I can see inside the gigantic gaping hole that is her mouth and smell the rotten flesh it's made out of.

"I am Ananya!" she roars and swallows me.

Acknowledgments

I think it's only fitting that after writing a story about badass bitches, I should start the acknowledgments by thanking the badass bitches in my life. To my Mr. Miyagi/Jack Sparrow/Yoda nanny, Dede—your stories shaped me. I listened to every word and I wrote it all down. Too bad dead people can't get royalties. Mommy and Ita—thank you for being my teachers in this world and beyond.

Tan, Lamb, Suzy, and Bron: Meryl is equal parts of each one of you. Since the days when we were figuring out *The Facts of Life* to surviving our own *90210* and now navigating the Seven Kingdoms, thank you for always believing and believing in my stories. To the rest of my soul sisters: Venla, Alisa, Rena, Shadia, and Liisa—thank you for a lifetime of unconditional love, unconditional encouragement, and unconditional wine.

Cheers to my soul bros Sasha, David, and Michael. Paul—thank you for advocating for me like I was a paying client. Markus—your expertise from countless hours playing video games, reading comics, and watching YouTube have helped me avoid more tired story tropes than my ego would care to admit. Oliver—thank you for reading that very first draft all those years ago and convincing me that I could do this.

It's been a twisted journey to get *Brown Girl Ghosted* published. Thanks to the incredible team at Versify for making it happen! For *BGG* to find a home with such integrity is beyond my wildest dreams. Kwame Alexander—I've fangirled you forever. I read the message you wrote about *BGG* almost every day and show it to every person that I meet. Margaret Raymo—thank you for getting *BGG* from the beginning and for not asking me to write about a zombie instead of a *bhoot* or suggesting I change the Midwest to the UK. Instead, you took *BGG* and used your brilliance, humor, wisdom, and warmth to help make it better. Thank you to my copyeditor, Tracy Roe, for her great work. Many, many thanks to Samya Arif for her gorgeous, vibrant cover and to Sharismar Rodriguez, the book's designer.

To everyone at Ferly who lets me whine, worry, demand, and drink in a way that's usually acceptable only for an author with much bigger book sales—thank you for *Storm Sisters* and for championing *Brown Girl* like it's your own. Laura N.—boss. Mikael—baller. Tuomas—my gentleman reindeer agent who always finds a way to open every closed door. Laura A.—thank you for using your invaluable storytelling expertise to clean up the mess of my "brilliant" first drafts. Cheers to number four and a lifetime more.

Much love and appreciation to the global Das-Koivisto family with its satellite offices around the world. To my Indian crew—I'm forever grateful to you for helping me find my

Assamese warrior queens. Koko—you taught me what it means to be an Assamese girl. To the Finnish branch—thank you to Pinni and Tarmo for setting the bar as creatives, parents, and people. To the American headquarters: Dada, Sarah, and Marlow—thank you for helping me stay connected to my midwestern roots by always keeping it real. Sne—you inspire me more than you'll ever know. Dad—your Shakespearean bedtime tales were my first lessons in storytelling, and your fearlessness was my most important lesson in life.

To my hometowns of Macomb, Illinois; Helsinki, Finland; and Assam, India—no matter how far I go, you'll always be a part of my stories.

Finally, to my husband, Kalle—you stay up with me until four a.m. figuring out plot twists; you find all the best hole-in-the-wall places on every trip; you make excellent palomas; you wake up every morning with a joke and a song; you follow me into secret caves looking for witches; you play in front of thousands of people and always stay cool; you let me buy too many bowls even if it means paying for extra baggage; you inspire me with your creativity, kindness, and brilliance every day. None of this would have happened without you. Too bad spouses can't get royalties.